THE
HEIGHTS

PETER HEDGES

 DUTTON

DUTTON

Published by Penguin Group (USA) Inc.

375 Hudson Street, New York, New York 10014, U.S.A.

Penguin Group (Canada), 90 Eglinton Avenue East, Suite 700, Toronto, Ontario M4P 2Y3, Canada (a division of Pearson Penguin Canada Inc.); Penguin Books Ltd, 80 Strand, London WC2R 0RL, England; Penguin Ireland, 25 St Stephen's Green, Dublin 2, Ireland (a division of Penguin Books Ltd); Penguin Group (Australia), 250 Camberwell Road, Camberwell, Victoria 3124, Australia (a division of Pearson Australia Group Pty Ltd); Penguin Books India Pvt Ltd, 11 Community Centre, Panchsheel Park, New Delhi—110 017, India; Penguin Group (NZ), 67 Apollo Drive, Rosedale, North Shore 0632, New Zealand (a division of Pearson New Zealand Ltd); Penguin Books (South Africa) (Pty) Ltd, 24 Sturdee Avenue, Rosebank, Johannesburg 2196, South Africa

Penguin Books Ltd, Registered Offices: 80 Strand, London WC2R 0RL, England

Published by Dutton, a member of Penguin Group (USA) Inc.

First printing, March 2010

10 9 8 7 6 5 4 3 2 1

 REGISTERED TRADEMARK—MARCA REGISTRADA

LIBRARY OF CONGRESS CATALOGING-IN-PUBLICATION DATA

Hedges, Peter.

The heights / Peter Hedges.

    p. cm.

ISBN 978–0–525–95113–1 (hardcover)

I. Title.

PS3558.E3165H45 2010

813'.54—dc22   2009020781

Printed in the United States of America

Set in Palatino with Trade Gothic

Designed by Daniel Lagin

PUBLISHER'S NOTE

This book is a work of fiction. Names, characters, places, and incidents either are the product of the author's imagination or are used fictitiously, and any resemblance to actual persons, living or dead, business establishments, events, or locales is entirely coincidental.

ALSO BY PETER HEDGES

What's Eating Gilbert Grape

An Ocean in Iowa

THE HEIGHTS

The list of those who have descended from the heights is long,
and only a few need be mentioned.

—JOHN KENNETH GALBRAITH

ONE

KATE

THAT MORNING WE WOKE TO FIND OUR STREET BURIED IN SNOW. THE STOOPS, THE sidewalk, the row of parked cars were a blanket of white; the trees looked as if they'd been dipped in frosting, and the whole of Oak Lane—with its impeccably preserved century-old brownstones—had the look of a vintage photograph. Only the loud scrape from an approaching snowplow betrayed what Tim, my history-teaching husband, would like to believe: Erase the plow, remove the light poles and the telephone wires, toss out all electrical appliances, and it could be any other Brooklyn Heights morning, circa 1848 or 1902.

Staring down from our fourth-floor apartment, I made out the faint prints from Tim's boots. Before sunrise, he'd crossed between two parked cars and trudged with his backpack full of graded papers toward Montague Street, where he'd climbed the steps to the Montague Academy. During the night, the thick flakes had fallen gently, but now it was morning, and the wind blew in gusts that rattled the windows of the living room/dining room/toy room where I was standing. I felt a chill.

Sam came running down the hall, his diaperless pants at his knees, crying, "Mommy, pee-pee! Pee-pee!" Teddy, newly four, followed, saying, "Sam made a mess!" Minutes before, I'd abruptly left the kitchen because, between the repeated calls of "More milk, Mommy" and "I'm hungry, Mommy" and "Mommy, Sam's hitting me," I knew either they'd stop, as asked, or I would snap.

With few places to look, it took no time for them to find me.

Teddy had been up early due to a bad dream, and Sam had eaten hardly any breakfast, feeding himself only the brightly colored mini-marshmallows from his favorite sugared cereal. "This will not do," I announced grandly. But, of course, it would. It did.

When Tim phoned from school, I had to shout over Sam, who was shrieking, while Teddy kept pushing the button that made the phone go on speaker. Tim asked, "How's it going?" more out of habit, I suppose, because one little moment of listening, and he'd know.

"Good, it's going good," I said, choosing not to tell him about a mysterious smell in the bathroom (the toilet was clogged and would not flush); the bar of oatmeal soap half-melted in the empty bathtub; the growing stack of unpaid bills; the clothes strewn, a Hansel and Gretel trail of little boys' pants and shirts and underwear; and how when I finally made it to the sock drawer to finish dressing Sam, no socks matched. I made no mention of how the winter wind was sure to shatter our front windows, nor my prediction that this was going to be the coldest day of the year. After all, Tim was hard at work. Better to spare him.

Later, in the vestibule of our building, I managed to open the stroller and carry it down the stoop, all the while coaxing the boys to follow. I belted Sam in, lowered Teddy so he could ride standing in back, and we began our walk. Both boys were practically smothered under sweaters and coats and scarves and hats, gloves, boots—only their eyes could be seen. Beneath it all, I could hear them crying, and when I leaned forward to ask what was the matter, Teddy sobbed, "My eyes are cold."

"I don't know what to do about your eyes."

Never enough. Never enough. A parent can never, ever do enough.

I had the makings of a song.

Gloveless, scarfless, with my down jacket still unbuttoned up top— I'd forgotten about me.

Soon after we set off, it became clear that, because of the snow, our stroller wasn't going to work. So, with the wind whipping and the need to think fast, I turned us around. Back home, I left the stroller in the vestibule and hurried to our storage closet in the basement to fetch

Tim's childhood sled. Outside, I wrapped the boys in an old blue blanket, set them on the sled, and pulled them behind me.

We were halfway down Hicks Street before I noticed other parents dragging their kids by the wrist, slipping and sliding, or struggling with strollers. Men and women, dressed for work, leaned into the wind as they headed toward the subway station on Clark Street, stepping gingerly, hoping not to fall. And here I came, pulling Teddy and Sam, the only children in the Heights riding to school on a sled. Glancing back, I could see them squinting in the way that comes only when they're smiling. And suddenly, that great unreasonable distance we traveled each morning to R Kids Count Learning Center became a blessing. Some children were getting rides in carpools, and others would be arriving by car service and taxi. But the boys and I were envied—one stiff parent, Chad the Wall Street whiz, surprised me by shouting from the corner of Pierrepont and Hicks, in a manner half amused, half in awe, "Now, that's the way to travel."

For once I was the clever mother, the only mother with this rather terrific idea, and my boys, Teddy and Sam Welch, were content.

These are the moments, I wanted to sing. *These are the moments.*

"Canceled," Maria (always perky) Spence called out from her Range Rover on the corner of Pineapple Street.

"But why?"

"Boiler. Broken. Call me. Playdate sometime." She had to go, her cell phone was ringing, and she drove on.

Teddy didn't understand why we were turning around.

"The school has no heat, sweetie," I said. "You'll freeze, and we wouldn't want that."

"But I wanna go!"

With my promise of hot chocolate, Teddy calmed down. As I pulled the sled up Henry Street to Montague, Sam said, "Daddy, work," and pointed toward the neo-Gothic ex–German Lutheran church that housed most of Montague Academy. On nice days, I often took the boys to the courtyard garden, where they climbed on the lower school's playground equipment. This was not to be one of those days.

Instead, we turned right on Montague and headed down to Muffins and More. Across the street, Starbucks was doing impressive business. I preferred, as did the other mothers in my circle, the locally owned Muffins and More, which, rumor had it, was in danger of going out of business, but not if we could help it.

Handfuls of rock salt had been scattered on the pavement outside Muffins and More. The ice and snow had begun to melt. I tied the sled to a parking meter and held Teddy and Sam by their mittens as we walked carefully toward the door.

Inside, sitting at a corner table—which they managed to commandeer every day at this time—Tess Windsor, Debbie Beebe, and Claudia Valentine drank their espressos and cappuccinos and decaf lattes.

"Kate will have an opinion," Tess said, picking up her parka, which had been lying across the only available chair. "Come over here, Kate."

Tess usually packed a child's activity ideal for bad weather. So it was no surprise to see her daughter, Maddie, who also went to R Kids Count, doing an origami project at a nearby table. Without prompting, Maddie offered to teach Teddy, who wanted to learn, and Sam, who seemed happy just to watch.

Debbie volunteered to go to the counter and get whatever the boys wanted. I gladly fished out a crumpled five-dollar bill, handed it to her, and plopped down in the open chair. Debbie was expecting her first in September. She often helped us with our children. "Practice," she claimed, although on this particular morning, I thought it may have been to escape the conversation I was about to join. Claudia said, "We were hoping you'd come by, we want your thoughts." Claudia has the throaty, smoky voice of a sultry movie star. "Tess and I don't agree. Debbie won't take sides."

"Because what do I know?" Debbie called from the counter before turning to order.

While Tess considered how best to phrase the question, Claudia blurted out, not whispering, because she never whispers, "What is it with little boys and their assholes?"

Tess winced. Debbie pretended not to have heard.

On that day, as far I was concerned, any of these women could say anything—talk nonsense, gibberish, even, and just so long as none of them called me Mommy or asked me to tie her shoes, I'd be positively giddy and, in no time, reborn.

Claudia continued, "Both my boys love to drop their pants, bend over, spread their butt cheeks, and say, 'Look, Mom!' I mean, what is that all about?"

Meet Claudia Valentine: loud talker, blunt thinker, eager playdate maker. I hadn't liked her at first—too brassy and needy, or so I thought—but after two of my favorite other mothers moved away last year, Claudia and I found ourselves increasingly the only ones left at what she called the dwindling party that was our life. What I always liked about Claudia was that she was the kind of mother who would kill for her kids. What I loved about her was she'd also kill for mine. Or any kid, for that matter. And if her Homer (yes, Homer) and Olaf (yes, Olaf) were to mistreat some other child, her justice would be swift and firm. She didn't tolerate unkindness or cruelty, and her children, while exposed to her many momentary lapses into volatility, had been given one of the true great parental gifts: They had been civilized. And if not, they wouldn't be able to blame their mother, for no one tries harder to be fair. Her tendency toward salty language and her unabashed capacity to speak her mind may have been off-putting to the Heights establishment, but I found her refreshing.

"It's a phase," Tess said. "Boys grow out of it."

"Do they?" Claudia countered.

"Yes," Tess said, looking toward me, hoping I'd join in.

Claudia again: "I don't think they do. I think it morphs. Their fascination with their own assholes evolves into their fascination with ours."

Tess giggled as she pretended to cover her ears.

Still Claudia: "What is it with men that they all want to fuck us in the butt?"

Please understand: I am no prude. I enjoy the occasional tacky sex conversation. But it was morning, and this was bar talk. I did my best to ignore the question.

But Claudia kept on: "Lately, Dan has been begging me, whispering in my ear, pleading. He even bought a book, written by a *woman*, about the joys of it, the supposed pleasure. I'm not convinced!"

I glanced out the window of Muffins and More just as Frida Fabritz from Heights Realty hurried into the coffee establishment across the street.

Frida Fabritz was the Realtor who, years earlier, rented us our two-bedroom apartment. That's a joke, considering one of the bedrooms is a small, windowless space, a glorified closet. Recently, we had one of the math teachers from Montague over for dinner. He admired how we managed in such "cramped quarters." I asked him to do us a favor and calculate the square footage of our apartment. Frida had listed it at approximately twelve hundred square feet, but I'd always doubted the figure. He paced out the apartment and, after a grim silence, said, "Well, you've got close to nine hundred square feet here, if you include the boys' room."

"Room?" I said. "You call that a *room*?"

That morning, as I watched Frida Fabritz enter Starbucks, I had an urge to chase after her. No, I wouldn't make a scene. I'd simply tell her what we'd discovered when a math teacher measured our apartment. I ached to make Frida buckle over with guilt. Luckily for her, she'd gone across the street for coffee. Luckily for her, I had both boys and was trapped in a conversation with my mother friends.

"Kate?"

I looked at Claudia. "What?"

"Where did you go?"

"I'm here, listening," I said, turning to check on Teddy and Sam, who sat entranced, watching Maddie fold a series of swans with the colored origami paper. Debbie held a corn muffin between them, breaking off chunks for them to chew.

"You're no help," Claudia said.

"I know," I said. "Sorry."

Claudia said, "Whatever."

"Where were we?" Tess asked.

"Assholes," Claudia said. Then she leaned forward and bellowed, "Oh, for the record, do you know which of our neighbors likes taking it up the butt . . . ?"

I escaped before learning the answer. Outside, Teddy, the willful one, struggled with me, using his winter boots to kick at my ankles. Both boys had wanted to stay, but I had errands to run, and Sam, gentle Sam, needed a nap. We set off for Key Food but stopped at the M&O newsstand for a box of cherry Luden's and a packet of tissues for the boys' runny noses.

"Kate, good, it's you."

I turned to find Frida Fabritz walking toward me, a forced smile on her face. "Sorry to grab you like this, but, please, I need a favor."

I tried to beg off her request, but Frida said, "I've got a prospective buyer with all sorts of questions about the neighborhood, and I thought, Who better—"

"You don't want me to talk to them," I said. "Not with the mood I'm in."

Behind her fake smile, fear was in her eyes. Perhaps for the first time, I was catching a glimpse of the real Frida Fabritz. In recent years, several large realty companies had moved into the Heights, and Frida had begun to feel the pinch. In that moment she appeared desperate, and I have a soft spot for desperate people. Besides, my thinking went, a Realtor in the Heights who owed me might one day be a good thing. So I pulled the boys back in the direction we'd come.

Once, during a job interview, I was asked if there had been anything in my past I regretted. At the time I couldn't think of a thing, not one single thing I wished I'd done differently, so I said lamely, "Sure,

I've made mistakes, yes, but I don't regret them because of what I've learned and I've been bettered from having made them." And while the person interviewing me was unimpressed, I knew my answer to be, if vague, sincere. Funny, now, what I remember thinking as I trailed after Frida—you see, she was already smiling again, which made me wonder if I'd been duped—and that was when I said under my breath: "This may be my first real regret." Frida turned back toward me and asked what I'd said. "Nothing," I replied. She paused before saying with cheeriness, "Great idea, by the way. The sled." Then she laughed nervously, a mixture of panic and glee. I'd never seen her behave this strangely, and then I saw why.

The woman stood just outside the doorway of Heights Realty, facing the other way, so I noticed her posture first. She had the long neck of a dancer. And when she slowly turned in my direction, she smiled as if she'd been expecting me. I may have gasped, because she was, quite simply, the most striking woman I'd ever seen.

"Kate, I'd like you to meet . . ."

The woman extended her hand. The leather of her glove felt warm and expensive; my gloveless hand was numb from the cold. She said in a whisper, "I'm Anna. Anna Brody."

"Anna's thinking of moving here," Frida said. "So I thought who better to tell her what it's like in the Heights?"

I don't remember what all I said, but when I finally stopped talking, Frida joked that I secretly worked for Heights Realty. "I don't work," I started to explain when Anna Brody smiled. "No, you don't work. You're just a mother." She said this with surprising affection and irony, and without saying it, she seemed to hint that we were the same.

"Oh," I said. "Do you have—"

"Yes, a daughter," she said. "Sophie. She's three."

"Well," I said, "it's a great neighborhood for children."

"So I see," she said, looking at my boys in their sled. I think she envied the sled.

It began to snow. Among the swirling flakes, I noticed the stream of exhaust coming from an idling black town car, double-parked. A driver in a uniform stood at attention, waiting for Anna Brody. But she was in no hurry. She slowly smiled at me and said in her soft, breathy voice, "You don't know what a help you've been."

I must have shivered because she undid her light blue scarf and draped it around my neck.

"I couldn't," I said.

"You must," she said, tying it for me. "Otherwise, you'll catch cold."

I wanted to say, "But it matches your eyes."

The driver opened the door. As Anna ducked into the back of the car, Frida shouted out that she'd be calling. Anna didn't look back, disappearing behind the tinted glass. I found myself waving stupidly as the sedan pulled away.

The rest of the walk home, I kept hearing the way she'd said it, as if it were a secret—*Anna, Anna Brody*. Like a stuck record, it kept playing in my head—*Anna, Anna Brody, Anna, Anna Brody, Anna, Anna Brody* . . .

The question became: How was I going to stop it? How was I going to drown it out?

Tim.

I imagined what Tim would say.

For six years my husband had been working on his dissertation. Titled and retitled countless times, it had turned into a large, sprawling work called "The History of Loss." On the rare good days, he called it "Loss and Its Many Friends," and on the frequent doubt-filled days, he laughed sadly and referred to it as "The Lost Cause." Given his own history and seen from the vantage point of his childhood, Tim's central thesis had been born out of necessity, a lifesaving theory that salvaged a lost boy, but, I had urged him to consider, what about the man? Wasn't it time for a new theory? Happily, not yet. Besides, all theories need to be tested. Here I found myself with the opportunity to try out Tim's.

And while many people found his approach depressing, I had lived with it long enough that I'd begun to find comfort in it. On that day, in those post–Anna Brody hours, it was Tim and only Tim I heard loud and clear. Often he'd couch it in historical anecdote, or pepper his conversation with apt examples, but the gist was: *Lose. Lose early, lose often. For it's how you lose that counts.* And you will lose. Your hair, your looks, your teeth, your body fluids and fecal matter; you will lose friends, your memory, and if you're one of the elite few, like Anna Brody, who expect to be remembered, give it time: Eventually, the world will lose its memory of you, too. *Anna who?*

I felt much better.

Still, I was in a sad, sad mood as I pulled Teddy and Sam down State Street. It had started with the scarf, an admittedly nice gesture, but enough already—now my tears were freezing to my face.

Back home, and in an attempt to shake myself out of my funk, I gathered Teddy and Sam in our living room/dining room/toy room, where we made a bed out of sofa pillows, stuffed animals, and the almost beanless beanbag chair I'd had since college. The three of us cuddled. I told them how happy I was and how much their daddy and I loved them. I kissed them on their forehead and on their soft, warm cheeks, and they sensed, I think, that if they didn't do something fast, I'd kiss them all over, so they began to squirm, push me away, and demand TV. We spent the afternoon watching animated and live action videos, all of which they'd seen numerous times. We had our own little film festival, and instead of making them lunch, I prepared a series of snacks that I brought out over the course of several hours. I made open-face grilled cheese cut into small squares. I made faces out of pieces of produce—grapes for eyes, a carrot stick for a nose, a banana split down the middle for a smiling mouth, and a handful of raisins, placed just right, to suggest a head of hair. I amused them and even myself, and for a few hours I was not only the mother I never had, I was the mother of all mothers.

TIM

WHENEVER I GIVE, SAY, MY ANNUAL LECTURE ON THE GETTYSBURG ADDRESS, WHEN I dress up like Lincoln, or recount the Cuban Missile Crisis from Castro's point of view, and whenever my students clap and cheer as I exit the classroom, and after I climb the school stairs to my cork-lined faculty office/cubby where I sit in my broken oak swivel chair, my heart racing, exhausted but elated from my brief dance with brilliance, and just as I'm about to announce to myself *I am the god of all teachers*, I usually have the good sense to do the following: I pull open my desk drawer, rummage through the assorted chewed-on pens and pencils, the packages of Post-its, the pair of green-handled lefty scissors, the loose change, and the leftover Halloween candy pilfered from one of the boys' orange plastic pumpkins, until the aging envelope is found—"Ah," I sigh—as I take out the single piece of crinkled, now yellowed paper and reread what a former student wrote a few years back:

> Mr. Welch, yore my faverite teacher ever.
> I don't care what anybody els says.

The writer of this note—who for obvious legal reasons will remain nameless—was not learning-disabled, dyslexic, or a product of the oft maligned New York City public school system. He was one of Montague's own. He is at present in his junior year at a swanky private northeastern college. His major? Elementary education. Soon he'll be teaching children. Maybe yours.

That day the above note failed to bring me back to earth. I was flying high and for good reason. Each class had gone better than the class before, culminating with sixth-grade American history, where I somehow pulled off a dazzling deconstruction of Francis Scott Key's lyrics for "The Star-Spangled Banner," managing vividly to set the scene, shape the context, and in forty-four minutes, turn eighteen sullen sixth-graders into *patriots*.

I'd lost all sense of time since that class, my last of the day, and now I sat in my office. *What now? What next?* I snatched up my office phone, hit 9 for an outside line, and punched the numbers that connected me home. There the phone rang, and Kate answered on the third ring, and I started to tell of my triumph only to be interrupted by Kate's squeal: "It's Daddy!" She handed the phone to Sam, who said something indecipherable. But by his tone, it was clear something big had happened, something worth celebrating, so I said, "Good, that's so good, Sammy," and Sam got more excited, babbling at a higher pitch, and I was cheering now, for what exactly I didn't know, but it was good, life was, yes, *wee-ha*, and then I said, "Let me talk to Mommy." Kate came on the other line, and so what if my good news was aborted, soon to be topped by Kate, who had quite a story to tell. So what if I'd left my guts on the classroom floor. So what!

"Did you get any of that?" Kate asked.

"Jesus, no," I said. "Tell me!" And she did. History had been made moments earlier when Sam woke up from some form of group family nap in the living room, wandered down our narrow hallway, stripped off pants and diaper, climbed up the helper step, sat on the toilet, and produced all by himself a single, perfectly proportioned poop.

Kate was ecstatic, recounting every step along the way, telling how Sam had told her as he'd pointed to the toilet, "Mommy, look what I made."

Oh, I had to laugh. Yes, I was calling because I'd had a triumph, too, and while it wasn't literally poop, it was a kind of metaphorical poop all the same.

"Are you crying, honey?" Kate asked.

She can always tell by the way my voice gets softer. The long, odd pauses between words.

"You know I am."

"Hurry home, okay? We won't flush until you get here."

After hanging up, I wiped my eyes and thought, *Life can't get better*. There was no person in history with whom I would want to change places. And I'm an ordinary man, which made this feeling all the more improbable.

Please understand I'm a great believer in lowering expectations. From a young age, I learned to speak the worst about myself, expect the least, and later, if lucky, be surprised to find out I'd been wrong. So am I ordinary? In the best sense, yes. Physically? I get a B, if I've bathed. "Unusual-looking" might be the most apt description: my frizzy mop of hair; my easy-to-read eyes hiding behind the tiniest of wire-rimmed glasses; my naturally straight teeth. I'm attractive enough that my students from time to time have had crushes on me, and yet not so attractive that you'll find me modeling underwear on a Times Square billboard. I've always thought this to be a good thing. Otherwise I could have been cruel and dull. Why? Because perfect-looking people are often cruel and dull. I was an odd-looking, gawky kid who grew up to be not such a bad catch, or so my wife has been known to say. I like to think my rocky start forced me to develop other key qualities—kindness, empathy for the underdog, a tendency to be enthusiastic for new and strange ideas. All of this, I'm now convinced, helped in my quest to be worthy of Kate Oliver.

Now, Kate Oliver is not inherently ordinary. But she aspires to be. At five-nine she's an inch taller than I am. Her straight blond hair, her kind green eyes, and her free-of-makeup face all combine to make this first impression: She quite likely could have been the love child of Joni Mitchell and Mick Jagger. Her hippie mother chased bliss and all its chemical and sexual equivalents for years. Her mother's addiction to drugs and drama seemed to inspire Kate to experience its opposite. Truth be told, Kate craves the ordinary. She longs for it. Often couples marry their own kind. In Kate's case, she married down, which was why from the first moment she appeared barefoot in her white lace wedding dress, that rip-out-my-heart moment when I saw her come around the stone column at the Chapel of Harmony in Big Sur, when I blurted out, "Oh my God," those first tears began to roll. I proceeded to cry nonstop, as if I'd sprung a leak. And it was why I kept weeping through the readings (Rilke; Rumi; First Corinthians, chapter 13), through Kate's mom, Ariel, singing/butchering "The Wedding Song." I sobbed, my back shook, a stream of clear snot leaked from my nose, and everyone except my father laughed as it became obvious I couldn't stop. Three of Kate's former lovers—Dr. Max Brown (Kate's geology instructor at UC Berkeley); Jeff Slade (yes, *the* Jeff Slade); and Solveig Knudsen (Kate's freshman roommate/lesbian activist/body double)—watched, stunned, wondering why it hadn't gone their way. It's clear to me now I couldn't stop because I couldn't believe my own sweet luck that she was marrying me.

Nine years and two boys later, I still had the ring. And what did Kate and I have? A great, ordinary love we both fought for and guarded. Somehow in these bumpy, broken early years of the twenty-first century, we had navigated our way to something good and simple.

That was what I felt as I sat in my chair. What a quiet confidence I possessed that afternoon—to own a feeling so great that for any price, it was not for sale. I closed my eyes, leaned back, *wah-lah* . . .

It was too perfect, I would later decide, the light rap of knuckles on the wavy glass of my office door. I ignored the knocking, but it persisted. I knew the hand. I could picture the chubby knuckles. I glanced toward the door and noted the odd-shaped silhouette pressed against the glass. Yes. Of course. It was her. Knocking. And I had no other choice but to open the door.

There she stood, all four feet nine inches of her, newly sixteen but still the same height as when she was ten, a forever pug-nosed little chunk of a girl, barrel-chested with mouse-brown hair and a cluster of pebble-sized pimples dotting her fleshy forehead.

"Mr. Welch," she hissed. "Am I disturbing you?"

"Always. What do you want?"

"I want to confirm that we're confirmed."

"Good-bye." I started to close the door.

"Mr.Welch,nextThursday,fourP.M.sharp,I'mlookingforwardtoit!"

The door shut, still the creature kept talking.

"Mr. Welch, I'll need an *hour*."

"Ten minutes," I said as my head fell against the wavy glass.

"Twenty!"

"Ten, and no more."

"Ten, *perfect*," she said, and then, thank God, she was gone.

Aw, fuck it. Against the strong advice of legal counsel, her real name is printed here. Bea Myerly.

Memorize the name and steel yourself. Should you meet her someday, remember—you've been warned.

BEA MYERLY

I love Mr. Welch. I love Mr. Welch.

KATE

THAT NIGHT, WHILE I WAS GIVING THE BOYS A BUBBLE BATH, TIM BURST THROUGH
the bathroom door, startling me. Teddy thrust out his sudsy arms, and
both boys shouted, "Daddy, Daddy!" I left them in the bathroom. There
was dinner to fix.

As sometimes happened, Tim had too much energy. Because he'd
left the house early and hadn't seen the boys yet, his day with them was
just starting, which explained his need to overcompensate. I knew from
the shouting and splashing in the bathroom that it wouldn't be easy
getting the boys to bed.

It wasn't, and later, I was the one insisting Teddy and Sam go to
sleep. Or else. Or else what? Or else there'll be problems. Or else no
special treats tomorrow. Or else no videos for a week. I was running out
of *or else*s. Standing in the dark hallway, Tim sighed heavily. I knew
what he was thinking—*You're too harsh*—but I would have none of it,
saying, "Easy to judge when you've been out all day." Finally, and that's
another part of this I always seem to forget, *there is always a finally*, after
a valiant fight, night won, and the boys were down.

It was past nine o'clock. A slant of light from the hall cut across their
tiny room, and Tim and I stood in the doorway. As we stared at the
boys, whose shapes could be vaguely made out, I remembered something Tim once said: Children fall asleep so you can love them again.

But there were dirty dishes in the sink, toys scattered in every room,
pillows and clothes and other general stuff that needed to be put
away.

PETER HEDGES

As we tried to finish straightening up, each chore led to another chore—bagging up the trash became sorting newspapers and plastic bottles for the weekly recycling pickup; sorting mail became paying bills, which became looking for the checkbook, which became calling our bank's automated phone line to get an accurate balance, punching in account numbers and codes, which became punching in the wrong password, which became hanging up and starting the process all over. When finished with the friendly tape-recorded voice, after having transferred nearly our entire savings account into checking, I wrote out checks for the bills we could afford to pay, left the unpaid bills for later, which led to a search for the newly purchased sheet of stamps, which were not in their regular spot, because we'd never decided on a spot for stamps. "I know they're around here somewhere," Tim said. Twenty minutes later, he found half a roll of stamps, but because of a recent postage increase, he had to paste two on each bill, muttering, "What's an extra stamp for rich people like us?," which made me laugh, although I could have gone the other way.

It was sometime after eleven P.M. when I came into our room and found Tim already in bed. He'd propped himself up with extra pillows and powered up our laptop and gone online. I put on my flannel night-gown, climbed in on my side, and waited for him to finish.

The best quality of the disaster that was my mother was her sincere interest in hearing about my day. So no matter where we were living, either in a tent, or at Willow Song (a now defunct commune just outside of Eugene, Oregon), or in the A-frame in Eureka, wherever she and I were, she made sure to find the time in those minutes before sleep to hear every detail of my day. It was our ritual, and Tim learned early on that it was sacred to me, so even now, at the end of every day, we tell each other what happened.

I fell in love with Tim one fall day in Berkeley. We'd taken a long hike in Strawberry Canyon. Tired, we sat down between two oak trees, and he rested his head in my lap. As he talked on and on (about what I don't remember), I watched him fighting off sleep, the way his legs and arms gave in, his eyes open at first, then closed. I liked especially how his voice seemed eager to counter the seemingly inevitable shutdown of the rest of him—his mouth, which is his most appealing feature, kept moving—he wanted, I realized, to tell me *everything*. As if to say, *Here, this is all of me.* He seemed worried it wouldn't be enough. And it wasn't that I expected him to tell me everything, but I loved that he was willing to try. And yes, in addition to the fact that I found him funny, and that he said I made him laugh more than anyone ever had, it was this willingness, this desire to tell everything—the muck, the petty parts, all of it—that sealed the deal.

Closing the laptop, Tim smiled, disappointed, and said, "They won."

"Aw, sweetie," I said.

"Terrible of me, huh? Wanting him to lose."

"No," I said. "It makes sense."

During basketball season, Tim religiously checked one particular women's NCAA Division III basketball score. The Cayton College Lady Revolvers were coached by the Ohio legend Jack Welch, Tim's father. Coach Welch had more wins than any coach in women's collegiate Division III history.

Tim rolled onto his side, facing me, and said, "Wait till you hear what happened today." Then he recounted his day of teaching, saying it was one of his best ever, and he was so sweet about it that even though I wasn't in the mood, I pulled off his pajama bottoms and touched him with my hands.

"But, Kate, you haven't told me about you."

I didn't stop.

"Not until you tell me—"

So I recounted the dullest parts of my day but whispered them as if these were my darkest, dirtiest sex thoughts. "Today I buttered toast. I licked the muffin batter off the wooden spoon. I pulled the sled in the snow." And after he came, I said, "So, that was my day."

Later, as we lay there, lit only by the glow from the Mickey Mouse night-light, what I hadn't told him began to bother me. It seemed silly, I thought, to withhold, so I said, "I met this woman today."

"Oh," he said.

Then I tried to describe her. The skin, the eyes, the gleaming Botticelli-like hair. The kind, unexpected gift of her light blue scarf. I did my best to objectively render the irrefutable astonishingness of Anna Brody, because to render her otherwise would be to deceive. This was my reasoning for why I had brought her into our bed. To my surprise, Tim said nothing, didn't even ask her name. Turning his way, I saw why. He'd fallen fast asleep and was, I think, already dreaming.

TIM

THAT TUESDAY, AT THE APPOINTED HOUR, BEA'S SIGNATURE KNOCK ECHOED THROUGH my office. Opening the door, I discovered she was not alone. Standing behind her was Jeremy Nathan. Tall and skinny, like taffy stretched too far, his bony shoulders rounded, his thick glasses magnifying his already large eyes, Jeremy was a curious mix of a beardless Abe Lincoln and a bullfrog.

"I hope we're not early," Bea said with a smile.

Liar, I thought, but said nothing.

Bea studied the scene. I had my winter coat on, my backpack zipped up, my desk unusually tidy—she saw I had other plans, plans that did not include her.

"Mr. Welch, you understand we have a deadline."

"Yes, Bea. Ten minutes, as promised."

"I worried you'd forgotten."

"Nonsense. I've been looking forward to it."

For weeks Bea Myerly had been leaving notes, making surprise visits in an attempt to pin me down. I'd postponed the interview twice. But she wasn't to be dissuaded, finally engaging the services of Mitchell Struck, the prissy assistant to the headmistress, who had explained in blunt terms that I was to make myself available for a face-to-face and that I should feel honored to have been chosen as the first faculty member to be profiled in the exciting new column entitled "Teacher Feature."

Bea explained the reason for Jeremy's presence that afternoon. As photographer for both the yearbook and the *Montague Missive*, Jeremy

23

had come along to take a photo. But because he'd recently broken his Pentax, he held in his bony fingers a yellow disposable camera.

Bea said, "Jeremy will be fast."

Confused, I looked in no particular direction as the camera suddenly flashed. Bea practically shoved Jeremy out the door while I vainly suggested a second picture be taken.

"Oh, no." Bea snorted. "Your time is *precious.*"

In quick succession, Bea produced a tape recorder, a handheld microphone, a pad of paper with several pages of questions written out, a bottle of water, and a plastic cup ("For when your mouth dries up from all the talking"). Then she pressed record and fired the first question.

I did my best to answer, saying yes, I was from Ohio, yes, I did my undergraduate studies at UC Berkeley, and yes, my dissertation was progressing nicely. I refused to answer her question about favorite historical figures, claiming there were too many to list and it would be a pity if we found ourselves out of time. "After all, Bea, the clock is ticking."

The way she nervously consulted her notes reminded me that I hadn't always disliked Bea Myerly. There was a time in those early days when I appreciated her hard work, her thoughtful questions and studious nature. Mostly, though, I pride myself on my fondness for the misfit student. Somehow, however, over time, Bea had imperceptibly crossed the line to become my least favorite student ever.

"Why did you choose history to be your life's work?"

"The truth?"

"Always."

"Well, Bea, I became a historian to escape the tyranny of being the small non-basketball-playing son of arguably the third-most-successful coach in the history of women's Division III college basketball."

"Do you care to elaborate?"

Apparently, I did. "History brought me comfort. No matter how bad things got when I was growing up, I knew somewhere in history there was a story or an account of someone enduring a worse experience."

"So for you, history was a way to feel good about yourself?"

"Well, we're talking about when I was eight or nine. Some kids set off fireworks or shot frogs with their BB guns. I read Herodotus. I read Gibbon. The Bible, even, although as an historical document, it's rather suspect. History helped me deal with it all."

Bea was too busy searching her notes for a next question, so I continued uninterrupted. "You see, Bea, the great gift we give others is the permission to change us. Please, enter my world, leave me bettered, leave me smarter, leave me more alive, but above all, *change me*. History is about how we change. History is about why we change. History is about what happens when we don't, when we resist. History is . . ."

A smarter man would've stopped. Me? Desperate for the right words, I flailed on: "History is . . . the great collective . . . ball of stuff . . . from which we . . . uhm . . ."

With that, Bea Myerly stood up and quickly gathered her things.

"Wait—is that it?" I asked.

"Ten minutes, Mr. Welch. You were very clear."

"But I could spare a few more minutes . . ."

A few? It was now one entire ninety-minute audiocassette later. I even stopped midsentence while Bea ran out to buy more blank tapes.

I have to give her credit. For the last hour and a half, she'd been listening with the contented smile of a lottery winner. And who could blame her? Not only was Mr. Welch sharing secrets, he seemed to be enjoying himself. I even joked at one point, "Oh, the catharsis of it all." Bea did her part, sighing along with me in the appropriate places, her eyes welling up as she heard how the coach's son couldn't dribble a basketball, how I was too short to play, how I was uncoordinated and bruised easily and was not inspired by the dank smell of locker rooms. So what did little Timmy Welch do? I became a scholar of the game. I learned the difference between a 2-1-2 zone and a 2-3 zone, the pros and cons of the four-corner offense, when to full-court press, the correct hand placement and wrist flick for a set shot. My bedroom became a shrine to the Cayton College

Lady Revolvers, and I became the ball boy/unofficial stat keeper/special assistant coach/unpaid team scout and the backup team mascot once I was tall enough to fill out the life-size foam-rubber silver bullet.

I told Bea everything as fast as I could remember it. How it was my older sister, Sal, who was the player. And what a player she was—15.6 ppg., 5.2 reb., 1993 Division III second team all-American. I told Bea about Game Day, the endless succession of Game Days, and the constant pressure in the house. Would the Lady Revolvers win? (We almost always did.) And when we did, the concern instantly became whether we'd win again. What about the occasional loss that occurred every other season? At age eight or nine, I would collapse on the gym floor in tears, until my mother remembered to scoop me up and take me home. But by age ten, I began to wonder if there was more to life. Surely there had to be. Then one day I flipped through a picture book of Matthew Brady's Civil War photographs and was transported. The Civil War. Finally, here was something worth getting upset over. I went from picture books to real books. I kept on reading. The War of the Roses, the War of 1812, World Wars I and II. So many wars! History brought the welcome perspective I craved. Plagues, revolutions, the long decline of the Roman Empire—these became my passions. For the first time, I felt balanced and free. Yes, I still had to attend the games, but somehow, sitting halfway up the bleachers, I managed to keep reading book after book, looking up occasionally to check the score, and usually only after my mother gave me a sharp elbow to the ribs.

It felt good to tell someone, even Bea Myerly. We were both laughing when the phone rang. I answered it. It was Kate, none too pleased. "Where are you?"

I looked at the small clock on my desk. *Uh-oh.* I was supposed to have been home an hour earlier.

Kate said nothing. She didn't need to. The boys were crying in the background.

I said, "I'm sor—" but she'd already hung up the phone.

———

That night, back at home, I was in even more trouble. Kate had left a not-so-subtle note: *Deal with this!*

In moments, I was clutching the final disconnection notice from the phone company, standing in our kitchen with the receiver wedged between my right ear and shoulder. This particular final disconnection notice was emphatic. Call immediately, make special arrangements, or else service would be terminated Tuesday. Well, it *was* Tuesday. And I'd been put on hold. I had a terrible thought—*They might even terminate service while I'm holding!* Just then a miracle, an operator—I'm sorry, a customer service representative—came on. She sounded pleasant enough, as if she had a sense of humor, so I said, "I'm sorry to hear about your troubles." She didn't answer. "Times must be tough," I continued. Phone company employee: "How do you mean?" "Tell me, will Verizon go broke or be shut down if you don't receive our $73.42 immediately?" Not amused, she explained my "option." (I was not aware that *one* possibility constituted an option.) We would need to pay the next day, in person, by five P.M., and only a money order would be accepted. Click.

Humiliated, I set the phone in its cradle and put the cap back on the pen with which I'd been doodling. Looking down at the back of the envelope, I saw the damage. I'd covered it with squiggles, blotting out a phone number Kate had written down and retracing a name I didn't know—someone Brody.

That night, after a war was fought to get both boys in bed, I knew what was coming. In bed with the lights out, Kate turned on her side, faced me, and attempted to discuss certain pressing budgetary matters. "How can we cut back, spend less? How are we going to survive another year on your salary?" She said it innocently enough, but her question cut. I said, "Oh, please, honey. Not now. Not after tonight with the boys, not after the Bea Myerly of it all." Kate: "I'm worried." Me: "But we have more stuff than ninety-eight percent of the world's population. Do you know how far my salary could take us in Kenya or Mozambique?"

I'd used this tactic before, but always with different countries. Kate usually countered, "Tim, we don't live in those places." And I'd say, "Yes, and we should be grateful," even though, I don't know, maybe those countries are the most magnificent places in the world to live. Maybe we'd be ecstatically happy walking among the naked peoples of wherever people are naked. Maybe we should be terribly sad and wake up weeping that not only did we not live in these places, we had never seen these places. If presented with this argument, Kate would sigh, "You're impossible," and I'd almost say, "Maybe we should move," knowing full well that Kate didn't want to move. She loved the Heights. She loved its panoramic view of lower Manhattan, its bucolic-looking streets with sweet idyllic-sounding names—Cranberry Street, Pineapple Street, Orange and Willow, Grace Court, Love Lane, Sydney Place, Garden Place, Willow Place—and most especially, that street of streets, our street, Oak Lane, that lone leafy block of dreamy childhoods and a favorite of Christmas carolers: The old brick fronts with the bluestone sidewalks and the original cobblestone paving gave a group of carolers the acoustic equivalent of Carnegie Hall. The sound, the bounce! Five singers felt like fifty. Bottom line: Kate didn't want to move, and it would be unfair of me to threaten it. Moving for Kate was equivalent to the abuse of children, for as a child, she had moved often, sometimes monthly, at least once a year.

Because Kate had heard my Mozambique argument before, I was disappointed when she provided no valid counterattack. Instead, she grew quiet and said, sniffling, "I was just trying to think of a way to make it easier for you, a way to relieve some of the pressure."

"There's no pressure," I said, lying. Kate covered her available ear with a pillow. Regrettably, I snapped, "Well, if you're so worried about money, maybe you should get a job."

That was when she let the pillow fall away. "It's funny you'd say that, because Bruno called. He wants to have lunch."

When we first moved to New York, Kate worked for Bruno Schwine at the Foundation for an Ethical Future. When Kate quit to raise our boys, Bruno left to start his own consulting firm, absurdly named Bruno Schwine Associates, even though he was the only employee. At the time Kate had scolded Bruno because he'd gone to work for the enemy, as a freelance adviser to that biotech behemoth, the Monsanto Corporation.

"He may have some ideas," she said carefully. "Maybe even a job offer."

"Bruno Schwine?" I snorted. "Fine, knock yourself out!"

KATE

ALL MORNING I WORRIED ABOUT WHAT TO WEAR. I TRIED THE GRAY PANTSUIT, THE beige silk shirt, and the pearl earrings; I tried the tan slacks, the light blue blouse, and my tiny teacup earrings; I tried the faded jeans, the striped pink sweater, and no earrings. After trying nearly every conceivable combination of my best and favorite clothes, I decided to start over from scratch. I was naked when the phone rang.

Part of me hoped it was Bruno Schwine calling to cancel, since this little decision of what to wear was proving too big for me. It wasn't that I was excessively vain; but I knew my choice of clothes would say a great deal about my intentions, and I didn't know what mine were. Was I a mother at this lunch, or a future employee, or was I, quite simply, an old friend meeting to talk about old times?

Picking up the phone, I heard static. It was a bad connection.

"Kate?"

"Yes?"

It was someone calling from a cell phone.

"Who is it?"

"It's Anna. Anna Brody."

Anna Brody who had left a message the week before, Anna Brody whose number I couldn't read because my husband had doodled on the back of the envelope where I'd written it, Anna Brody who wasn't listed in the Manhattan phone book, the Brooklyn phone book, or with directory assistance. "Oh," I said, "I've been wanting to call you."

"It's all right."

"No, I can explain. See, one of my kids scribbled on the piece of paper where I'd wrote your number." *Wrote?* "I mean written."

"Is this a bad time?"

I'm naked, I'm late, and you're not Bruno Schwine calling to cancel. "Yes," I said. "It kind of is."

"I'm sorry to keep calling . . ."

"No, no, it's no bother."

"I just wanted to ask you something about the neighborhood."

"Go ahead," I said as I stepped into my underwear.

"Philip's worried . . ."

Philip, I decided, must be her husband.

"He's worried I'll be bored."

"When my Teddy says he's bored, I tell him he's not bored. He's *boring*."

"You do not."

"No, but I will when he gets older, because it's what I believe. Or what I've been told to believe."

She laughed.

"We absolutely love it here," I told her. "The people are nice. It's beautiful. You can walk pretty much everywhere. Best part is even if one of your distant relatives dies, your neighbors will bring you homemade soups, cookies, and trays of lasagna. You won't have to cook for weeks. And since you have money . . ."

I stopped midthought. *Oops.*

But Anna seemed completely at ease. "Go on, Kate," she said. "Since I have money . . . ?"

"There's no end to what you can do here." I checked the clock by our bed. *Late, so late.* "Maybe we could speak more later?"

"Not necessary. You see, the truth is . . . ?"

"Yes?"

"You more than answered my questions."

"I did?"

The signal momentarily faded.

"Kate, can you hear me? You know this isn't . . . connection. Look, I'll call ag—sometime. Soon."

Until Teddy was born, I worked with Bruno at the Foundation for an Ethical Future. We were a ragtag, indefatigable bunch of futurists. We were never about predicting what would happen. We merely tried to imagine what could. Our work was to help our clients "rehearse" their responses to a variety of possible futures. As our fearless leader, Bruno had the idea to use the scenario-creating techniques developed by the RAND Corporation in the 1950s that had been modified for business purposes by Royal Dutch/Shell after the 1973 oil embargo. Bruno's genius was to apply these same techniques to various nonprofits. We didn't have much money, but we had the belief that these organizations and community groups (the Vera Institute of Justice, the Eliot Feld Ballet, etc.) were as important as weapons of mass destruction and our addiction to oil, and, more important, we had that most underrated and essential of currencies—the belief that we were right.

When I arrived at Siggy's Good Food on Henry Street, I looked right past the bone-thin man waving in my direction. I was embarrassed about not recognizing Bruno right away. But he didn't look well. His cheeks were hollow, and he was much too skinny. Still, he smiled as I sat down. "Pictures, please," he said.

I brought out the pocket-size photo album I carried of the boys. Bruno fawned over each picture, noting that Teddy looked just like Tim, and Sam had some of me.

I asked if he was well.

"Better now that I'm with you." He paused, but not long enough for me to ask what was up with his health. "Kate, question: Have you heard of Louis Underfer?"

"Can't say that I have."

"Have you heard of Cortez?"

"The conquistador?"

"No, the corporation."

"Sorry," I said. "But I'm well versed in Barney and Big Bird."

Bruno laughed faintly, took my hands, and said, "I want to make this as easy as possible for you." He had just returned from his fortieth high school reunion in Webster Groves, Missouri, where he had reconnected with his childhood adversary, Louis Underfer, the billionaire founder/CEO of Cortez.

"Google him, and you'll learn more than you need to know. Anyway, Louis is almost as rich as he is guilty. Which is good for us."

Bruno went on to explain that during the reunion barbecue, in front of several former classmates, he had attacked Louis about the dangerous and irresponsible actions of giant corporations like Cortez, accusing them all of "careless disregard for the children and the children's children." Louis walked away in a huff, but apparently, Bruno had gotten under his skin, because Bruno said proudly, "He called me when I got to New York and offered me a job. I hung up. When he called back, I said, 'Why should I work for you?' And this is what he said: 'You're right, Bruno. I'm a blessed man. I can do more, but I need your help. Make me better.'"

Bruno explained that Louis Underfer already had a foundation in place. He wanted Bruno to help him figure out where to give his money.

"So I named my price, and also named yours, insisting that I'd only be willing to work with him if I could hire the brightest, most tenacious, and most ethical person I've ever encountered."

Like my mother, Bruno tended to exaggerate. But he was convincing, because he nearly made me a believer.

He went on, "We can go over the details later, but basically, we'll be seeking out worthy organizations and award them grants." He added with a wink, "We'll be Santa, but without the suit."

Bruno was the most flirtatious homosexual I'd ever known. At times he seemed to have a crush on me. The sweet kind, though, much like how a boy feels toward his best friend's little sister. Innocent.

Nothing sexual. Other times he exuded a kind of paternal pride, as if I were the daughter he'd always yearned for and never had.

"Think about it."

I promised I would.

"Oh, I hope you'll like this—we won't be starting until the fall. And since we're giving away Louis Underfer's blood money, here's what I imagined for your salary." He wrote down an amount on the back of a paper napkin and slid it my way.

After my lunch with Bruno, I was too wound up to head straight home. So I walked to the Promenade, still clutching the napkin. My mind was racing. Maybe because I was both giddy and scared, I made up a little poem. I even sang it to myself as I stood in my favorite spot and looked across the East River to Manhattan.

> Bruno Schwine is sick
>> The sky is clear blue
> Anna Brody called me
>> Look at this view

That was what I wished I had told Anna Brody: *It's the view. You can't be bored here because of the view.*

To this day Tim believes he did the convincing. As we walked over the Brooklyn Bridge that first time, he tried to dazzle me with the history of its construction, the story of the man who'd designed it, his son who'd built it, and the son's wife who'd made sure it was finished. But in truth, it was the view. Not from the bridge—no, it was the view I saw once we'd made it to the other side. Sure, I'd seen it in photographs and often in films and on television. That day, standing on the Promenade, a slight breeze blowing, the whoosh of traffic racing below on the BQE, looking across New York Harbor at majestic Manhattan and where the Twin Towers had once been, I had the distinct feeling this place could be home.

Tim already knew the view. He'd paced the Promenade just days earlier in the moments before his interview with Dr. Millicent Vandeventer, the controversial headmistress and founder of Montague Academy. It was a quick interview, and he was hired, because Dr. Millicent Vandeventer was in desperate need of a teacher. Had she more time, Tim believed, she'd have kept looking; had a car not crashed into a restaurant window in Cambridge, Massachusetts, running over nearly twenty people and killing four, one of whom was Sadie Brier, the recent Phi Beta Kappa graduate from Harvard, who had been hired to teach history at Montague. Had this not happened, Tim never would have gotten the job, nor would he have formulated one of his most popular teaching games—Bad News/Good News. An example: It was *bad news* that William McKinley was assassinated. It was *good news* that Teddy Roosevelt became president. Or: It was *bad news* that they crucified Jesus, because it's not nice to kill God's only son. It was *good news* that they crucified Jesus, because He had the good fortune to be God's only son, and if they hadn't . . . and so forth, so on, etc. Tim's idea is that one way to soften life's cruel blows is to understand that your bad news is quite likely someone else's good news. But the reverse is also true: Our good fortune came at the expense of young Sadie Brier, who never got to teach at Montague. And now, to add to the pile, I had just been offered a tasty job at a rather inflated salary, while my former boss, Bruno Schwine, was not only facing a summer of treatments for colon and prostate cancer, he also had a constellation of suspicious moles on his backside that may very well have been melanoma. Bad news, indeed.

That afternoon when I returned home, I found the boys standing at the top of our stairwell, begging me to hurry up the steps. "You got a box!" Teddy shouted. The boys hoped for toys, but Tim knew better, because the box was a crate, and on the side was stamped HEIGHTS LIQUOR.

Tim said, "It was just delivered."

"Mommy, open it, open it!"

Tim used the claw from our hammer to pry open the crate. Inside were twelve bottles of expensive wines, reds and whites. Inside a second, gift-wrapped smaller box was a bottle of Cristal. "Yippee," Tim said, pleased, because he drinks only champagne.

Disappointed, the boys returned to the living room/dining room/ toy room, where they had been watching a video. I wanted to tell Tim about Bruno's proposal, but he insisted I open the small envelope taped to the box, so I did. The note was written on Frida Fabritz's personal stationery.

Kate—

For the biggest single home sale (by far) in the history of the Heights, I have you to thank. My client says that you, and you alone, made the difference.

Enjoy.

TIM

OH, WE WERE DRUNK, AND IT WAS LATE, AND KATE HAD BEEN CRYPTIC AT BEST. AND I, barely a drinker, kept draining the champagne from my flute (really a glass) while begging for details. Since the work was with Bruno, it would be important but low-paying. "Au contraire," Kate said. The money? Spectacular. How much? Kate was almost embarrassed by the figure. How was she to wrap her mind around the fact that by quitting work to have children, that by virtue of being out of the loop for a fistful of years, she would have increased her value threefold . . .

Ha, there it was.

Her value had increased threefold!

"Wow," I said.

"I know," Kate said, not believing it herself.

Even this drunk husband couldn't help but notice the change in his wife. The six-figure job offer had given Kate a renewed sense of her own worth. It was all over her. Mostly, it was in her eyes.

The possibility of it all must have been too much for her, because Kate started turning off the lights and said, "Let's talk about it tomorrow."

"What's to talk about?" I said, following her. "Take the job with Bruno Schwine, work hard for a year, make buckets of money."

"But the kids. What about the kids?"

"What about them?"

"I can't leave them with a babysitter."

"You don't have to. I'll take care of them."

"What about your teaching?"

"I'll take the year off. It'll be like a sabbatical."

"You'd be willing to do that?"

My mind began to race with this new possibility. I could finish my dissertation. And enough with teaching other people's children. What about *our* children? Even Sam had begun to complain about the size of our home. And hadn't Kate sometimes joked, "Something has to give."

So now here it was—life was giving.

"You'd really take care of the boys?"

"It's my turn to be the one at home."

Kate, later, in the dark: "Are you sure?"

"Yes," I said as we fucked. *Yes.*

And so it was decided.

TIM

SOME DAYS YOU FEEL LIKE YOU'RE IN A MOVIE. THE DAY I DECIDED TO BREAK THE news was one of those days.

All of April and much of May, I'd been in a teaching slump. Why? Was it the decision Kate and I had made? Or that it was still a secret?

When I woke up that particular Friday morning, I knew it was time. Bad news was best delivered on Fridays. Give the students a weekend to recover. It was only fair.

What I didn't expect was how different it would feel that day. As I climbed the stone steps to the academy, it was as if I'd been given a new set of eyes, as if my head had been wrapped in soft gauze. Each student, my fellow teachers, even Dr. Millicent Vandeventer appeared warm and fuzzy and backlit with an auburn glow. It was as if behind every move I made, every word I spoke, an orchestra played.

A faint, lone oboe caressed the air as I typed my resignation letter on my Underwood No. 5 manual. Enter flutes and a French horn as I was ushered into Dr. Vandeventer's oak-paneled office. A chorus of fifty German singers hummed as I requested a leave of absence for one year, during which I would "study and reflect" on my experience at Montague and "yes, absolutely, finish the dissertation." I expected Dr. Vandeventer to be upset by this request, particularly with it coming so late in the year. To my dismay, she seemed elated. She nearly shot out of her wheelchair to a standing position; she nearly danced on her desk.

Before her stroke, Dr. Vandeventer had been a bright, vital force but was, truth be told, a rather nasty person. After the stroke, apart from the wheelchair and a tendency to slur words, only one aspect of her changed: She got nastier. She had long suspected—and I didn't agree—that her history department suffered from a lack of diligence and rigor. Here was her chance to change all that, to find the next Sadie Brier, whose ghost probably kept appearing before Dr. Vandeventer, reminding her what could've been. Born Vera Milhinkowitz, Dr. Vandeventer had chosen her new name, it was believed, just days before she crossed the platform to receive her doctorate from SUNY Buffalo. An Ivy League wannabe, she loved nothing more than to crow about the high number of Montague graduates attending the Harvards, the Yales, the Princetons. The rumors, if true, told of the former Vera Milhinkowitz and her wild bohemian youth. Among her conquests: two ambassadors, a recent president of Dartmouth, a Nobel laureate economist, sundry award-winning poets, and a female Supreme Court justice. Oh, the stories—men, women, men *and* women—here was someone, pre-stroke and post-stroke, who'd eagerly fuck a great mind. If you were sexy and stupid, she had no interest. Or if your dissertation topic didn't appeal to her.

(During that first interview, as I described my work on the history of loss, her brow wrinkled up and her mouth pulled back in horror. "It seems rather unformed," she said. "It's early," I said. "Young man," she said, "it's never early." Then, as she stared at me with her cold, bloodless eyes, she said, "I have a feeling the students here are really going to like you." I thanked her. "It's not a compliment," she said. "To me, it'll just mean you're doing something wrong.")

That morning, as she wheeled me to the door, she positively glowed. She extended her hand, and I held it. How cool and smooth and soft was her skin. She looked up, smiled slightly, and cooed, "Timothy, your going away will be good for all of us." I couldn't believe what I did next. I bent down to kiss her. Unfortunately, she saw me coming and had already started to wheel herself back to her desk. Finding only air, I made a smacking sound with my lips so we'd both know I'd tried.

Fifth period, World History. Bea Myerly was in the middle of her oral presentation on the obscure Gnostic rites of the Byzantine Empire. It was to be only a five-minute talk, but Bea was in minute twelve with an inch-high stack of index cards left to get through.

"Excuse me, Bea?"

She kept talking at her usual debater-like clip.

Others in the class had to help shout her down. "Bea. *Bea!*"

"Can we finish this up Monday?"

"But—"

"Thank you, Bea."

Sulking, she gathered up her note cards, her audiovisual aids, the poster board with the Byzantine time line printed out in five colors of ink. She clomped to her desk and sat down, part pissed, part humiliated.

This did not faze me, as I knew who was in charge. I also knew that it was important to finesse the delivery of my disappointing news. My plan was to simply tell them the truth. Leave enough time for the impact to land. Then, when the bell rings, exit fast. Easy.

But after checking the clock, I saw that I'd left too much time. "Hey," I said, as if hit with a terrific idea. "Let's talk. What's on your mind?"

Nothing, it seemed. No one spoke up.

"We've got a few minutes left. What do you want to talk about?"

The only sound was Bea slumping down farther in her chair.

"Come on, now's your chance. Ask me anything. Max? Joni?"

A short, fleshy arm rose slowly, the plump hand and stubby fingers stretched high.

"Anybody?"

The lone arm in the air started to wave back and forth like a metronome picking up speed, making it even harder for me to ignore that front-row sitter, that extra-credit doer, that proverbial burr in my ass.

"Yes, Bea?"

"What's the most important thing you ever learned?"

I have a weakness for the sincere question. And Bea Myerly seemed sincere.

"That's a pretty broad question, Bea. Could you be more specific?"

She smiled. "Yes, in fact, I'm glad for the opportunity. What's the most important thing you learned *in high school*?"

"That's easy. There's really only one useful thing I learned in high school. I use it all the time. And it may actually be the only thing I truly believe."

I had their attention now.

"Wow, Mr. Welch. Will you please tell us?"

"Sorry, can't."

"You can't?"

"Oh, no. If I told you, I'd lose my job."

"That's not fair!" Bea shrieked.

"And that was the second most important lesson—life is not fair."

Bea and the others were not pleased.

"Okay, look, after you graduate, I'll tell you."

More groans.

Bea: "But we don't graduate for another year!"

The others: "Tell us! You won't lose your job! We won't tell anyone!"

I checked the clock. Under a minute left. *How to segue, oh boy.* Then it came to me. *Perfect,* I thought. *I'll drop it in a subordinate clause.*

I couldn't have planned it better.

"How will I know you won't tell anyone? Next year, *while I'm away on a leave of absence,* I won't be able to keep tabs on—"

Before any of the others could register a reaction or ask who was taking my place, Bea let out a gasp. One loud gasp, like a cannonball in the gut.

I looked around at the others. They needed more time to process.

That was when Bea let her head drop. It thudded on her textbook.

Well, it was embarrassing—she let out a cry so loud, so long, that none of the other students could express their own feelings.

The bell rang, and while the other students gathered their things and hurried off to their next classes, Bea Myerly didn't move and cried well into the next period, which, of course, was my free period.

"Please, Bea," I said. "Be happy for me."

She looked up and, with tears streaming, said, "Mr. Welch, this will be your undoing." Then she gathered up her things and fled the room.*

---

* What follows is the most important thing I ever learned in high school. I'd like to thank my high school Driver's Ed teacher, Mr. Rex Lambo, who told me what I'm about to tell you while we both guarded the punch bowl at my senior prom.

Imagine you find someone attractive. Are you picturing a person? Good. Now imagine you have the good fortune to give this person a hug. Are you hugging him or her? Nice, huh? Now, if, during the hug, this person pats you on your back or your shoulder, you can be sure of one thing: This person will never sleep with you.

I should add that if the person doesn't pat you, it does not guarantee he or she will sleep with you. It merely means he or she might.

Also, if you're a man and you're confused by the above, I've simplified it for you—if she pats, you'll be left holding your own bat.

There you have it. The truest thing you'll ever hear.

TWO

KATE

WHEN SUMMER CAME, EVERYONE FLED—WELL, NOT EVERYONE, JUST THE ADAIRS, the Adamses, the Alexander-Lowells, the Baxters, the Boydens, the Brills, the Cahills, the Carpenters, the Cass-Wentworths, and the Davis-Hargroves, to list a few, to their country homes, their oceanfront beach houses, their rented rustic cabins on glacial lakes, with destinations as varied as the Vineyard, the Cape, Sag Harbor, the Hamptons, Bucks County, the Adirondacks, the Berkshires, the islands Shelter, Fire, and Block. Mothers and weekend fathers and children loaded up their SUVs, strapped bicycles to the rack, drove away the minute school let out in early June, not returning until after Labor Day, not until they were tanned, with sun-drenched hair, pink-peeling noses, and bodies lean and limber from aerobics, tennis, and sailing. Others went farther—Ireland, Italy, Greece—others farther still, and where were Tim and I during all this extravagance? At home with the kids in our un-air-conditioned apartment, where, except for one unfortunate weekend, we had a terrific summer—the best ever.

For Tim, however, it began with a bump. In previous years, within days of turning in final grades, he'd speak of his great ache to be back in the classroom. That summer I thought he'd ache more than ever. Fortunately for us but sadly for him, any desire to teach disappeared the moment he opened the end-of-school edition of the *Montague Missive*. He'd mentioned in passing that a feature interview/article would be appearing. One night while we were sharing a bath, he admitted his eagerness to read it, for even though the interview had been conducted

by his least-favorite student ever, he had found the conversation surprising, far-ranging, thrilling, even. I thought it was cute how he confessed to waiting for the mail each day. (The last edition of the *Missive*
is mailed each year after graduation to students, faculty, alumni, and
the board of trustees.) I even overheard him phone Lucinda Watts, the
school secretary, to ask if she knew when the *Missive* would be put in
the mail. "Soon," she assured him.

Too soon, it turned out. On the day it arrived Tim had already left
for the library. I opened the *Missive* to find that the entire interview/
article had been excised, leaving just a photograph—arguably the worst
picture ever taken of my rather nonphotogenic husband. There was
Tim, his face filling an entire page of the paper, Tim, looking up from
his cluttered desk, Tim, his eyes half closed, his mouth half open, stupidly, as if midyawn. Below, in large emphatic block print, was this
caption: HISTORY. And then under it, typeset in tiny script: *Mr. Welch
takes a leave of absence to finally finish his dissertation. Bon voyage!*

Debbie Beebe had called to warn me it was coming, and Claudia
Valentine, who was with me at the time, needed only a quick peek before she wondered out loud if we could sue. When Tim arrived home,
I tried to pretend I hadn't seen the photo, but one glance at my pained
face and he knew. He understood the awkward circumstance I was in,
as there was no bright side to the photograph, no argument to be made
that might give a welcome perspective. Tim returned to the photo,
squinted for a long moment, then quickly balled up the paper and
tossed it heroically into the trash. Done. Forgotten. It was agreed. We
would never speak of the picture again. But it had to hurt. "No," he said
after I asked him. "I'm not bothered a bit." Disbelieving, I studied his
face as he looked away, and in a brief flash of something very real, I saw
a sense of relief. To his credit, he didn't mope or pout. Rather, the insult
of it all seemed to energize him. He worked a good portion of each day
on his dissertation. But even better, when he was with the boys and me
that summer, he was with us.

Fourth of July weekend, we rented a car and traveled to Gettysburg. Hearing my husband attempt an explanation of the Civil War to his two sons, the older four and a half, the younger nearly three, made me want to undress him. Not because he did it well (he didn't) and not because they understood all that he told them (they didn't) but mainly because he tried, grasping at phrasings, stuttering as he attempted to boil America's bloodiest battle down to its preschool essence. "You know how you and Sam sometimes fight?" Tim resorted to saying. Teddy, his mouth discolored from a red, white, and blue Popsicle, nodded between licks. "Imagine you and all your friends fighting. Can you do that?" Tim must have known Teddy had no interest. But this did not stop him. And I didn't want to stop him, because the minute he gave up his premature history lecture would be the minute we'd have to climb back in the rental car and drive to the Gettysburg mall parking lot and locate Booth 48, where my mother, Ariel, and her common-law husband, Hal, were displaying my mother's artwork for sale.

My mother is an artist. Part of me would like to leave it at that. Leave you with your own idea of what an artist is. But to say she is an artist, while kind, is to mislead you. Greater specificity is required. My mother—the ex-hippie, herbalist, cigarette-smoking vegan—is a driftwood artist. Meaning: Three months each year, she combs the beaches of both coasts (especially the log-strewn great Northwest) where various shapes of certain saltwater-logged woods wash ashore. The first time she explained her process, I listened closely. But after realizing that a chasm existed between her description of "the work" and the reality of said work, I chose to forget what she tried to explain. Simply, and it's all rather simple, this wood washes ashore, she collects it, she dries it out (the larger pieces take a few weeks), and she "listens" to the wood. Not literally. She looks at the wood and waits until the shape suggests itself to her. For instance, the most common of shapes to suggest itself is a coiled snake. Or the half-coiled snake. Or the slithering snake. Listening to the wood is basically a process of determining where to place/ glue the two plastic eyes, for the amazing thing about driftwood, and I use *amazing* in the most limited sense, is that without the eyes placed just so, the wood stays any old wood. *You see, Katie* . . . (My mother calls me Katie whenever she's proud of herself and wants me to be proud of her, too.) *You see, Katie, it's the eyes that make all the difference.*

But that's already too much about her.

The truth was, after that unfortunate weekend in Gettysburg, our summer got increasingly more glorious. This was due, I believe, to the approaching first Tuesday in September when I would resume working full-time. We knew to appreciate those few hot months. Tim coined the perfect phrase for it: "Never-to-be-again time."

BEA MYERLY

Dear Mr. Welch,

There are no words

Dear Mr. Welch,

It has taken me most of the summer for me to realize the error of my

Dear Mr. Welch,

Voltaire was right when he wrote, "Regret is

Dear Mr. Welch,

According to my sophomore-year journal, you said the following while lecturing on reparation attempts made to Japanese Americans interred during World War II: "Sometimes saying sorry just isn't enough." I fear this may be one of those times. Still, I am very, very, very, very, very, very

Dear Mr. Welch,

I hoped that if I kept my distance, if I gave you space, time would be our friend, and any ill feelings we have for each other might mend. Which is why I never bothered you all those summer afternoons you labored on your dissertation in the library. Or when you'd take your short breaks and sit on the park bench at the end of Pineapple Street, eating your sack lunch. I may have followed you, but I left you alone!

But it occurs to me all is not well between us.

Please accept this gift-wrapped box as a symbol of my sincere regret. But before you open the box, I better explain. Writing you this letter has been *impossible*. If you only knew! So therefore I am sending you every attempt I've made. As you can see by the numerous crumples of paper (over thirty in all), I have tried and tried and tried. Perhaps you'll get what I'm clearly not able to say. Well, there's no way around it . . .

Forgive me! I did a terrible thing! What was I thinking? Deleting your interview and not even telling you was one thing! But then to run that unbearable picture! What can I say? I will repay you. Someday, and I know this may be hard for you to imagine, *you will need me*. You will turn to me for a favor. And Mr. Welch, whatever—and I cannot emphasize this enough—*whatever* you want, whatever your wish is, I will do all in my power to grant it. I believe, as the Stoics believed (was it the Stoics?), that forgiveness freely given is meaningless. Forgiveness is earned through action.

> Your forever student,
> if you'll still have me.
>
> BM

TIM

LATE THAT AUGUST, WE RECEIVED A HANDWRITTEN INVITATION FROM JANICE
Wellfleet, one of those neighbors on Oak Lane we vaguely knew, inviting us to her annual Labor Day dinner party. Flattered and yet with no idea why we'd been invited, we decided to attend, because one should. We arrived to find the Wellfleets positively giddy over their good fortune. Their youngest daughter, Polly, had just finished her first week at Princeton. "And neither of us went there!" Janice Wellfleet crowed. Barton Wellfleet couldn't contain his pride about their oldest, Becky, who was traveling in some remote corner of the Galápagos Islands, using her new cell phone to call everyone she knew. Before disappearing into the kitchen, he said with awe, "And the reception was as clear as if she were calling from down the street!"

I called out with a false enthusiasm only Kate would catch, "Now, *that's* progress!" Across the table, Kate smiled. We'd been seated at opposite ends of an absurdly long, oval cherrywood table in the narrow dining room of the Wellfleets' 1860s Federal-style brownstone.

"Meat, anyone?" our host said, appearing with a large ceramic platter covered with generous slabs of prime rib.

"Beef, honey. Beef sounds better."

"Here's the rare, the medium-rare. Well-done is coming up."

I looked over at Kate and made a face as if to say, "Can we go now?" But she stared off blankly, and I knew where her thoughts were: with the boys, and how tomorrow was her first day of work, and how she hadn't wanted to leave them minutes earlier, how she'd bathed them and dressed them in their matching pajamas, their hair wet, smelling of strawberry shampoo, and how, more than anything, she wanted to be home with them, cuddling with them, forever home.

Meanwhile, our hostess was in midmonologue: "Just for the sake of argument, let's imagine a small chemical weapon is detonated in the center of the Heights, say at Starbucks, and only this neighborhood is wiped out. There goes most of the brains of Wall Street, much of publishing; gone are some of the brightest lights of this brightly lit city. That cartoonist for *The New Yorker,* that food critic for the *Times,* the managing editor of *The New York Sun* . . ."

"Janice, what on earth are you talking about?"

"I'm saying there's no place quite like the Heights. Barton and I have lived everywhere. London. Sydney. Hong Kong. Berlin when it had the Wall. And honestly, there's no place I'd rather live."

Everyone sitting around the table seemed to agree.

Our hostess: "The history alone here . . ." Then, turning to me: "Who am I talking to? You are well aware of the history here, aren't you?"

I shrugged.

"Excuse me, why is he so well aware, as opposed to, say, you or I?"

"Because he's a history teacher—"

"Was. I mean, I'm not presently—"

"He was a fantastic history teacher—"

I started to protest.

"You're modest. He's modest. He was the premier history teacher at the Montague Academy for the last umpteen years!"

"What does he do now?"

"He's a stay-at-home dad."

"I wish I'd have done that."

"Done what?"

"What he's doing."

"What, who?"

"This fine young man to my right . . ."

"Tim—I'm Tim Welch."

"And do you know what he's doing? He's being a dad."

"And finishing his dissertation," Kate added.

"So he stays home with the kids?"

Kate, passing a plate of asparagus: "Yes, when they're not at preschool . . ."

"More beef! Here's the well-done!"

"How great that you can do that, that you can *afford* to do that."

"Well," I said, "you'd do it, too, if your wife got a job with Bruno Schwine."

A pause. No one seemed to recognize the name Bruno Schwine.

"Bruno who?"

I'd started to explain Kate's new job when she interrupted, "We work for Cortez."

For one man down on the other end, the mere mention of Cortez was a conversation stopper.

"That Cortez stock is astonishing, at a time when few stocks are. Philip tipped me off, said it was going to be big . . ."

"And was he right?"

"In the last six months, the stock has split maybe four times. Earnings are up seventy-eight percent last quarter, so yes, Philip was right. But that's no surprise."

"I hope they're giving you stock options."

Kate smiled. (They weren't.)

"What company are you talking about?"

"Cortez. They have their finger in every pie. But they made their first money in biotech. Genetically enhanced crops. Super hybrids. This corn, for instance, undoubtedly is an example of what Cortez does best."

"God, this corn is beautiful, the most perfect-looking ears . . ."

"Funny," I said, "I find it has no taste."

"Corn this beautiful doesn't have to taste good!"

"Okay, I've got a pen finally, I've got a piece of paper—say the name of that company again."

Many in the room, in near unison: "Cortez!"

"I've never heard of it before."

"You will," I said, looking at Kate, who sighed, half smiling, half already home.

"Not everyone is as sold on Cortez as you are, Nathan."

"They're just jealous they didn't buy in. Philip says it's just the tip—"

"Who is this Philip? You keep talking about Philip. We all want to know Philip."

"Philip Ashworth."

"I haven't heard of him."

"And only because he wants it that way. I mean, take Donald Trump. He parades around with his ninth wife, combs his sad hair in that nasty, nasty way—he's all hype. But Philip Ashworth is the polar opposite of Donald Trump. He's discreet, humble. He glides under the radar. While others, including The Donald, inflate their worth, Philip Ashworth downplays his."

"Then why did he buy that house?"

"What house?"

"Not a house—it's *the* house on the Promenade."

"Oh, well, I heard he bought it for her."

"Wait a minute. Philip Ashworth bought a house around here?"

"That's what I've been trying to tell you."

"He's moving into the neighborhood?"

"Yes, he is."

"That house, have you been in it, oh my God, *that* is *the* house!"

"And now he'll be our neighbor."

"I heard it's his wife who made him buy here . . ."

"Oh, her. Everybody's talking about *her*."

Kate perked up. "What do they say?"

"Well, for starters, she's unapproachable. Cold. And she clearly has no problem spending his money."

"I've heard she's impossible to please. Architects come and go, she fired the designer Tad Keith, she was rude to someone, I can't remember who . . ."

"She sounds like a piece of work."

"Yes, a piece of work who's had a lot of work done. People just don't naturally look that good."

"I heard Amber Goodsleeve say that Rebecca Plant had heard . . ."

"Well, I heard . . ."

Somewhere around the tenth *I heard,* Kate began to laugh. And some laugh it was. Harder than I could ever remember. Laughed so hard she nearly slipped out of her chair. Laughed so hard tears sprang from her eyes as she covered her bright red face with her available hand. Laughed so hard I was afraid she'd pee her pants.

The conversation stopped as the others watched. Our hostess: "What's so funny?"

"All of you," Kate said, wiping her eyes. "You haven't met the woman, you don't even know her name. None of what you say about her is true!"

"How do you know?"

"Because," Kate said, standing to leave, "she's my best friend."

KATE

NOT LONG AGO TIM EMERGED FROM OUR TINY BATHROOM WITH A LOOK OF ABJECT horror on his face. When I asked him what was wrong, he refused to explain. "Tim, please," I begged. "No," he whispered as he wiped the tears from his eyes. I moved close to hold him, and he confessed. He'd farted in the bathroom, and devastatingly, the smell was unlike that of any fart he'd ever let fly before. The smell, he claimed, had "a certain middle-aged texture, a tangy thickness, a queer persistence." Surely he wasn't serious. Then he explained how this particular fart was identical in smell to those of his father. Hence the tears. I laughed, because how absurd, right? But the smell for Tim evidenced what he feared most. No amount of good intentions, no wishing it were otherwise, can prevent the inevitable slow drip of our parents back into us. We repeat their sayings, we yield to their petty theories, we perpetuate their quirks and facial tics and even their fart smells. It can't be stopped. Muted at times, perhaps. Redirected, maybe. But they win, parents do, in ways we haven't even yet imagined.

Tim and his fatherlike fart came to me as we climbed the stairs to our apartment after our hasty departure from the Wellfleets' dinner party. For as much as my life has been a direct retaliation to my mother and her wild ways, my behavior moments earlier had reminded me how I hadn't shaken her motherly imprint. Whenever I exaggerate, I am most like her. *Best friend?* Why did I have to reach so far? Couldn't I have said, "Well, that hasn't been my experience. I rather like Anna Brody." The truth was, other than one meeting on a snowy day and a brief phone call last spring, I didn't know her. The truth was, I wanted to know her. I was *dying* to know her. But for all I knew, everything those party guests had been saying could very well be true. Maybe they were being kind!

At home, Tim apologized to Pearl, our babysitter, for our early return. He paid her for the hours she'd been promised, walked her to Clinton Street to hail a taxi, and then came home and found me already in bed, under the covers, wide awake, agitated.

"Look," Tim said, sitting on the bed and pulling off his socks. "Forget the Wellfleets—we swim in different waters."

Funny, I hadn't even been thinking of them. And of course, they'd been insulted. Our abrupt exit had been rude, at the very least. Now the Wellfleets were added to my worries. It was safe to assume that in the weeks ahead, I'd see them frequently, and it would be awkward—from now on; forever, probably. But what worried me more, and what I started to tell Tim, was that I had greatly exaggerated my relationship with Anna Brody. He would have none of it, stating how proud he was of me for defending my friend.

"But you don't understand—the words *best friend* were completely ludicrous."

"Nothing else would have stopped them—"

"But to say *best*—"

"Okay, so maybe you were premature."

"What do you mean, premature?"

"So she's not your best friend now, but maybe one day up ahead she will be. And as Bruno likes to say, Kate, you have an innate capacity to envision the future."

Then he kissed me, rolled over, and fell fast asleep.

How I envied the ease with which he did it. I was far from sleeping. The next day was to be my first day of work, and I felt nervous, with a tight knot in my stomach, and was plagued by a faint inner voice that said, *Well, this is going to change everything.*

Unable to sleep, I got up and checked the radio for the weather forecast, laid out my clothes, then ran a bath and used the boys' Mr. Bubble. I even used their baby shampoo. If I smelled like them, then maybe they wouldn't feel so far away. As my hair dried, I paced the apartment, finally sitting down at the kitchen table, where I wrote a note for the boys in crayon, explaining my whereabouts and how they were to have fun with Daddy and that I would be home soon, taking the fastest train I could.

The offices for Bruno Schwine and Associates were in Manhattan, on the ground floor of a pre–Civil War brownstone on Eleventh Street, just west of Fifth Avenue. Recently, Bruno had evicted a few therapists who had been renting office space for years. Bruno had lived upstairs since 1974. He'd bought the brownstone for one hundred and thirty-five thousand dollars: as he liked to say, "A fortune at the time." Now it was worth millions.

I buzzed. While waiting, I looked through the wrought-iron grille-work of the downstairs windows. The front room was packed full with stacks of boxes and random pieces of furniture still wrapped in plastic. It became quite clear that my first days—weeks, even—would be spent more as office manager. Phones would need to be installed, walls painted, office supplies purchased, the works. There was much to do, and I had overdressed.

Bruno came out the parlor floor door and stood on the stoop, holding a cup of tea. Dressed in jeans and a cotton dress shirt but still wearing slippers, Bruno looked rested, with a dark tan, his salt-and-pepper hair dyed a deep reddish-brown. He'd gained back at least half the weight he'd lost. He looked terrific, and I told him so right away, and he said, "Well, I feel terrific."

"So," I said, smiling back, "then it's a good day to begin."

The summer had been rough for Bruno, another round of chemo-therapy and radiation that had resulted in his being hospitalized at

St. Vincent's in early July. I was stunned at this news, but he laughed it off, saying he hadn't bothered me because he'd wanted my summer to be "interruption-free." I learned all this (and more) during the breakfast that turned into lunch that we shared on my official first day. Bruno did most of the talking, repeating some of what we both knew. A generous allowance had been provided for office space, travel (when necessary), staff (me), all with the singular goal of helping Louis Underfer's private charity, the Lucy Foundation, award grants to needy organizations.

I knew only what Google and Wikipedia knew about Cortez. Based in St. Louis, Cortez was the brainchild of chairman/CEO Louis Underfer, a former high school biology teacher, who started Cortez in an effort to make money after his first child, his only child, Lucy, was diagnosed with an extreme form of autism. It may be apocryphal, but Louis Underfer worked in his garage/laboratory and, over many months of late nights, developed a rare everything-resistant hybrid for seed corn. One thing led to other things, none of which I bothered to remember, only this: Louis Underfer and his wife, Sheila, had lived in the same house in a nondescript St. Louis suburb for the last thirty-five years. Apparently, any move from their modest split-level on their typical suburban street would irrevocably disrupt their daughter's sense of place. She would come undone. It would be devastating. So here was a man, admittedly one of the most successful in our time, who could afford any home imaginable, who couldn't ever move, who wouldn't ever even think of moving, all because of his great love for his daughter. In a word, he was decent. And yet the Cortez Corporation was anything but.

Bruno laid out my schedule for the next few weeks. My mornings would be spent getting our office up and running. Afternoons would be for reading and research.

Bruno didn't know how much money we would have to give away; he said he'd be going to St. Louis soon and would have a better idea then. "In the meantime, Kate," he said, "think of this as jazz."

"How so?"

"We're making it up as we go along."

The best part of that first day was going home.

What a mess. Our apartment looked as if a series of bombs had been detonated. I could hear Tim in the kitchen, wearily insisting that Sam eat a carrot: "At least try it," he said. I called out faintly at first, then louder until they heard me: "I'm back." This was followed by a sudden silence, then the boys appeared at the end of our narrow hall, racing toward me, arms outstretched. I squatted down to catch them.

That night Tim, Teddy, and Sam presented me with a gift that had been wrapped in newspaper. The boys helped tear off the paper. It was a large blank journal with Monet's water lilies on the cover. I tried to be gracious, but I didn't want a gift. I wanted to be the one giving. Tim urged me to open the journal. I did and saw that he'd written an entry. I promised to read it later.

September 6th

8:32 A.M.—Kate kissed both boys good-bye. And left for work. Boys called out from window. She turned and waved. She wore a dark blue pantsuit, a cream-colored blouse, her new comfortable shoes. Before she left, Teddy said, "Mommy, why are you so pretty?"

8:45 (approx.)—Kate called from subway platform to see if we were okay. And we were! Teddy was helping with dishes while Sam had curled up on the kitchen floor, wrapped himself in his blanket, thumb stuck in his mouth.

9:00ish to 9:28 exactly—art project. Made *Welcome home, Mommy* sign for front door and *Congrats on first day of work* card. Teddy did a good job printing his name.

9:30 to 11:00—errands, stopped at Muffins and More, where each boy picked out his favorite muffin/bagel/treat. While we were out on errands, Mommy left two messages. The first to check in, the second to tell Teddy and Sam a secret. She asked me to leave the bedroom, which I did, but kept my ear to the door so I could hear. She'd hidden a bag of jelly beans for them under . . .

The entry continued in that vein for two-plus pages. Where and how Tim had found the time to write it, I do not know. But it was a kind gesture, and I knew what he was trying to do. It was his way of making it seem I wasn't missing anything.

Later, after the front door had been double-locked and the lights turned out, Tim, almost asleep, said, "Oh, I forgot. Someone called for you."

"Who?"

"That woman from the Brooklyn Heights Association."

"Oh, it can wait," I started to say, but Tim sat up and turned on his bed light. "It sounded important," he said as he reached over to the answering machine and pressed *play*.

ABIGAIL HOSFORD

HELLO, THIS IS ABIGAIL HOSFORD, PRESIDENT OF THE BROOKLYN HEIGHTS ASSO- ciation, calling for Katherine. Hi, Katherine, I'm surprised we've never met. The reason for my call is that I understand from my associate Pamela Wyeth-Bacon that you are a close friend of Mrs. Ashworth's, although I don't believe she uses her husband's name. Might you call me ASAP at the office or at my home (we're up late!)—we need to know the name she goes by, and perhaps, and I'm hoping this won't—

It's Abigail again, simply wondering if you might arrange a proper introduction of sorts. All of us at the Heights Association would love to welcome your good friend to the neighborhood. Thank you in advance for making this happen. Hold on . . . oh, right, yes . . . we're looking forward to meeting you, too? Eager for your call. Cheers.

TIM

ALL THOSE YEARS TEACHING HAD OBSCURED ONE SIMPLE FACT: NOBODY ELSE'S children are as interesting as your own. Or as perplexing, sure, or as frustrating.

That was the gist of what I tried to write one early October afternoon. I'd been diligent with journal entries. Lately, though, it was proving more difficult. To be the recorder of Teddy and Sam's histories seemed a tall order, considering what else was required: to be a frequent referee, both judge and jury, to navigate the treacherous terrain of *sharing* and *turn taking*, to covertly implement my own intricate system for bribing them (which meant establishing a complex yet comprehensible program of snacks and treats), to amuse/inspire/educate them, to keep them from harm's way, and somehow, while juggling all of the above, manage to look happy. However, this cannot be emphasized enough—*I'm not complaining*.

Not that I didn't have complaints. I did. I had one big one. Names. How was I to remember all the names of all the mothers and babysitters and nannies and the oh-so-many children? It was impossible to differentiate between little Sam Blumenthal and even littler Sammy Plant and chubby Max Steiner and not so chubby Maxwell Silverstein and Ruben and Rhonda and Rebecca and Rory . . .

Right away I had to abandon any fantasies of posterity. This journal wasn't for historians. It was only for Kate. So I developed a kind of shorthand, starting with a story about What's-Her-Name, a mother whose name I'd forgotten yet again. She had accosted me on the playground about the boys not wearing warm enough clothes. As I tried to tell Kate about the incident, I was nearly derailed by my inability to conjure up the woman's name. "You know the mother I mean," I said in a pre-Alzheimer's panic.

"No, I don't," Kate said. "There are so many mothers."

"You're telling me!" I couldn't snatch the name from the place in my brain where names were stored. Then I remembered the conversation. Not what was said but what happened when What's-Her-Name turned her head at a particular angle so that the sun, which was setting over the Manhattan skyline, backlit her face, revealing a rather unfortunate field of blond facial hair. When hit by that late-afternoon light in Pierrepont Playground, What's-Her-Name became known as Mom with a Beard. Oh, sure, she had a name, but for the time being, Mom with a Beard would have to suffice. Even better, Kate knew exactly which mom I meant.

She also knew Milk Mom, who, rumor had it, still breast-fed her five-year-old boy, Jett. I had proof, having watched the boy named Jett pester his mother in the children's section of Book Court. In fact, he bothered her so much that she led him between History and Biography, lifted up her shirt, exposed her tired and overused nipple (long like a straw), and let the boy take a few quick sucks.

There was Nazi Mom—incidentally, not a German mother but a stern Southern woman who said to her son in a thick Georgia drawl, "Honey, get your little butt over here before I spank it *red*."

There were Flicka, National Velvet, and Misty of Chincoteague—a cluster of equine-featured women who seemed inseparable, always moving en masse with their kids in strollers, all with long manes of hair, wearing similar leather boots that clacked like hooves as they walked.

There were Eager-to-Please Mom, Best-Dressed Mom, Grateful Dead Mom, Cindy McCain Mom, Pippi Longstocking Mom, and Mom with a Man's Voice.

Kate preferred the nice nicknames to the cruel ones. But sometimes

I could get her to laugh out loud against her will. Dad Without a Clue, Mom with Beaver Teeth, and Momma-licious.

There was one nickname that I waited to reveal, holding out for a moment when Kate would need to laugh most.

The Weasel.

His real name was Wendell. But he was dubbed the Weasel the first time I met that odd, short man with the Dutch-boy haircut, his dyed-black bangs cut straight across his flat forehead. The Weasel had an extremely small head, three-quarter-size, and the tiny hands of a ten-year-old, except they were hairy. Indeed, the Weasel was an immensely hairy creature, with bug eyes and a faint ring of white foam around his perpetually chapped, cracked lips. His teeth had a tinge of black—due, or so the story went, to an excess of medicines he had to take as a baby. Rumors about the Weasel were rampant. Some claimed he had a thick, long scar that traversed his chest from a radical open-heart surgery performed on him when he was a boy. His bluish skin tint was explained by a lack of circulation. In fact, Martha Stewart Mom and Mom Who Knows More About You Than You Do had told me the Weasel had a condition that at any moment could claim his life. They competed to explain: "That's why he has all that energy! That's why he's so joyous!"

I remarked with sarcasm too subtle for some, "Oh, I agree. When I see him, I'm reminded of life's beauty! And suddenly, I don't feel I deserve to complain!"

Surely, though, there was a cost. Perhaps my secret world of nicknames and character reduction kept me at arm's length from the others. Maybe I appeared more the observer and less the partaker. I felt ostracized. No, not by the nannies. I knew they liked me, and lately, I'd made inroads with the au pairs. But to the mothers and the handful of other fathers, I was not to be trusted.

Of course, I didn't tell this to Kate. Why worry her? And yet it was hard to watch the Weasel charm the other mothers each afternoon on the playground. Even a small gesture, like Dad Without a Clue offering a stick of Juicy Fruit and a Wet 'n Wipe to Casual Mom, threatened me. So I clung to that hard lesson of life that history teaches: It's all cyclical, really. One day the Weasel will reveal his true nature and fall out of favor. Dad Without a Clue will flake out and forget to pick up his kid. And maybe one day I will be the Dad with All the Answers.

Still, I'd begun to doubt myself. Then one morning—*wah-lah*—a minor miracle occurred. It happened the same morning I'd dropped off a note from Kate to this Anna Brody person. The note was simple, sweet, saying basically, *Welcome to the neighborhood.* Kate had asked me to hand-deliver it to the Ashworth-Brody house. *House* was an understatement. It was easy to find, what with all the workers—the painters, the plasterers, the plumbers, the men on the scaffolding, the roofers; most of Brooklyn seemed to be hard at work transforming the building, which up until the previous March had been divided into eight apartments, back into the newly restored circa-1848 Pierrepont Mansion.

Kate's note was received by a pert-looking, officious type who seemed to be overseeing the delivery of a rather large painting. It must have had some value, for she had security guards with her. Before taking the note, she asked me who I was. I said, "No one." She looked at me suspiciously. I continued, "It's from my wife to Anna. They're old friends."

She said nothing and turned to go back inside.

I couldn't help but ask, "When will they be moving in?"

"Soon, wouldn't you think?"

I headed toward Muffins and More, where I squeezed into my favorite corner table and began to work, which meant reading the *Post,* the *Daily News,* and the *Heights Press* before hunkering down to reconceive the middle section of my dissertation.

Later, I fell asleep with my head in my hands and woke to hear the following from a voice I recognized: "He's turned up the heat. What was an occasional drunken request is now an almost daily beg."

It was Mom with Moxie (aka Claudia Valentine) talking to Martha

Stewart Mom and Pretty-in-Pink Mom. They were huddled at their regular corner table, and Mom with Moxie needed comforting.

Martha Stewart Mom said, "Well, forget Dan for a moment. What do you want, Claudia? What do *you* want?"

Claudia looked around at her girlfriends and said, "That's easy. I'm sick of not having enough money. The husbands in this neighborhood with their hedge funds and their cushy Wall Street bonuses. At the start of the longest bull market ever, who did I marry? Dan the Bear. Mr. Better-Safe-Than-Sorry. He sold our Microsoft back in ninety-six, he bought a bunch of AOL–Time Warner right before the bust, and he balked at Chad Bixby's tip to get in on the ground floor of a little company called Google. For the last several years, our entire nest egg has been sitting in a money market account, making squat in interest."

I started to transcribe her words, thinking Kate might enjoy hearing the kind of conversation she was missing.

"So this morning he tells me that Chad Bixby made a crisp four and a half million last week from his hedge fund, and then he asks me if I'd please let him try butt sex just this once. I mean, he's begging for it, so I make Dan the Bear an offer: 'Fine, sweetie. Make a million by Easter, and you can fuck me in the ass.'"

The other mothers gasped.

"Then I told him, 'Make ten million, and you can stay in there permanently.'"

Some men wait their whole lives to overhear this kind of conversation.

Unfortunately, it was time for me to go pick up Teddy and Sam from preschool, so I stood up to leave. From the stunned expressions on their collective faces, it became clear that while they hadn't noticed me before, they noticed me now.

"Don't mind me," I said, scooting past.

But there was no denying I'd heard everything, so to put them at ease, I turned and said, "Forgive the intrusion, but what happens if he doesn't make the money?"

Claudia paused. "I haven't provided for that."

"My suggestion, for what it's worth?"

"Yes?"

"If he doesn't make the million by Easter?"

"Yes?"

I had their attention.

"Then *you* fuck *him* in the ass."

There was a deathly silence. *Oops,* I thought. Then Claudia slapped her knee and roared triumphantly, "Yes!" The other mothers laughed nervously. I hurried off, smiling to myself, sensing I'd just passed a crucial test. I had entered the inner circle. I was now an honorary mom—albeit a mom with a penis—but an honorary mom just the same.

Arriving late with the boys, I noticed right away that all the children at Angus Strubel's fourth birthday party were in costume except for two, and those two were mine. I'd hurried out of the house knowing I'd forgotten something, and now I remembered what it was. As I stood in the Strubels' doorway, Veronica, my favorite of the Jamaican babysitters, came up the steps with little Benji Walker, who was dressed in a store-bought clown costume. I smiled at Veronica, hoping for but not getting any sympathy. From across the room, in a voice louder than necessary, Gail Strubel shouted, "I told Kate it was a costume party!"

I shrugged as if to say, *It's news to me.*

"Kate said she wrote it down on the calendar!"

The calendar. That faithfully prepared document. The master schedule. How Kate labored to make sure all playdates, activities, phone numbers, and especially parties were recorded there. "Without this," she'd said only days earlier, "we won't get through the year." Somehow, in addition to working too many hours a week for Bruno Schwine, Kate found time to wash and fold clothes, precook and freeze meals, and pack snacks. Not only did she wear the pants, she was the über-mom. She missed playing the mom part. And for the Angus

Strubel party, she couldn't have made it easier. *Just dress them according to the following instructions,* she'd written on the note for that day.

I remembered it all now. But by the time I could race back home, gather up their costumes, hurry back, and dress them, the party would be nearly over. What would be the point?

I turned to see Teddy trying to pull off little Chip Bigelow's Darth Vader mask. "No, Teddy," I said, but it was too late. Teddy had the mask, and Chip didn't seem to mind. Sam clung to my leg until Angus's father, Dale Strubel, dressed as Frankenstein, appeared in the doorway to announce, "The haunted house is no longer haunted. But up on the roof, we have a *witches' brew* and a *hunt for the missing mummy's finger* and a great view of an *almost full moon!*" As he led the charge up the stairs, a cluster of kids followed, including Teddy, wearing the Darth Vader mask, and an eager Sam.

I felt the reproachful glare of Wilma Strubel, Gail's mother-in-law. "My fault," I said. "My wife made two terrific costumes."

Which was an understatement: Teddy's pirate costume was an elaborate affair—a curly black wig, one of Kate's old blazers (bright blue), a red sash, his black L. L. Bean rain boots, a plastic sword from the Toy Attic, a makeup kit for drawing on a mustache and applying a latex scar, and a rubber hook to hold in his left hand. Sam's ghost was simpler but was exactly what he wanted: a sheet with the head hole cut and hemmed, white sweatpants, brand-new, all-white tennis shoes, and a gray-white pancake base to cover his face.

When I started to describe the costumes, Wilma raised her freckled hand and said, "You don't have to convince me."

"I'd go get them," I said, "if we had the time. Anyway, the boys seem fine about it."

Wilma grunted, then moved into the kitchen, where the other Strubels—each of them large and lumpy—sat around a circular table, eating second and third helpings of the Big Bird cake.

Wanting to escape, I considered going up to the roof. But the sounds of Dale and the sugar-laced children laughing and stomping convinced me I was not needed, at least not yet. So I went on a quest for some candy I could pocket and snack on later. I made my way to the abandoned basement and found that synthetic cobwebs had been stretched over the banister leading down the stairs. Other webs had been strategically woven around the room. Cardboard witches and bats and pumpkins had been taped to the walls. And on a hidden stereo, a CD of ghost sounds, banging doors, and creaking floors filled the musty air. Many kids had left unwanted stickers and candy wrappers scattered across the shag carpet. A bowl of potato chips had been knocked over, and the chips had been stepped on, crushed into little bits. In the corner, on a plenty big enough TV, a video played of a recent animated extravaganza from Walt Disney. And when a trio of unfortunate-looking animals appeared to sing—mercifully, the TV had been muted—I slumped into a child's beanbag chair and had this thought: *Too many guests, too many presents, too much candy and cake for any one kid.*

I closed my eyes, though not for sleep. I closed them because I couldn't bear looking at the well-intended decorating effort any longer. It depressed me. But closing my eyes didn't help, because I pictured the grotesque stack of presents upstairs, most of them bought at the last minute from the same toy store on Pineapple Street. Most frightening of all was the image of Angus Strubel's privileged frosting-coated fingers tearing off the wrapping paper of his many presents.

When I opened my eyes, I was startled. Standing before me, her face merely inches from mine, was a young girl dressed in a lacy white dress. Her blond hair had been pulled back with a festive pink ribbon. She was either Cinderella or Goldilocks. She had these almost unreal curls, her big eyes were maple-syrup brown, and her lips were lined with chocolate. In her raised left hand, she held a book.

She stared at me with a kind of otherworldly wisdom. I thought, *This may be the most beautiful child ever.* She kept staring. Unnerved at first, I did my best to stare back, determined to outlast her. I was about to ask her name when she handed me the book to read. Then she crawled onto my lap, rested her head and those curls on my shoulder, and waited for me to start.

Five pages in, I was overcome: This girl, light in my arms, made for a feeling unlike any I'd ever had with a child. It was disarming. My boys had no capacity to be this still, to give in. They fussed and kicked and wiggled. But she was so light, as if she were warm air, and I read in a near whisper until, the next thing I knew, a woman said, "Somebody's got the touch."

I looked up and found a woman standing before me. "Oh," I said, "You must be the mother . . ."

"Yes."

"I'm sorry. She just climbed up . . ."

"She's very particular."

"Apparently not," I said.

"Nonsense. I should thank you. She needed a nap."

That was when I realized the little girl had fallen asleep.

I introduced myself.

"I know who you are," she said, smiling.

Really?

Upstairs the kids were bashing a piñata. The party was almost over.

"Well," I said, lifting up the daughter to her mother, "we didn't get to finish the book."

"Next time," the mother said.

"Yes," I said, even though I remember thinking, *Who said anything about there being a next time?*

KATE

DURING THOSE FIRST WEEKS, IT BECAME CLEAR: FOR THE SAKE OF MY BOYS, I would have to learn how to leave work at work. So each day at five P.M. sharp, no matter what Bruno and I were discussing or whatever obscure foundation I was researching, I would stop cold, put my desk in order, leave promptly, and head toward the subway.

But my arriving home at a consistent time didn't guarantee a smooth transition. The boys had acute radar for when I was physically present but mentally elsewhere. It wasn't easy to quiet my mind after a day of drinking in so much information. The innumerable charities worthy of support had begun to overwhelm me.

So here was what I learned to do. Each evening, on the packed-like-a-sardine-can Number 2 or 3 train going downtown, instead of continuing the conversation with myself, I'd pick my people. To the man in the gray hooded sweatshirt flaunting his new Air Jordans, I imagined telling him about two competing charities—One World Running and Sole 4 Soles—both dedicated to providing new and gently used shoes to the needy everywhere. To the young angry girl with multiple piercings, I mentioned that what makes me mad are the hundred thousand new chemicals that have been unleashed in our environment in the last five years. And what we are we going to do about it? To the pasty white businesswoman who boarded at Chambers Street clutching a bottle of Evian, I stunned her with this unacceptable fact: Almost one-third of the world's people don't get enough iodine from food and water. This can result in mental slowness and the needless loss of more than a billion IQ points around the world. And to everyone on the train, I shouted about how with the Micronutrient Initiative, we can iodize salt for only two to three cents per person per year! By imagining these conversations, I could quiet my racing, over-excited mind and for a brief moment feel that these needy causes weren't just mine to champion. They were *ours*. Then, bing-bong, the subway doors opened, I stepped out with some others, climbed the eighteen steps, turned right, and walked toward one of three eleva-tors that lifted me up to the street level of the Clark Street station, pushed through the turnstile, emerging outside with the sweet sense that my brain had been drained. The twelve-minute walk home through the Heights was used to clear out any leftover bits that might still be bouncing about. I made it all about breathing and walking at a moder-ate speed, gently directing all thoughts toward the approaching mo-ment of the key in the door, deadbolt turning, the breadwinner's victorious return home.

In terms of Tim, I had to make room for the disappointment factor. No doubt the house would be much messier than I'd like. Toys scattered throughout, dishes stacked in the sink, a handful of half-finished activi-ties, all of which pointed to what was becoming abundantly clear: Tim's basic inability to handle the task. But it wouldn't help to point this out. What helped me most was to picture worst-case scenarios—the tub overflowing, broken dishes shattered on the checkerboard linoleum, the kitchen on fire. These catastrophic imaginings made it possible for me to accept whatever I found with an easy smile.

Mostly, though, I didn't want Tim to feel defensive. Without a doubt, he was doing the very best he could. Besides, as his favorite historian says, and I paraphrase: "Most of us suffer from unreal expec-tations."

I feared I was guilty of this, too.

"I'm back," I called out. That day what I found inside made me gasp. The living room/dining room/toy room was immaculate. The hallway, pristine. Everything was in place, and everything that wasn't in place was in a better place. Teddy once asked me, "Mommy, am I dreaming this?" I had to wonder if I was dreaming.

No one was home. Then I remembered my family was at Angus Strubel's birthday party.

I went back and found the kitchen spotless. Well, not spotless, but as spotless as our kitchen ever gets. On the table, there were two Scooby-Doo plates that must have held cookies, and two plastic cups half filled with now warm milk.

So maybe the world is going to hell, but not the Welches here on Oak Lane, no, we're on the way up . . .

That was when I pulled open the door to the boys' room and saw the costumes. All laid out. Waiting to be worn.

The sound that erupted out of me defied description. Surely our neighbors heard it. Furious, I called over to the Strubels' and learned that Tim had just left with the boys. Gwen asked if everything was all right. I lied and said, "Yes." By the time they got home, I had shut the door to our room. Tim found me there, seething, bloodthirsty. He told me to wait, saying he could explain.

I heard him start a bath for the boys. When he opened the door to our room again, he asked first thing, "Is this because of the costumes?"

I glared at him. "That, too." Then I snapped, something about being disappointed and hurt and that if we didn't fucking need the money, I'd quit my fucking job right now, which wasn't exactly true.

Tim said he was sorry.

I said, *"What will it be next time?"*

He tried to calm me down by claiming the party had been a disaster and the boys hadn't minded and the costumes were going to be a knockout, best on the block, and if they'd worn them that day, they wouldn't wear them on Halloween, and then he said, "You see, Kate, sometimes even you are wrong."

"I'm not wrong."

"Yes, you are. Case in point . . ." That was when he told me he'd met Anna Brody.

"She was at the party?"

"She came at the end."

"And you talked to her?"

"Briefly. I spent more time with the daughter, though."

"What'd you think?"

"Of the daughter? Well, she's maybe the cutest, most adorable girl in all the world."

"Figures."

"But Anna Brody? No thanks."

I waited for him to explain.

Basically, Tim said she seemed nice enough and that she was defi-nitely unusual-looking, but she wasn't as advertised. She was all bones and hard edges. Something about her unfortunate profile. I think I liked best what he said about me. That I was much more beautiful. That I was in rarefied company, and the way he saw it, Anna Brody was not in that company. Then he said, "I was expecting someone breathtaking. But you know what she is?"

"Tell me."

"She's just rich."

The boys called from the bathroom that they wanted bubbles. Tim left the room to oblige them, and when he was far enough away, I said so he couldn't hear: "Okay, then. You're forgiven."

I don't remember why, maybe I wanted a change, but the next day I decided to walk home up Hicks Street instead of Henry. The corner of Montague and Hicks is often windy, but that day the wind was so strong it felt as if I were about to be swept up myself, which was why it took both hands to hold my hat on my head, and why I turned to walk backward, which was why I happened to see in a window of the

Heights Café that Anna Brody was waving at me. Now that she had my attention, she gestured for me to come inside.

By the way, Tim had been wrong about Anna. She was even more beautiful than I remembered. The only conclusion I could draw was that Tim didn't have very good taste.

Anyway, she met me near the front door.

"Look, I'd love to talk," I said. "But my boys are waiting . . ."

"Please," Anna begged, "you have to save me."

I remember thinking, *Oh, right, as if Anna Brody needs saving.* I was about to ask, "Save you from what?" when she pulled me toward the back of the restaurant to a table of well-dressed women, all midmeal.

"Ladies, I trust you know Kate."

None of them did. But they went around the room and introduced themselves. Lynn Auchindale. Valerie Snelling. Pamela Wyeth-Bacon. The last woman, with the clenched jaw, smiled a fierce, cold smile and said, "And I'm Abigail Hosford."

Oops. Her call was one I probably should've returned. I had expected someone much older. Abigail Hosford may have been all of thirty.

Anna slipped on her coat and said, "Kate and I have a previously scheduled engagement. Nice to meet you girls, thanks." The ladies glared at me, clearly blaming me for breaking up their party. Anna left quickly, and I trailed after. Outside, Anna said, "I owe you."

"But I did nothing."

"You have no idea. They were never going to let me go."

I tried to place Anna's accent. It seemed to come from both nowhere and everywhere, as if she'd been born and raised over an ocean at thirty-five thousand feet.

Anna went on, "Oh, I met your husband yesterday. He was a big help with my Sophie."

"Yes, he said you two had met."

We both stood there for a moment, unsure what we were doing next. Then Anna said, "Would you like to get a drink?"

"Yes," I said, forgetting about the boys back home.

At Jack the Horse Tavern, while we waited for our drinks, Anna said, "Your husband is really good with kids."

"You think?"

"My daughter is very shy. And she took to him right away. The way I took to you. Except I didn't fall asleep in your lap."

Our drinks arrived. Anna took a slow sip and continued, "I suppose I should've been concerned—my daughter in the lap of a man I'd never met. But when I put it together he was your husband, I thought, Well, of course."

I wasn't quite following her.

Then Anna asked, "How did you two meet?"

So I told her about the first time I met Tim Welch from Cayton, Ohio, on the campus of UC Berkeley. How he was skinnier then, all bones, and his hair was short, and when he spoke, he had a sibilant *S*, so he sounded like a bicycle with a slow leak. That he seemed so excited by the thought of everything, the possibility of everything, and this enthusiasm combined with an excess of energy and a tendency to cry made me certain that the Ohio boy following me around must be a homosexual. "Which was good news," I told Anna. "Otherwise I'd never have befriended him."

"Why?"

"Because at the time, I'd had enough of boys and professors, and I was looking for a way to unsmoke all the pot and, uhm, unsex all the sex."

Anna smiled as if she understood.

"Tim was innocent in a midwestern sort of way. He knew nothing of the world, it seemed, and I knew too much, and because I thought he'd be attracted to his own kind, I felt safe."

"Of course."

"But before the start of his sophomore year, he came back two inches taller and ten pounds heavier. He'd even begun to shave selected areas of his face—the chin, above his top lip. He looked sexy in a goofy kind of way. This was bad news for me, because I wasn't as frosty toward the idea of a relationship, and the one boy I fancied was never going to be interested in me. But then he asked to meet for a late-night 'sssssnack' at a local diner."

I worried I was talking too much, but Anna said, "Don't stop."

So I continued: "I arrived late, having spent, to my surprise, too much time primping in front of my dorm room mirror. That night, over cheese fries and a shared vanilla shake, Tim admitted his feelings for me, saying that he had liked me first thing. He said I reminded him of a blond Patty Hearst. I said, 'Thanks?' Then he said no, it was more specific than that. He took out his wallet, unfolded a photocopy from an old newspaper, saying, 'This is because I don't have a picture of you.' It was that famous Patty Hearst photo where she was wearing a beret, holding a machine gun while robbing a bank."

"That's sweet."

"So I brought him back to my room that night, and after we slept together, he cried . . ."

"He cried?"

"Yes, and said, 'Thank you ssssso much.' "

Anna laughed and said, "So he wasn't gay."

"No, he was just enthusiastic, and a crier, and for one night, at the very least, he'd made me feel like Patty Hearst."

Neither of us said anything. I felt I had revealed too much.

"Philip never cries. I don't know if he even has tear ducts."

I asked how they had met. Anna sighed and said, "It's not interesting. Not like you and your husband."

"Oh, come on."

"He bought me. Basically, I was for sale."

"What? Were you a prostitute?" She didn't blink at my inappropriate question.

"No, I was poor. And he was anything but. And he wore me down. Philip is, if anything, persistent. And persuasive."

We had so much left to talk about, but my cell phone vibrated. It was Tim.

"I'm on my way," I told him. I flipped my phone closed and signaled for the check.

"Gotta run," I said. "Dinner's ready."

"So he cooks?"

"He boils noodles and heats up sauce . . ."

"Still."

When the check came, Anna wanted to pay. "No," I said, putting down my credit card, "it's on me."

Outside, we said our good-byes and headed off in separate directions.

Turning back, Anna called out, "Maybe you'll come for dinner sometime."

I said, "Yes, we'd like that." And I thought, *It can't be soon enough.*

JEFF SLADE

I HOPE I'VE GOT THE RIGHT NUMBER. KATE? KATE OLIVER? IT'S SLAKOWITZ. JEFF Slakowitz. Did you know I changed my name? They made me. I go by Jeff Slade. But I'm still the same old Slakowitz. I don't know when we last talked. Was it your wedding? I hope you remember me, Kate Oliver. Because I'll never forget you. This machine is probably going to cut me off. Hey, remember your theory that in order to be famous, you need to have a big head? Well, you'll never guess what—

As I was saying, remember your theory about bigheaded famous people? Well, you were right. Because Jay Leno's head is huge. The head of a bulldog. I just taped Leno. I'm on Leno tonight. It airs tonight. [Pause.] Damn, you probably don't even have a TV. You always hated TV. Did you know that I've got my own series? ABC. Sunday nights. Look, I got some more calls to make. But I just wanted you to know—

Cut me off again. I'mjustgoingtohavetotalkfaster, aren't I? [Laughs.] I heard you have kids—two, how great is that? Kate, I'm proud of my new show. It's very *family*. One more thing—I'm on at the very end of Leno. And I talk about you. What am I saying? I'm talking about you when I'm talking at the end. [Pause.] Hey,greattalking. Hopeyou'rewell. It'sgreatyouhavekids. Oh, and, of course, please say hey to Tom.

TIM

WHAT WAS I THINKING, TOSSING MY RATTY BLACK OVERCOAT TO THE MAN IN THE tuxedo who opened the door? It was a sudden, arrogant impulse, but it took Kate digging her heel into my shoe for me to realize I'd been rude. "Thank you!" I hurried to say. The Man in the Tuxedo said, "You must be Tim." Impressive, I thought, for a cater-waiter to know me by my first name. He was a classic cater-waiter type—mostly handsome, well mannered with two perfect racks of large, square white teeth. Then it occurred to me that I might have met this man some years before. Was he perhaps one of those actors Kate had bedded back in Berkeley? I'm not suggesting she had withheld telling me about this man—I sincerely believed she'd simply forgotten him, because he seemed rather much a type: the not-so-bright handsome-guy type who wanted to be famous but, in his quest for fame, developed no quality whatsoever that made him vivid in the long term. Then again, one need only consider the meteoric rise of Jeff Slade, *the* Jeff Slade, on-the-cover-of–*TV Guide* Jeff Slade, who, had things been different, easily could have been working this party as a cater-waiter himself, because what is vivid about Jeff Slade? Apart from being the most famous bad television actor in the world, apart from his highly publicized dalliance with that nasty ex-junkie rock star, apart from his recent release from the Betty Ford Center, and apart from the fact that the motherfucker still calls me Tom, guess what's so vivid that sets Jeff Slade apart from all the other cater-waiters of the world? Jeff Slade is still in love with my wife.

Was this why I had tossed my ratty coat like a hot tamale and shouted, "*Catch!*" as it sailed through the air? Perhaps. Or maybe I was simply overcompensating for how small I felt. Earlier that evening, as I stood staring into our cluttered closet trying to decide what to wear, I made a decision. *I will dress how I dress. I will be me.* So I pulled from the closet my well-worn tan corduroy blazer; my scuffed brown loafers; my mohair sweater vest, a bird's nest of orange and yellow and light green threads of wool; and yes, later from the hall closet, I yanked from a hanger an old favorite article of clothing, my trench coat, purchased my senior year of college for six dollars at the Goodwill store in North Oakland.

When Kate suggested I wear something nicer, I gave my usual knee-jerk response, bastardizing Thoreau: "Beware the occasion that warrants a new suit." Knowing me to be stubborn when it comes to clothes, Kate didn't press the issue. I had prevailed.

We were quiet and reflective during our crisp walk across the Heights. Only the click-clack of her black heels underscored the scene. But as we approached the house and saw the chauffeur-driven limousines out front, I regretted my choice. Even before we climbed the bluestone steps to the majestic cream-colored house on Columbia Street, before entering the candlelit vestibule, before hearing the string quartet of recent Juilliard graduates carve the air with Beethoven, Vivaldi, and Bach, as the music floated across the exquisite and polished original parquet floors, bouncing off the walls as thick as buffalo, faintly echoing through all eighteen fireplaces, each cut from the same Italian pink marble; even before I met the other guests—of which there were only six, and before I realized who those six were—and certainly before I realized that the cater-waiter who caught my coat and carried it down the hall as if holding a priceless fur was not a cater-waiter at all but our host, Philip Ashworth, before all this and more became exceedingly clear, I had the wherewithal to sense that while Kate was dressed and ready to impress, we were both in way over our heads.

KATE

TO UNDERSTAND THE INAPPROPRIATENESS OF WHAT TIM THEN DID, ONE HAS TO fully appreciate fine wine.

When Philip Ashworth announced he was opening a bottle of '59 Romanée-Conti Richebourg, Penelope Winston, the ex-supermodel/ linguist, turned to me and whispered, "It's a monster wine. Simply devastating. Had it once in Venice. Said to be one of the best burgundies you'll ever taste."

Philip Ashworth swilled it, sipped, and said, "Disappointing."

"Oh, come on, Philip," Wally Walker, the crown prince of publishing and Philip's roommate from Yale, called from across the room, cigar in hand. He insisted on tasting it. He took his turn, lightly smacked his lips, and said, "It seems tight to me. But just a little."

Against the objections of the other guests, Philip had the bottle taken away. He sent for two different bordeaux, and when the cater-waiter returned, Philip announced a '61 Haut-Brion and a '66 Le Pin and said, "We'll taste them against each other."

Wally Walker moaned in anticipation and said, "This is why we love you, Philip."

I knew enough about wine to know that these were fantastic, once-in-a-lifetime wines. And as the wine goblets were filled to tasting depth, a large glass of orange juice was carried by another caterer on a tray and presented to my ridiculously underdressed nondrinker of a husband, which was bad enough, but then he joked, "And what year were these oranges squeezed?"

No one was amused. Tim gave out a high-pitched honk of a laugh, and I joined the others in ignoring him.

Anna Brody sat across the room in the bay window, near the crackling fire, blowing her cigarette smoke toward the chimney. I didn't know she smoked. On careful study, I saw that she didn't inhale. She was a social smoker. And the way she did it—the slow draw, the grand exhale into the updraft—made me wish I was smoking, too.

Philip very much wanted to know our thoughts.

Rene Scarlata, the bone-thin coloratura and consort of Dante Calibrini, the venture capitalist, favored the Haut-Brion. "But I could go the other way just as easily," she said. The men—Lancaster Group CEO Benjamin Wirtz, a banker from Hong Kong named Wai Jen, and Goldman-Sachs asset allocation genius Walter Clyde—all championed the '66 Le Pin.

Taking in the room, I realized that these were all Philip's friends. We'd been invited to be Anna's.

Turning to me, Philip said, "Kate, which do you prefer?"

I looked around the room. All eyes were on me. "Which do I prefer?"

Everyone was waiting for my answer.

In one of the articles I had read on Louis Underfer, he'd been asked, "What is the key to a successful person?" His answer: "The ability to make a choice and, if it's wrong, then make another."

I felt blood rush to my face. *Make a choice.*

I am, by nature, not a person who seeks the spotlight. But something about that room, those guests, and such fine wine made me want to stretch this moment, make it last.

Philip said, "Kate, take a leap . . ."

The truth was I wanted to gush about all three, even the burgundy that we'd been forbidden from tasting. "Well," I said, "I would have to say—"

That was when Tim, out of nowhere, decided to tell an unrelated story. It was about a famous writer who suffered from depression and decided one day, because living was so hard and terrible, that he was going to kill himself.

The guests looked around. No one knew what to say. There had been no transition whatsoever. After a cold, dead silence, Wally Walker spoke. "Who was the writer?"

"I don't remember," Tim said. "But he's famous."

I had to laugh.

Tim went on to explain that this famous writer *whose name he couldn't seem to remember* had taken elaborate steps to prepare for his suicide. When asked what those actual preparations entailed, Tim didn't know! "But it's really beside the point," he said, digging his hole even deeper. "Because just as the famous writer was about to kill himself, he happened to hear on the radio the Four Last Songs by Strauss. The irrefutable beauty of the music made it impossible for him to do it. Suddenly, he wanted to live!"

Tim might as well have strapped a bomb to his own body. Not only was he committing a kind of social suicide, he was taking the party with him.

"And your point?" Wally Walker asked as he cut off the tip of a Cuban cigar.

"It's not a point. It's a question. What is it in life that you value so much—what work of art, what piece of music or building or natural wonder—could you imagine having a similar effect on you?"

Someone: "That's awfully deep."

Someone else: "Too deep for me."

Philip passed the humidor.

I wanted to shout: *These people rule the world. They have no concept of wanting to kill themselves!*

"Well, okay, then," Tim continued. "Forget the suicide part of my story. Just think about what you find beautiful."

Philip sounded bemused when he said, "Are you asking what we *like*?"

"I'm asking what you, uhm, hold in awe."

"This wine," Penelope Winston joked.

"And my cigar, Philip, it's like smoking God."

"Yes," Philip replied, "if only God could be smoked."

The evening went on to a discussion as to whether Croatia was the new Prague and what to do in Dubai if you have only a day, and then Anna Brody, who sat opposite us, her face flushed from the wine, her eyes partially closed with the glazed look of a really good buzz, spoke: "The cry of a baby."

"What was that, darling?"

"Bach. Sophie, even on a bad day."

Except for the slow rolling clouds of cigar smoke, everything seemed to stop.

Anna closed her eyes and kept going. "A first kiss, my father's cologne, the Gettysburg Address, de Kooning's *Woman I,* the top of the Chrysler Building, a swim in the warm Caribbean sea or any warm sea, baby teeth, Rilke and Rimbaud, thinking of or touching the giant clams in Palau, the cathedral at Chartres because it's unfinished, Monet's haystacks, a ripe peach . . ."

I didn't speak to Tim during our walk home. He asked if I was all right. I said nothing. He wondered if I'd had a good time. He asked if I was mad.

"Mad is a child's word," I said. "Can we just not talk?"

Apparently not, because one block later, Tim started up again: "Hey, didn't it feel like we were invited as some kind of entertainment?"

"And didn't you play your part perfectly?"

"The clown?"

"Clowns are funny. You were something else. Shakespeare couldn't have dreamed you up."

"I think Philip Ashworth will survive."

"Of course he'll survive. He doesn't give a damn what you think of him."

"I think he liked my irreverence."

I sighed.

Watching Tim attempt battle with Philip Ashworth and his friends had made me almost irreconcilably sad. Tim had never seemed smaller, like a schoolboy outnumbered and outsized, circled by bullies, except this time I found myself rooting for the bullies. David deserved to be crushed by Goliath. And this time David was.

"We were guests," I reminded him as we walked home. As usual, my legs moved faster than his, and he lagged. But I felt he was testing me to see if I would slow down and walk with him. I didn't. I may have even increased my speed.

TIM

THAT NIGHT, WHILE TAKING A COLD SHOWER, I KEPT REPLAYING ONE PARTICULAR moment from the Ashworth-Brody dinner party—not that bumbled exchange when I'd interrupted my wife, nor how the light from the fireplace had bathed Anna's face, not the all-alone feeling I'd had during the long silence after I asked the question, not even the flash of relief I felt when Anna gave her poetic and perfect answer—no, what haunted me was the surprising moment after the putting on of winter coats when I turned to Anna Brody, offered my hand to shake, and she pulled me into a hug.

Instinctively, I employed my preemptive strike. *Start patting from the moment of contact. This way, when she pats you, you'll know you patted first.*

The hug that night was nice and long, and what was funny—or maybe not—was how the more I patted, the more Anna Brody didn't.

THREE

KATE

POOR TIM.

The call came in the middle of the night. His sister, Sal, forgetting, I suppose, the time difference, was phoning from the Australian outback, where she and her lover, Red, were in the middle of a monthlong camping trip. "Called when I could," she told me. I passed the phone to Tim, who was now sitting up in bed.

Bad news likes to come at night.

"What happened?" he said into the receiver. He listened. Then, as if punched in the stomach, he said, "No, no." He said so many *no*s, I wondered who had died.

I turned on my bedside lamp. Tim grimaced, either from what he was being told or from the sudden light, or both.

After hanging up with his sister, he called the airline, bought an open-return ticket (not cheap) for the following morning's first flight to Toledo via Chicago. I helped him pack. His best suit. (Really, his only suit.) Enough clothes for three days. Tim couldn't understand how it was that his sister had gotten the news first. Especially considering how findable he was. "Why didn't they call me?" he asked as he zipped up his suit bag. "She had to be tracked down. In Australia!" I tried to comfort him, but whatever I said seemed to be wrong. I stopped midsentence when he covered his ears with his hands.

Seeming more stunned than sad, he said, "You expect your parents to die. You rehearse for it. You even practice hearing the news."

"But no one died," I reminded him.

"True, but isn't this worse?"

TIM

FOR MY FATHER TO RETIRE MIDSEASON MEANT ONLY ONE THING: HE'D BEEN FIRED.
How did I know? Jack Welch would never quit. He was arguably the
third-greatest coach in the history of women's collegiate Division III
basketball. In 1990 he'd been named by then-president George H. W.
Bush as one of America's Thousand Points of Light. In the special mil-
lennium issue of the Cleveland *Plain Dealer*, he'd been listed as one of
Ohio's living legends, along with former astronaut/senator John Glenn
and Dave from Wendy's.

As I got off the plane at the Toledo Express Airport, Coach jerked
his arms above his head and, in Richard Nixon fashion, gave an awkward thumbs-up. Normally, I'd be embarrassed, thinking, *Why can't my
father be like other people?* But that day it didn't bother me. I barely noticed he wasn't wearing his usual pink and powder-blue Clayton College Lady Revolvers sweatsuit. In fact, I was so deep in thought, I
almost walked right past him. What was I thinking? The same thoughts
you'd be thinking if Anna Brody hadn't patted you.

"And that's how you greet your father?"

"Oh," I said, snapping out of it.

Coach was standing before me. "Where's your sister?"

Sal would not be attending the hastily organized retirement party
and testimonial dinner. "First of all, it was so sudden," she had explained over the phone. "Of course, if it was a funeral, or to take him
off life support, then I'd come. But an honorary dinner, *please*." I had
begged Sal to attend, arguing that only one of us kids needed to go. "I'm

a disappointment to him," I said. Since he liked her better than me, she should catch the first flight back to the States. The argument was moot, though, because Sal couldn't make it back even if she'd wanted to.

"She's in Australia, Dad. That's on the other side of the world."

"Her loss," Coach said with a chuckle. "Let me carry your bag."

I marveled at the ease with which Coach slung my overnight bag over his shoulder. It should have been no surprise. Dad was a brick. Hard, lean. A Jack LaLanne type. Sixty-five years old, but if you looked at him from the neck down, you'd swear he was thirty.

"What do you have in this bag?"

"Books. My dissertation so far."

"Oh, *that*. It's a little light, don't you think?"

Funny, I found the bag almost crippling in weight.

I started to say, "Well, I only brought a section of it . . ." But I stopped, because what was the point? In moments we'd be talking about Coach and only Coach.

"So, Dad, what happened?"

"It's easier to understand if I show you."

He slapped an arm over my back, and we moved quickly through the airport terminal. A well-wisher called out, "Thanks, Coach. Thanks for all the memories." A janitor pushing a mop said to me, "You must be proud of your old man." I nodded, longing for the moment when we'd be alone, for surely Coach had been staggered by the recent events. I secretly hoped that I'd get a glimpse of the broken and defeated man, the authentic man.

Fired? How can you fire Jack Welch?

My father liked to say: "A man becomes a man when he becomes a father." Or: "When he pays taxes the first time." Or: "When he marries his high school sweetheart, buys a house, and coaches an undefeated team all in the same year."

That day I wanted to say, "Dad, a man becomes a man when he loses everything he loves."

"You were only three and two, they shouldn't have let you go."

"They didn't fire me, son. I quit. And I'm about to show you the reason why."

What became apparent, and why I longed to board the first plane back, was that Coach Jack Welch had already rewritten the events of the last twenty-four hours. His forced retirement had been repositioned as a victory. He was going out on top. "I still have my mind, my health," he said, pleased. "My memory," he half whispered as I noticed my mother, Bobette, sitting in the backseat of the family Cadillac.

"You left Mom in the car?"

"Tim, relax. She prefers the car. But brace yourself—it's gotten worse since your last visit. I'm sure she'll recognize you, but mostly, in public, she panics, worried she won't remember names or faces. I mean, if truth be told, it's why I'm quitting."

"Oh," I said, as that sinking feeling, the Great Disparity, returned. Caught between what would be wonderful if it were happening (retiring because of his devoted love for his dear wife, Bobette) and what was actually happening (fired for a three-and-two record), I felt the squeeze.

"Hi, Mom," I said.

She smiled as if hearing the news that she was a mother for the first time.

"I've missed you, Mom."

"Aren't you sweet?"

No, I wanted to say. *"Sweet" visits. "Sweet" calls often. "Sweet" is nothing like what I am.*

"You won't believe who's coming. I'm so touched by the outpouring."

"Just a minute, Dad. Hey, Mom, how are you—"

Coach, interrupting: "Guess who's coming?"

I sighed and then began to list the players most likely to return for the quickly planned festivities.

"Trisha McGuiness?" (5' 9", 145 lbs., All Conference, 14.6 ppg.)

"No," he said, as if the thought of Trisha was preposterous.

"Riley?" (Riley Haliburton, a 90 percent free-throw shooter—"Man, could she pass.")

"Not Riley, no."

So I mentioned my father's best players, his favorite players, and finally, Coach snapped, "Stop it! Most of those people live far away."

"But I live far away . . ."

Coach ran over my words, listing five players, two of whom I didn't remember, and I thought I remembered them all, and the three I did know were below-average players, but all of whom still lived in the Cayton area: Tami Long, Karin Hickok, Cheryl Porter.

Meanwhile, I drifted off to Anna Brody Land.

"Did you hear me?"

"Oh, did you say something?"

"I expect you'll want to speak at my party."

I moaned like a disgruntled teenager forced to do a chore. "No, Dad . . ."

"You have plenty to say, I think. From a family perspective."

"I'd rather not."

Coach's smile turned icy. "You—will—speak." Each word said with equal emphasis. There was no choice. I glanced to the backseat. There sat my mother, who had found her own way to manage. I understood now. It wasn't chemical or explainable by a lack of iron or an overexposure to lead. It wasn't dementia or early Alzheimer's. It was pure wisdom. The way to beat the oppressor is to forget his victories, to vanquish all glory moments to an early grave. Bobette Parker Welch had found the ultimate revenge. She'd left without leaving. She'd forgotten because—for some people—if you don't remember, you win.

"Tim is going to speak," Coach said loudly to Bobette.

"Oh," she said. "Who?"

"Tim, your son, is going to speak about how proud he is of me."

He turned the Cadillac out of short-term parking. We passed two middle-aged women, one of whom hit the hood hard and shouted at my dad: "Pervert!"

"What did she say?"

"Just another grateful fan," Coach said.

I glanced out the back window, and this time I was able to read her lips as she shouted it again. *Pervert!*

"See, son? People love your old man."

KATE

"ARE YOU THERE? PLEASE BE THERE. PLEASE BE THERE."

It was Tim calling from Ohio. I had let the machine answer, and for a moment I didn't want to pick up.

"Dammit, I wish you were there . . ."

Out of guilt I lifted the receiver. "I'm here."

"Oh, God. Oh, thank you, God!"

"Sorry, didn't hear the phone—"

"You can't believe how bad it is here, Kate. It's horrible. You know how I thought he was being fired for his record? Well, I was wrong." Tim continued, spitting out half-formed sentences, hinting at something horrible but not explaining it clearly. And then he said something about how, in a few hours, he had to address a packed room. "He wants me to speak. And I don't know what the fuck to say!"

I tried to listen and sympathize, but ultimately, it was his family, his father, his speech to give.

"And, Kate, I found out the real reason . . ."

In my defense, whenever Tim visited his dad, there was always a crisis. Still, I should've listened better.

"The Athletic Director pulled me aside—"

"Honey, I have company. Anna's here."

"Who?"

"Anna Brody."

"She's there? Oh, why didn't you say?"

"Because you haven't stopped talking."

99

Tim was quiet. "You better go, then."

"Look, we can talk a few more minutes. I'm only saying—"

"No, Kate, I'm fine. I'm actually doing great. Believe me, I am. And be sure to tell anyone who asks."

Click.

Earlier that morning, right after Tim left for the airport, I called Bruno to explain why I wouldn't be at work for the next few days. "A family emergency," I said. Bruno, ever concerned, asked, "Is everything all right?" "Yes, here at home. But for Tim and his dad, not good." Bruno wanted details, but I told him I'd have to explain later because Sam had wandered into the kitchen, having just crawled out of bed.

The breakfast/get dressed/brush teeth rituals all went smoothly. Sometimes it's just easier with one parent. I made pancakes in the shapes of animals and, according to Teddy, did "better than Daddy." While the boys watched a few minutes of TV, I called Claudia to see if she wanted to meet for coffee, but she and Debbie Beebe were off to Pilates.

At drop-off, stay-at-home-dad Wendell Carson was talking with a mother whose back was to me. I always wanted to laugh when I saw Wendell. Not because of Tim's nickname for him—the Weasel—which was perfect, by the way. No, it's because lately, Tim had taken to imitating Wendell, and he had him down pat: his pursed lips, his fey gestures, and his annoying tendency to poke you repeatedly in the arm while talking with you.

That morning Wendell was gesticulating wildly, having cornered, I soon realized, none other than Anna Brody. I eavesdropped while he described a "fffabulous" play space in Chelsea where he had taken his son, Jasper. As expected, Wendell poked Anna in the arm twice for emphasis, and as he started in for a third poke, she moved slightly aside so that his finger stabbed the air. I must have laughed out loud, because Wendell turned to look at me. "What's so funny?"

"Nothing," I said. "I just thought of something my husband said."

"Oh, by the way, tell him to call me. We're starting a men's group. And we need men."

"I'll tell him," I said as Wendell hurried off.

Anna said, "How lucky." (Meaning, I thought, his leaving.)

"Yes," I said, turning toward Anna. "Hey, are you doing anything now?"

As we climbed the stairs, I worried that this was a terrible idea. I started to apologize for what she was about to see, but for some reason, I stopped myself. I'm unable to explain why. Maybe I was testing her.

After following me into our apartment, Anna looked around but said nothing for the longest time. When she finally spoke, it was something about the advantages of a small home. I believe the word she used was *intimate*. She mentioned how, in her house, it seemed all she did was look for one of Sophie's lost socks or the house keys. "Same thing with us," I said, proving the thesis of a book from some years back that argued men by nature compete and women seek consensus. Anna moaned about the upkeep of a house (as if she genuinely did the upkeeping). I nodded as if I knew how she felt. In an attempt at humor, I demonstrated how, if one cleared off the table in the living room, it became a dining room. I demonstrated how, by moving the movable bookshelf in the wall unit (which Tim had designed and built), it allowed that same room to become a home office.

I hoped she would laugh.

She didn't. She said almost too sincerely, "What a great place."

I wondered whether to believe her.

Where I saw a much too small bedroom for two growing boys, she saw the walls covered with their watercolors, crayon drawings, and art projects of my own invention. She noticed the homemade picture frames made of corrugated cardboard that the boys and I had painted. She said, "Nice," and in an effort to be completely honest, I admitted the idea for the frames had been appropriated from an arts-and-crafts magazine. "Still," she said, meaning I had done it. Yes, she was impressed, and not because it was my idea but because I'd taken the time to find and implement someone else's good idea.

Where I saw the trundle bed Tim had built for the boys as a kind of primitive configuration of white pine, she admired the ingenuity of the design, the care he'd taken, the charm of the names painted on the headboards.

To my surprise, the opposite of what I'd expected occurred. I saw our home with her eyes, and for the first time in a long time, I liked what I saw. The evident care taken, the make-do practicality, the creative touches. The art in our home was the simple art of our children. Still, I nearly gasped when she said, "There's so much love here."

I smiled and said, "That's kind."

"It's not kind. It's what I see."

I left the room to compose myself, wipe my eyes.

I was in the kitchen boiling water for tea when Tim called. As I described earlier, he was in a panic. As I half listened to him, I checked to see if Anna was all right. "Don't worry about me," she said from down the hall, where she was looking at the framed photos on our wobbly bookcase. The teapot whistled. After I hung up with Tim, I asked Anna to come back to the kitchen. Using a yellow sponge, I wiped the breakfast table clean.

"That was Tim," I said, gesturing for her to sit in the good chair. "He had to leave town."

I straddled a stool. Because of the metal security gate that covered our kitchen window, the morning sun cast fractured shadows across both Anna and me. She seemed much too bright and vibrant for our little kitchen. Rather akin to Greta Garbo in Kmart. But she didn't seem to mind.

She asked where Tim had gone.

"Back home," I said. "A family crisis."

I explained that Tim had a complicated relationship with his dad and that it was hard for me to have sympathy because I never had a father.

"Oh," she said with a sad smile. "What's the problem with his dad?"

There were countless stories about Coach that I could have told, but for some reason, this is the one I chose.

That previous Christmas he'd sent Tim a box of Cayton College Lady Revolvers swag—a light blue and pink warm-up suit, tennis shoes, even a team jacket, all with the Nike insignia prominently displayed. This was his gift. Pissed, Tim promptly threw everything in the trash. Several days later, while walking across the Heights, he saw a man decked out in Cayton College athletic apparel. Shocked, Tim approached the man to ask if he'd gone to Cayton. But then he realized the man was homeless, and the clothes had been the ones Tim had thrown out.

"Perfect," Anna said.

I went on to brag about Tim, saying that ever since that day, he had taken special interest in the homeless man, whose name was Lenny. He became Tim's charity project. Every so often Tim gave him money to sweep our building's stoop, or bought him slices of pizza, or gave him a Cayton College stocking cap.

"Your husband is a good man," Anna said.

"Yes, I think so."

"A good, good man."

Later, after she was gone, I realized she hadn't touched her tea. Maybe because I'd forgotten to pour it.

Downstairs, I found the mail scattered on the vestibule floor. Bills, mostly, and junk mail, and a large manila envelope that I opened. Halfway in, I realized what was inside. I'd forgotten that I'd even ordered it. It was easy to do, and I'd done it from work. When the woman from *The Tonight Show* asked where to send it, I had to think for a moment. My first impulse was to give my work address, but then I thought, *I have nothing to hide.* So I gave my home address, telling myself that if Tim found it, I'd explain.

All it took was a phone call and payment by credit card. I didn't even need to know the airdate. Did I know the guests? I knew only one, I said. One was all they needed. "And the guest's name?"

The transcript read like your standard late-night interview. Small talk: *You look great. It's great to be here,* etc. I confess to skimming it quickly, looking only for my name, thinking that he must have mentioned me. Hadn't he said on our answering machine *I'm talking about you when I'm talking at the end*?

I didn't find my name, but he was right. It was at the end. When I found the section, I had to read it twice.

JEFF SLADE: Well, Jay, I'm basically a normal guy. I go to work. I love my dog. But like all people, I have my regrets.

JAY LENO: Can you give us an example of a Jeff Slade regret?

JEFF SLADE: Actually, I can only think of one.

JAY LENO: Just one?

JEFF SLADE: But it's big. And she's probably not watching.

JAY LENO: Aw, we're out of time. You promise to come back and tell us all about your one big regret?

JEFF SLADE: I'd like that, thanks.

So I was Jeff Slade's one big regret. *Now he tells me.* I tore the transcript into pieces, stopped at a neighbor's garbage can, and buried the scraps deep in the trash.

TIM

"CAN YOU HEAR ME? CAN EVERYONE HEAR ME? JUST RAISE YOUR HAND IF YOU can't.

"Good evening. My name is Tim Welch. I'm the son. What a privilege it is for me to speak with you tonight. And what a remarkable turnout, especially considering the short notice. There's so much one can say at a time like this. Hey, wasn't the video presentation terrific? Excuse me while I look for my notes. Oh, here. On behalf of my sister, Sally, and our mother, Bobette, we'd like to thank the Cayton College community for your rousing send-off of my father. Several of you have mentioned your surprise at learning Coach Welch had a son. This, I think, reflects the intensity with which Coach—yes, even I call him Coach—went about his work. A tough man to label, Coach was more than a father, a friend, a teacher, more than a taskmaster, more than the Great Motivator—he wasn't just any one thing.

"For those of you who don't know, I am, by profession, a history teacher. So hopefully, not only can I bring the family perspective to tonight's celebration, but perhaps the historical perspective can be illuminated as well.

"I would like to tell you about a memory of my father that I didn't quite understand until this very day. It happened when I was seven, in our basement. Our basement is wood-paneled and, over the years, has basically become a museum to Coach's unprecedented career. Framed team photos hang in sequence along the walls—plaques, medals, certificates, lighted trophy cases, large squares of illuminated Plexiglas that house the five hundredth Victory Ball, nets from the eight national championships, framed letters from Richard Milhous Nixon, Ronald Reagan, and George H. W. Bush. There's even a display case I made in ninth-grade Wood Shop for his lucky tie—the light blue one with an American flag set off in bold relief . . .

"But I digress.

"I was only seven years old, so I didn't understand what my father's erect penis was doing in the mouth of Linda 'Minus' Callahan (13.2 ppg., 3 to 1.2 assist-to-turnover ratio, All Conference honorable mention). Is Linda here tonight? I didn't think so.

"Anyway—confused by what I had seen and perhaps a bit shaken—I asked him what he was doing. He said that Linda was having problems, and he was helping her out. Now it turns out he's been *helping out* a succession of young women for over forty years.

"Only five—five so far—have come forward, five who are participating in the lawsuit— Oops, wasn't supposed to mention that. Yes, the rumors are true. The college wants to keep it hush-hush. Many more of you could receive a nice chunk of change. You see, the college hasn't realized that for every one of you who has come forward, there are ten or twenty of you who yet could. So spread the word. Close the school down. Most important, let's gut the motherfucker . . ."

Regrettably, I didn't give the above speech. I was either too chicken or still too stunned.

Earlier that night, while we drove toward the governor's room of the Holiday Inn North in Toledo, Coach asked for a copy of my prepared text. I told him I hadn't written anything. He asked if I thought that was a good idea. He was understandably nervous about what I was going to say, especially since I'd gotten wind of the real reason for his retirement. I explained that it was too difficult for me to put into words the enormity of how I felt about him. He nodded, looking dubious.

The crowd that had gathered was much smaller than he had imagined. The room was decorated with photos on foam core. Bouquets of light blue and pink carnations added to the occasion's funereal feel. As featured speaker, I would go last. After the twelve-minute video presentation set to Queen's "We Are the Champions" and Dionne Warwick's "That's What Friends Are For," I walked to the podium with no idea what would come out of my mouth. What did I say? Nothing for a good long time. Then I said, "The facts." I proceeded to recite his career statistics. That took a good ten minutes. At the conclusion of the endless litany of his triumphs, applause broke out, and someone threw a handful of confetti.

Then I said, "And what do they mean?"

I felt my father shift in his seat. The air in the room grew cold. Pin-drop silence. Here was my chance to speak truthfully. But somehow, when I opened my mouth, a piece of confetti lodged in my throat. People thought I was choking up when, in truth, I was just trying not to choke.

"Coach is my father. I am—his—son. What else—is there—to . . . ?"

Something about how I was trying to spit out the fleck of confetti gave the impression of my struggling with great emotion. The guests broke into applause, and Coach ascended the small platform, slapping me on the back so hard I still feel the sting. As the Cayton College jazz band played the fight song, more confetti continued to fall, and Coach shouted over the music and the cheering, "Thanks, son. I couldn't have said it better myself!"

On the small plane from Toledo to Chicago, I smiled as the flight attendant used the microphone/intercom to go over safety procedures. There were only a handful of passengers, but the flight attendant was behaving as if we were on a 747 headed to Milan. As she dutifully pointed out the emergency exits, I noticed her carefully coiffed hair, her excessive makeup, how hard she was trying, and I couldn't help but think about how hard I'd been trying to not be my father. I would do anything to not be my father, especially now.

As the flight attendant pushed past with the beverage cart, I surprised myself by asking for a Bloody Mary. She was handing me the miniature bottle of Absolut when the pilot asked all passengers to be seated and belt themselves in, as a bumpy approach was expected. We were, it turned out, already on the way down.

As the plane jerkily made its descent, yet another inappropriate Anna Brody thought came to me. So I gripped the armrests and tried to beat back that thought by repeating to myself: *I am not my father, I am not my father, I am not my father . . .*

Late that night, after my return home, Kate ran me a bath, and I climbed in. She sat on the toilet seat with the lid down as I told her everything. And she heard my every word.

Before she went off to bed, she kindly quoted what a wise woman (Kate) had once written to me on a birthday card: "Growing older—contrary to what everyone tells us—is one of the nicest parts of being alive. Growing older, and not becoming our parents, but rather, slightly better versions."

As she left me alone in the tub, she called back, "So tell me, Mr. Welch, can we safely conclude that we're both already that?"

KATE

MY FIRST MORNING BACK, BRUNO GREETED ME WITH THE NEWS THAT HIS TRIP TO St. Louis had been an unqualified success.

"So it went well?"

Bruno coughed his recurring tubercular-like cough and held up his hands in victory. He'd gone to visit Louis Underfer to achieve one simple goal: finding out how much money we have to give away in the near future.

One point five million dollars.

"We can work with that," I said, pleased.

"It has its peculiarities. Thirty-five grants—for up to thirty-five thousand dollars each—announced in St. Louis at Cortez Headquarters on the thirteenth of June."

"Why St. Louis? Why the thirteenth of June?"

"Underfer doesn't fly and it's his daughter's thirty-fifth birthday."

"Okay, it's a little cheesy, but it's a start."

Bruno wasn't fooling himself. "At some point," he told me, "we resign ourselves to the fact that while we may not irrevocably alter the world, we will have at least tried."

He asked why I was smiling.

"Irrevocably alter," I said. "Two of Tim's favorite words."

Suddenly, we had purpose. Contacts needed to be made. Site visits planned. Bruno wanted my dream list of who would be ideal as our first grant recipients. I told him he'd have a list ASAP.

So much to do, so little time was my thinking when Claudia called, wanting to meet later for a drink.

I didn't go straight home that night. I met Claudia at Sample on Smith Street. She had promised interesting news.

"Jill the nanny. You know the one I'm talking about?"

I didn't know Jill. "I'm happily out of the loop, Claudia."

"Jill, the whitest, spunkiest, most impressive nanny ever in the history of nannies. Anna Brody's Jill. Rumored-to-be-receiving-a-six-figure-salary Jill. The same Jill who had been once, most notably, the live-in nanny to billionaire Ronald Perelman's daughter Caleigh and also the nanny to the children of a very famous Hollywood couple with Scientologist affiliations. Jill whom Dan the Bear described as 'the Julie Andrews of nannies.'"

"Okay, Claudia," I said, stirring my drink. "I get the picture."

"Well, guess who had these miniature high-tech video cameras installed all through her eighteen-room house?"

"Anna Brody."

"Yes. Isn't that terrible?"

"Videotaping the nanny? Not if you have reason to believe there's something wrong going on."

Claudia told me what the videotape had revealed. Jill was bright, attentive, creative at free play, that Sophie especially loved Jill's story about the swans. Apparently, Jill was firm when necessary but never cruel, never raised her voice, never shamed, often sang beautifully to Sophie, and was teaching her how to count in French.

"So what's the problem?"

"Anna fired her."

"On what grounds?"

"No one knows. But my theory? Maybe she felt a wee bit threatened. You see, if Jill were to stick around, Sophie would never be happy with Anna."

"That's awful."

"Not for Jill. She got her whole year's salary for just two weeks of babysitting. Not bad work, if you can get it."

I didn't know what parts of this story to believe. I wasn't about to call Anna and ask her myself. The very next day, however, and new to her role as a nannyless mother, Anna Brody called me instead. I was surprised she knew where to reach me. Then I remembered having given her my work number, probably with the thought that she'd never call.

"Is this a good time?" Anna asked.

"Yes, it's a good time."

I can't remember the reason for those first calls: activity suggestions, maybe directions to the Children's Museum, it didn't matter. The conversations were brief and, individually, no big deal. For weeks I'd wanted to be this kind of girlfriend to Anna Brody—her confidante, advice giver, favorite friend—and how unfortunate that when she finally showed an interest, I no longer had the time. Still, it wasn't until the fourth call that day that I might have sounded impatient with her.

"Me again," Anna said. "Is it still a good time?"

"Yes. Well, actually, I'm kind of busy . . ."

In the background, I could hear Sophie crying.

"Well, then," Anna said quickly, "I was just wondering if your boys could come over for a playdate."

"Ask Tim. That's his domain."

"I thought I should ask you first."

"No need. Just give him a call."

"Oh," she said after an odd pause, "I just didn't want you to feel left out."

"Don't worry about me feeling left out." Truthfully, for me, feeling left out was a new and welcome feeling. Then I noticed Bruno standing in my office doorway, looking concerned.

"I have to go," I said to Anna.

I hung up the phone and laughed, but not for funny reasons.

"Kate, I couldn't help overhearing . . ."

"What?"

"Your mention of feeling left out."

"Oh, please," I said. "Don't worry, it's not about work. It's this new mother in our neighborhood. She's a strange one. She wants permission to call my husband to arrange a playdate . . ."

"Maybe she's just sensitive to your situation."

"What situation? That I get to have a career? Is it terrible of me to enjoy working? Because I love coming here. I love dressing up. I even love the parts of my job I'm not supposed to enjoy. The crowded ride on the subway. Even the lack of mission . . ."

"Do you think we suffer from a lack of mission?"

"Well, yes, I did. Up until yesterday I didn't quite know what we're doing here. And even that was okay. I trust you, but I was beginning to doubt Louis. Now that we're about to have actual money to give away, I admit it, I'm giddy! About all that we can do. And that we get to do it together. But mostly, what I'm saying is that for one day my friend Anna should have real people's problems."

I explained about the staff, the eighteen-room house, the rich, handsome husband.

Noticing the clock, I went to the hall closet and slipped on my coat. "Anyway, it doesn't matter, Bruno, because you and I . . ."

"Yes?"

I couldn't help but smile. "We're about to change the world."

TIM

KATE HAD GONE TO WORK EARLY, THE BOYS WERE GRUMPY, AND I WAS IN A BAD WAY
when the dreaded phone call came from my mentor, Dr. Jamison Lamson of St. Bernard's College in Queens.

"Where is it?" he said. Meaning: my dissertation.

I wanted to tell him I'd lost momentum, that my father had thrown a wrench into things and I would be done if Dr. Lamson had been my dad, but I lied and said, "Good, it's going good."

"When, then?"

I gave him my stock line: "No one wants it done more than I do."

"Well, Timothy, I'm standing by."

Later, I was pushing the boys in the stroller down the Starbucks side of Montague Street when I saw Joni Kirtley and Max Weiss, two of my star former students, enter Muffins and More. Time for a detour. I whipped the stroller around, checked for traffic, and zipped across the street.

Teddy said, "No, Daddy, I don't wanna go there."

But I was not to be stopped.

Inside, Joni and Max had disappeared up to the mezzanine level. I asked a nice-seeming woman if she'd watch the boys while I ran upstairs to use the bathroom.

Truth be told, I didn't need the bathroom. I needed to see my former students, and more important, I needed them to see me.

Upstairs, maybe ten or twelve of Montague's best and brightest had pushed several tables together, making one giant study area. Backpacks were slung over chairs, textbooks cracked open, laptops powered up.

"Hey, guys," I said, feigning surprise upon seeing them.

The kids were polite, but there was something restrained about their response, something guarded. In order to cut through this weird tension, I introduced myself to the one student I didn't know. "I'm Mr. Welch."

"Yes, I know," the new student said.

Oh, I thought. *He's heard of me.*

He extended his cold, damp hand for me to shake and said, "I'm Dr. Thorne."

I did my best to hide my reaction, but a jolt shot through my body as if I'd stepped on a live wire and been subjected to a thousand volts. There he was. Dr. Prince Thorne. The youthful, strapping, lightly freckled, redheaded wunderkind who was my replacement.

Rumor had it that when Dr. Millicent Vandeventer first introduced Dr. Prince Thorne to the student body of the Montague Academy, and after reading his lengthy educational pedigree (Yale, Princeton, Harvard), the honors, the accolades, and after holding up the galley for his first novel, entitled *Planet Stasis,* she said the following: "I want to be perfectly clear—I got him to commit for one year. Now it's up to you to convince him to stay forever."

On your best day, you think you're irreplaceable. You think no one can do what you do better than you do, especially when you're doing it in the way that only you can. (Diagram that sentence, Dr. Thorne!) But then one day you realize you were wrong.

In those brief moments as I stood before them, it was clear: These students all revered him, and they didn't miss me.

I excused myself by saying, "Sorry, I hear one of my boys calling." Of course no one was calling. But it got me out of there.

So I was at sea, lost, and in a foul mood when I clacked the large iron knocker at the Ashworth/Brody house. When a frazzled Anna Brody answered the door, she smiled nervously and called out to a crying Sophie, "Honey, they're here!"

From far off, Sophie let fly with a wail like a World War II air-raid warning.

Anna sighed and said, "I'm sorry, it's just been one of those days."

Clearly. Some pudding or jelly had spilled on Anna's cashmere sweater. Her left cheek was bright red, as if it had been pinched. I mentioned we could come back at a better time.

"No," Anna said, "please stay."

Sophie appeared at the bottom of the grand staircase.

Anna knelt down and said, "Come say hello to your new friends."

"Noooo!" Sophie scrunched her face and grabbed her mother's hair and started to pull.

Anna held Sophie's wrist firmly. "She's never been—this—bad," Anna said. "Do not pull my hair. You do not pull hair."

So Sophie started to kick at her mother.

My boys stood in the vestibule, motionless. They were meeting Sophie Brody-Ashworth, and already they were scared.

I had experienced my share of meltdowns, but this was one for the ages: the kind where there was no fixing it, no going back, no making it right.

As her daughter's tantrum showed no signs of letting up, Anna seemed to shut down. She had no idea what to do next.

But when a flailing Sophie smacked her forehead on the banister, I saw an opening. As a maid ran for ice and Anna tried to comfort Sophie, I played one of Kate's games—Boo-boo Be Gone—wherein I badly mimed gathering up her pain, packing it into a pretend snowball, and throwing it deep, deep, deep into space. I even included appropriate sound effects. The result was miraculous. Sophie stopped crying and stared at me. Her tear-stained face broke into a big smile.

Anna said, "Wow, you're good."

The rest of that first playdate remains a blur. While the boys and Sophie played quietly, I shared with Anna some strategies for dealing with a feisty kid. Time got vague, fuzzy—soon it was dark out and we needed to get home.

This much was clear: That day, in Anna's mind, I became the Picasso of parents. Funny, I know. But more important, and I didn't understand this until later, she made me feel like a teacher again.

KATE

THE HEIGHTS CAFÉ WAS PACKED FULL WITH PEOPLE I DIDN'T KNOW. ARRIVING LATE, I looked around until I found him sitting in the corner booth, his back toward the other customers. He held a menu but didn't appear to be studying it. He hadn't seen me yet.

I'd come straight from work, stopping at the Starbucks up the street to use their bathroom for a hair/makeup check. Surely I'm not the only one who, when having dinner with an ex-lover, spends an uncommonly long time at the mirror. Part of me found my behavior vain, but a bigger part of me wanted to look my best, as if to say, *Fuck you—this is what you missed.*

This would be my first encounter with Jeff since he'd changed his last name from Slakowitz to Slade. Years ago, when I last saw him, he was a paralegal working the night shift at Skadden, Arps. He moved to L.A., changed his name, and in his first audition, was cast in a supporting role on a forgettable show on FOX. It ran half a season, was canceled by Christmas. Discouraged, he wisely considered a career in carpentry, cabinetmaking, that sort of thing. He enrolled in a woodworking course north of Santa Barbara only to reluctantly audition for and land the lead on a new ABC series about a sexy single dad who helps people find love, rediscover love, redefine love, and there is a mystical component: the sexy single dad is an angel.

In truth, I wouldn't know. I don't watch the show.

Now, if Slade was anything like Slakowitz, he wasn't going to ask me about my new job that night. So I was determined to tell him about the Lucy Foundation and how I was getting to use my background as a scenario creator to look ahead and imagine various futures that might occur, all the result of choices made now. What I wouldn't tell him was that on the train ride back to Brooklyn, I had done a bit of scenario creating of my own. What if I had become Mrs. Slakowitz/Slade? One version had me living in a Malibu beach house, my hair bleached, my car a convertible, my breasts silicone. That one made me laugh. Another version had me divorced already, embittered by his brutish male behavior. A third scenario had me blissfully happy, living in southern Vermont with my carpenter/cabinetmaker hunk of a husband who'd stopped auditioning not because he'd discovered that he wasn't much of an actor but because he didn't need the acclaim of millions, the *TV Guide* covers, when he had me—I was enough—we were enough—it was enough to wear flannel and homeschool our children and run naked in the snow while we tapped sap from a cluster of maples on our own twenty-two-acre plot of land . . .

This last scenario was more elaborate than the others, which concerned me. If our dreams at night reveal what we're most afraid of, then our daydreams tell us what we'd most like our lives to be.

Still, I convinced myself, it would be good to see this particular ex-lover in the flesh and to crush for all time any lingering regrets, his or mine, regarding what might have been. Eager to finish the job, I scooted across the room toward the corner booth.

"Excuse me?" I said when I got close enough.

He didn't look up, probably thinking I was an autograph seeker.

"Hey, Slakowitz."

This got his attention. He looked up. "Oh, Kate, hi." He quickly slid out of the booth and stood to greet me. "My God, you look fabulous."

I kissed his cheek. He smelled of a mixture of cigarettes, cologne, and too much soap. "Jefferson," I said. "How good to see you."

"You really do look fabulous."

"You seem surprised."

He helped me off with my coat. I removed the furry earmuffs the boys had given me last Christmas and took my place across from him. He'd dressed casually. Too casually, I thought. A loose-fitting black sweater, faded jeans, brand-new black leather tennis shoes.

"I was hoping we'd have some time alone," he said.

"We're alone right now, Jeff."

"Yes, but," he said, pausing to smile, "he's in the bathroom."

In all the rush—and I'm not proud of this—I'd forgotten Tim was coming. This was particularly troubling because I had insisted that he join us. He was worried he'd be in the way. I said, "Nonsense, you're my husband," something like that, something obvious that didn't really express why I wanted him there. But I was firm, and finally, he relented.

Jeff glanced back over toward the men's room. "He's been in there a long time."

"What? Oh, he's funny that way."

"Yes, but he's been in there a really long time. I mean, I hope Tom's okay."

"Tim. It's *Tim*."

"Since when?"

"It's always been Tim."

"Aw, you're kidding." Jeff brought both hands to his face. "Aw, man. I wondered if I had the name right. You know that feeling when you don't know if a name is right? You kind of hesitate but hope. And when he didn't say anything, I kept saying Tom."

"It's his own fault, then. He should have said something."

"I feel bad."

"He'll be okay."

There was an awkward silence during which we looked at each other. Others would say he was more handsome now. The short, spiked hair, the day-old beard, the same real teeth, now bleached a blinding white. But I preferred the longer-haired Jeff, the less buff, perpetually stoned, in-need-of-a-bath, roll-his-own-cigarettes Slakowitz that I'd lusted for once upon a time.

Taking my hands in his, he said, "I feel terrible about what happened with us. There's so much to say. So much I'd do differently. Like that was a vulnerable time, right before the wedding, and I wished I hadn't . . ."

Jeff Slakowitz came to our wedding, even though I had wanted to uninvite him. But since my sudden desire to uninvite him might have exposed what had occurred, he remained on the guest list.

"It's behind us," I said.

"You *say* that, but . . ."

Okay. Two weeks before the wedding, we'd shared a bottle of wine, smoked some cheap pot, and Jeff's playful pleas for me to call off the wedding grew more desperate and pathetic. He agreed to quit begging if he could have one last kiss—which seemed a sweet idea except for the lack of time limit we placed on it, because this last kiss led us to a bland room in a Motel 6 outside Bakersfield, where it almost turned into one last time. My maid of honor said it didn't count because Jeff never entered me and it was all over quickly. I needed Tim to know about it. You see, during that last month of our engagement, he'd been telling me everything. Funny things. His first French kiss. Not so funny things, too. Two students he'd slept with in his student-teacher days. He'd been so forthright that I knew I had to tell him. Also, he deserved to know the person he was marrying. I was struggling to explain it when Tim held up his hand for me to stop talking. "Listen," he said, "I'll forgive you your past if you forgive me mine."

"But I'm trying to tell you what happened yesterday."

"Yesterday included."

How cool was he. It was one of those moments when I knew I was marrying the right man.

But now Jeff Slade, TV star, was sitting across from me, struggling to find the words so that I might forgive him our past.

"I was rotten to you," he said.

"Really, I don't remember it that way." I was lying.

"Part of my program of recovery is that I make amends to the people I've hurt. And you are my last person. And I want to thank you for giving me this chance . . ."

The beauty of this particular narcissist is that while he believed he'd changed and learned and grown, he forgot that so had the person sitting across from him. Yes, he hurt me, and yes, it took a long time to recuperate, but time and distance had been my friends in this regard: If there had never been the frequently drunk and wasted Jeff Slakowitz, the three-timing, deceit-riddled Jeff Slakowitz, that hollow/shallow/ soulless thing of beauty, I never would have found Tim. Jeff made Tim possible in the same way that any person's mistakes inform his or her future choices. I can't count the times I've wanted to tell my husband, "Without Jeff Slade, there would have been no you."

I had the above thoughts while Jeff Slade kept on talking: ". . . was awful to you. And boy, do I know it now. The monster I was . . ."

Also, I wanted to thank him for single-handedly altering my aesthetic sensibility. Because of him, my idea of what beauty was changed from the washboard stomach, the chiseled cheekbones, the Adonis-like figure, and the love of mirrors to dependable, decent, humble, funny, gentle, generous. Slakowitz was my transition. He was my vapid, gorgeous fuck buddy. Tim Welch was my future.

"I hurt you, and I wish I could . . ."

But now, to mess with my head, Jeff Slade was midway through making his amends when I realized what he'd become. Dependable, decent, humble, funny, gentle, generous. And also newly sober.

"I'm basically trying to say I'm a changed man. And I wish I'd changed sooner—"

"I get it. I got it. Don't say any more."

But it appeared Jeff was just getting started when I heard a vaguely familiar male voice go, "Oops."

We both turned to find Tim, who had finally emerged from the bathroom, standing there. I didn't recognize him right away.

"Do you two want more time alone?"

That was when I started to laugh, partly from guilt (because I did maybe want more time) but mostly because of how he was dressed. He wore his professorial cardigan sweater with the brown moleskin elbow patches. He'd slicked back his hair in such a way that it made him look younger and more vulnerable. What especially got me was the rose-briar pipe (empty of tobacco, of course) that he held in his hand and occasionally stuck in his mouth. He looked retro-fifties, like a loving father from one of those black-and-white TV shows. It was off-putting at first, but it quickly grew on me. *Bravo*, I thought. Tim was the real actor that evening. Award-winning. He hadn't wanted to attend the reunion of two ex-lovers, but he'd come along because I'd insisted. And for better or worse, he'd come on his own terms.

My only objection was his choice of where to sit. I'd made room for him next to me, but he slid in on Jeff Slade's side. It was the oddest feeling, the two of them next to each other, both facing me. I thought of that *Sesame Street* song about how one thing is not like the others.

Before we ordered from the menu, Jeff announced that this would be his treat. I started to object, but Tim said, "Kate, don't be rude." I shut up because Tim was right.

Jeff ordered what I ordered, the grilled chicken salad, and Tim went for a bacon cheeseburger with twice-dipped fries.

During the meal, Jeff talked all about Jeff. He spoke about his show, which Tim claimed we'd seen and liked. "It's your best work," Tim said. Jeff looked in my direction. I nodded.

"You don't know what that means to me," Jeff said.

We saw plenty of pictures of Jeff's new dog, the ineptly named Korky, a Great Dane with a disturbingly large penis. We saw pictures of his new car—a Mercedes-Benz SUV—and his new house, a 1920s Spanish villa–looking structure, red tile roof, once home to none other than Zsa Zsa Gabor. It was your typical movie-star mansion. What was atypical was that it belonged to someone we knew.

"It's just a house," Jeff said with humility. "It doesn't make a person happy."

I wasn't sure if he believed that to be true.

Tim listened intently, appearing fascinated by everything Jeff Slade had to say. On several occasions, during our Jeff-dominated conversation, Tim found a way to segue in my direction—from a discreet mention of my work to what the boys were like and how we enjoyed life in the Heights. Later, Tim became so frustrated that he out-and-out bragged about the grants Bruno and I were going to give away. Of course, Jeff countered that he'd been recently approached by Make-A-Wish, which caused Tim to snap and say, "But Kate is actually doing something . . ."

I reached under the table and squeezed Tim's knee.

It was that kind of night. Annoyed one moment, relieved the next. But it went well, considering, and it probably would have continued going well if it weren't for a cell phone. When it rang, Jeff flipped open the receiver and pushed talk only to realize he and I had the same ring.

Digging through my purse, I found my phone. The caller ID was flashing our home number, and I answered. Pearl, our babysitter, sounded worried. Teddy had come down with a fever, and while she was taking his temperature, he'd thrown up all over his pajamas. I asked if he was all right, and she said, "He's doing fine, considering," and that he was asking for Daddy.

I told her I'd be right home.

TIM

HUBERT HUMPHREY, FORMER VICE PRESIDENT, EX-SENATOR FROM MINNESOTA, AND Democratic candidate for president in 1968, was a patient at the Mayo Clinic in Rochester on and off in the spring of 1978, while undergoing radiation and chemotherapy for a quick-spreading cancer of the bladder that would soon claim his life. One evening while being visited by his devoted wife, Muriel, and other loved ones, he said he was feeling very tired, so they hugged and kissed him good night. On the way out, Muriel informed the nurse that the vice president was not to be disturbed. Desperate for sleep, Humphrey himself dialed up the switchboard to make sure they would turn off his phone. With the promise that they would, he fell quickly asleep. Ten minutes later, the phone rang. Startled and annoyed, Humphrey fumbled around for the phone and answered it, none too happy, only to discover that Richard Milhouse Nixon, his opponent in the '68 election, was on the other end of the line, calling from his house in San Clemente, California, where he'd been living in disgrace since resigning the presidency on August 8, 1974.

That night these two men—Humphrey dying, Nixon wishing himself dead—spoke on the phone. What did they talk about? No transcript of their conversation exists, but it stands to reason they spoke about how the vice president was feeling. Perhaps they discussed their loving wives, their wonderful and supportive children. Nixon may have talked about the recent birth of another grandchild. Maybe they voiced admiration, regrets. Maybe they had old friends in common to discuss.

Maybe Nixon said something that made Humphrey laugh. We'll never know. But this much is certain: What had likely been intended as a brief call to a former adversary turned into a two-hour conversation.

I thought about Nixon and Humphrey in those moments after Jeff Slade had excused himself to take his turn in the Heights Café men's room. Kate had been gone half an hour at that point. I know it's a stretch—Nixon/Humphrey, Slade/Welch. Still, I couldn't help but wonder: Were the feelings between me and Jeff Slade somewhat like what Nixon and Humphrey felt that night after hanging up? The surge of warmth in the veins, the sense of uplift that comes when your enemy is no longer your enemy, that what kept you fierce and burning no longer needed to be fed.

Yes, this was like that.

Now it wasn't that I'd instantly become Jeff Slade's best friend. But I found myself kind of liking the guy. What had happened? One moment, I later realized.

It came after Kate had hurried off to tend to Teddy. Our waiter was turning the pepper grinder, and the pepper was floating down over Jeff's grilled chicken strips on mixed greens, when he said, "Look, I know I'm lucky." It wasn't the words, exactly, but how he said them. The look of humility in his eyes. The complex contradictory tones. *I know I'm lucky.* The subtext of it all being: *I know what I'm not. I'm not a good actor. I'm overpaid to do something that ultimately keeps the masses fat and sedated.* I believed everything that ran under those words. That was the moment when I started to like Jeff Slade. That was the moment when I felt the cost of nursing such an intense hatred, those times I'd turned on the television and thrown the boys' stuffed animals at the screen whenever the camera cut to a close-up of that symmetrical face and those bee-stung lips.

We'd both won, after all. Jeff Slade got the money, the fame, the fast cars, the endless sex, the house in Hollywood, the Lakers tickets (courtside), and what did Tim Welch get? I got the girl. This thought brought the beginnings of a smile to my face. That was when I noticed a young couple sitting at a nearby table, staring at me. The young wife leaned over and whispered to me, "I'm sorry to bother you."

"Yes?" I replied, sensing what was about to come.

"Can you tell us—" She gestured toward where Jeff had been sitting. "Is it him?"

Oh, yes, it's him, and he's in the bathroom taking a crap, just like you or me.

But I said no such thing. I nodded and said, "Yes, and isn't he the best?"

"Yes, we love his show." Then the wife punched her doughy husband in the shoulder and said, "See, I told you."

What fun this was, dining out with the famous. What did sitting in such close proximity with Jeff Slade intimate? I must be someone, too.

Later, after much of the café had cleared, Jeff Slade and I had the following conversation while waiting for Kate, who was not to return.

"So, Tim, have you spent much time in L.A.?"

"No—"

"It's incredible. It's a wild place."

"I bet."

"Who do you want to know about?"

"What do you mean?"

"I find lots of people are curious about celebrities, stars. Is there anybody you want to know about?"

"Not particularly—"

"Who's nice, who's not so nice? Who gives the best head?"

I coughed up the water I'd just sipped.

Jeff Slade smiled. "Hint: It's a famous director's actress wife. Before her, it was a TV actress of some note who pretty much blew everybody. She does infomercials now. I'm not going to say their names, because I think that would be rude."

"Yes, it would be. Rude."

The decline in this conversation seemed to work in concert with the dimming of the lights in the dining area. Jeff was now mostly lit from a single large flame flickering wildly from a votive candle he had moved closer to his side of the table. The candle cast a menacing light across his chiseled features.

The waiter appeared with dessert menus. "Not yet," I said. "We're waiting for the rest of our party to return."

When the waiter disappeared, Jeff leaned forward and grinned. "Okay, you twisted my arm."

"I twisted what?"

"True story. Early in my career, I'm shooting a TV movie in Canada, staying at the Hyatt in downtown Vancouver. I've finished shooting for the day, I'm back in my room, and my hotel phone rings. I answer. Guess who it is?"

"I wouldn't know."

"It's Angelina Jolie. Now, I first met Angie years ago at the infamous ear-biting Tyson/Holyfield fight in Las Vegas. I was catering at a prefight cocktail reception, and she bummed a cigarette off me. On my break, we stood in a corner and talked and clicked in that way people click. Do you know what I mean?"

I just nodded, because what was I supposed to say?

"So, where were we? Vancouver. The Hyatt. I'm on the phone talking to Angelina Jolie. This is in her post–Jonny Miller, pre–Billy Bob phase, before the blood vials around their necks, obviously before Brad Pitt and their United Colors of Benetton family."

"Oh," I said, as if interested.

"So I say, 'Hey, Angie, this is a surprise.' She says, 'I'm in town.' And I say, 'No way,' and she says, 'Yep,' and then she tells me what hotel. It's the Sutton Place, which I can see from my hotel room window. And she says, 'I'm only here for one night.' I start to say, 'That's too bad' (because I'm about to have dinner with my mom, who's up visiting from Florida), but I don't finish my sentence because she tells me she's checked herself in under a certain name, Trammel—which she points out was Sharon Stone's character's last name in *Basic Instinct*—

and she tells me to write down her room number, and then she says, 'I'm leaving in the morning. And, Jeff, I want to be perfectly clear. This is a onetime offer.'"

Jeff Slade paused, for he knew he had my attention now.

As nonchalantly as possible, I said, "And so what did you do?"

Jeff suppressed a smile as he used the small red straw to stir his Shirley Temple. "I don't know if that's your business."

"Oh, come on."

"A gentleman never speaks of such things."

"You know what? You're absolutely right."

"Okay, I'll tell you . . ."

I waited as Jeff Slade took his time. Then, finally, he said: "I did what you would've done."

When I got home that night, Kate met me with news of Teddy. "What's more heartbreaking than a small child throwing up? They take it so personally. At least Teddy did. Between dry heaves, he was crying, saying, 'But, Mommy, I did nothing wrong.'"

Only after scrubbing the small throw rug in the boys' room, only after Teddy's pajamas were hand-washed in the kitchen sink, and only after we started to get ready for bed did Kate and I speak of the earlier part of the evening.

Kate, while looking for her nightgown, said, "Was he upset when I didn't come back?"

"Disappointed, but I think he understood. He said something about how he can relate now that he has Korky . . ."

"You mean the dog?"

"Yeah, his dog. That dog with the giant dick."

Kate either ignored the dick remark or didn't hear it because she was busy pulling her nightgown over her head. "Did you have a nice time after I left?"

"Oh, pretty much the evening fizzled without you there."

"You're nice to say so."

"He said he comes to New York a lot. He said we should go out again. He said he was very tight with the owner of Nobu."

"That would be Robert De Niro."

"He didn't say that."

"Only because he's discreet."

I had to laugh. Kate asked why I was laughing. "Well, Jeff Slade is anything but discreet." To prove my point, I told her Jeff's Angelina Jolie story.

"Okay," Kate conceded, "so he's not discreet."

"So do you think he slept with her?"

"First of all, it's not our business—and yes, of course he did—and what do I care if he slept with Angelina Jolie?"

"Liar. You're lying."

"No, really, I don't care."

As I lay there next to Kate, I reheard Jeff's words: *I did what you would've done.* This prompted me to ask, "Aren't you the least bit curious about what I'd do?"

"It's beside the point, though, honey, isn't it? I mean, she would never . . . not you . . . especially now that she's the biggest movie star/coolest mom in the entire world. But if she were to ever throw herself at you, I only hope you'd ask if I could roll around with Brad."

Then Kate turned out the light.

In the dark, I stewed over what to say. Should I be insulted?

Kate broke the long silence when she sighed contentedly. "He's turned out to be an okay guy."

"Yeah." I sighed back.

An even longer silence followed.

Then Kate: "Is there something you want to ask me?"

Actually, no, there wasn't, but maybe there ought to have been, so I started to think only to be interrupted by Kate, who said, "Look, I won't lie. There's a lot about his life that is attractive. But the answer is 'No, not for a minute. I'm more certain than ever I married the right man.'"

Funny. I didn't even know that was in question.

No doubt about it. A storm was coming. It was more a matter of when. But that particular afternoon, the Pierrepont Playground was overflowing with moms and nannies and babies and half-day kids. I stood on the fringe, over by the swings, pushing Sam as high as he could go.

A mother I'd just met—Squeaky Voice Mom—and I had been discussing the ominous sky over New Jersey and how the storm appeared to be heading our way. Others must have noticed the mammoth black clouds, the repeated flashes of fractured light. But Squeaky Voice Mom and I seemed to be the only ones worried. I figured the storm would hit within the hour, but that may have been wishful thinking. Squeaky Voice Mom thought sooner, and what followed was the first low rumble of thunder.

Most impressive was the amount of lightning. Squeaky Voice Mom said, "It's like that laser light show at Epcot. Except at Disney World, you don't get wet."

"Wouldn't know about it."

"You haven't been to Disney World?"

"No," I said, "but it's been a dream of mine." Which was true. Kate swore we'd never go there, arguing that it was redundant, since our boys had been weaned on *The Lion King* and every other Disney extravaganza. We'd either rented or owned every Disney animated movie, and we had more than our share of Disney treasure, the *Finding Nemo* toothbrush, the Simba blanket. While we weren't a religious family, the case could be made that for our boys, Disney had been their church.

Squeaky Voice Mom (or Minnie Mouse Mom): "We go every year. Six years running. And we still haven't seen everything. You really should take them. Take them while they still believe in things."

I lifted Sam out of the swing, left that corner of the playground, and headed toward a cluster of familiar mothers. Claudia Valentine, Tess Windsor, and Debbie Beebe sat on their regular park bench, sipping large cups of aromatic chai.

"We were just talking about you," Claudia called out a little too loudly.

I smiled, assuming it to be a good thing.

"We were just saying how nice you look today."

Normally, I would have appreciated the attention. But not that day. So I waved it off, thanked them. "It's no big deal," I said. And then I offered up my idea of a joke: "I bathed."

"We're not used to seeing you so put together," Claudia said. "It's not your usual style."

I should have seen it coming. Claudia sometimes liked to give what appeared to be a compliment. But as usually happened, her warm words slowly revealed their true intent. I have a name for her technique—the Reductive Compliment. Kind-seeming words said kindly, which some-how results in the diminishment of the person being praised. I knew better than to engage with her. Why couldn't she just leave me alone?

"So, Tim, you're keeping something from us. What's the occasion?"

Was it that obvious? Okay, so maybe I'd actually washed and combed my hair that morning, as opposed to my usual ritual of shower and shampoo later in the day, and yes, I'd worn a button-down shirt that brought out the best in my blue-gray eyes, and yes, I'd worn slightly baggy cargo pants, Converse high-tops, and a beige/brown fuzzy/furry pullover. My look was casual but classy. The only true indulgence—other than the newly purchased roll of wintergreen Breath Savers in my pocket—was the faint application of my favorite and only cologne, Chanel for men.

"I think he's up to something."

"Are you turning red?"

I needed the ladies to leave soon, for I was about to be busted. And because they'd made such a to-do over my combed hair and my burgeoning fashion sense, I knew they'd know the real reason once Anna Brody arrived with Sophie.

So I tried to use the weather to my advantage. Any roll of thunder, any distant flash of lightning, I'd ooh and ah and uh-oh and say, "Did you see that? Did you hear that? Looks like it's gonna be a big one!"

While I appeared concerned about the weather, the other mothers were more concerned about me.

This was to be Sophie and the boys' fifth playdate in as many days, but unlike the previous four, this one would take place in public, our first out in the world.

Playdate #1 has been previously described.

Playdates #2–4 took place on the garden floor of the Ashworth-Brody home, a vast, cavernous space with an oversize stuffed bear, a miniature toy kitchen, enough foam building blocks for an entire pre-school class, cushioned floors, a ball pit, white and pink girlie furniture and a minibar for snack time.

Playdate #2 was all about a box I found in the Ashworth/Brody utility room. It had held a large flat-screen TV and hadn't been flattened yet. With a sharp knife, I cut into the corrugated cardboard, slicing out a door that swung and windows with shutters (flaps), and dragged it into the middle of the great room. I covered the base with an array of pillows. "It's all yours," I said to the kids.

Anna watched as they went wild. "Brilliant," she said.

"Let's save *brilliant* for Einstein and Marie Curie. To say it's a good idea—yes, it was a good idea. Thank you, Kate."

Anna said, "So it was Kate's idea. But you're the one here helping me."

"I'm just saying that these good ideas usually aren't my own. I learned from the best."

Anna, holding up a cup of lemonade, gave a mock toast: "To Kate, then."

"To Kate."

Playdate #3 began with my giving all three kids a ball of string, which Anna and I helped them unwind and wrap around the toy furniture, light fixtures, and doorknobs. Soon we'd turned the downstairs children's wing of the Ashworth-Brody house into a giant cobweb.

Anna was amazed that something so simple as string could keep kids busy for an entire afternoon. "Wait until we do the colored pipe cleaners," I said. "They can be bent into any shape imaginable. Or make our own Play-Doh. Or mix our own bubbles. As the great Dr. Seuss wrote, *Oh, the Places You'll Go!*"

Anna smiled at the thought.

Playdate #4: Anna and I sat in Sophie's ball pit among countless brightly colored plastic balls while the kids climbed all around us. Anna confessed that our frequent visits had become the highlight of her day. Or so she said. Repeatedly. And I, for one, believed her.

She knew she was lacking as a mother, but she wanted to improve. I was useful to that end. She paid me with compliments, and it was cloying at first, all the praise. But I grew to like it. She also had a quality charismatic people often possess. When she spoke to you, you felt as if you were the only person in the world.

She was also a bit erratic and could say something impulsive and inappropriate.

For example, while we were in the ball pit, she said, "I bet you and Kate have great sex."

I liked my answer. "That would be Kate's and my business, wouldn't it?"

"I'm sorry if I made you blush."

Dammit.

"I guess I just need to believe that someone out there is having . . ."

"Okay," I said, "we have great sex."

"I knew it."

I neglected to mention: *About once every six months.*

I began to notice a pattern: If I talked about history, Anna appeared bored. Any mention of my dissertation induced a yawn. But whenever I talked about Kate's and my relationship, Anna got interested. She loved the details, especially in regard to our domestic life. She loved our joint bank account, how we divvied up the family responsibilities. She especially loved the coin jar and how we'd roll pennies to go out on a dinner date once a month.

It was at the end of Playdate #4 that Anna said: "Do you know your eyes get wet every time you talk about Kate?"

"Every time?"

Anna nodded slowly and said, "How come there aren't more men like you?"

Character, my father told me, is what you do when no one's looking. But during those playdates, character was what I did when Anna Brody was looking. Because when she wasn't around, I was just an average dad with average ideas. All those times when we met up with Anna and Sophie, didn't Anna know my best self was on display?

So that day (Playdate #5) when the rain came, it came hard, and it did what I couldn't do. It cleared the entire playground. Tess Windsor, as she put the plastic cover over her younger child's stroller, called out for me and the boys to meet over at her apartment at 2 Montague Terrace. Hot chocolate was going to be served.

I said, "No, thanks," and Teddy, Sam, and I stood against the shelter in the playground, having decided to stay. The cold rain fell hard and at a slant, and I thought that because the drops were so big and fat, the storm would be brief. I told the boys, "We're going to wait this one out."

Teddy whimpered for a moment, after everyone was gone, saying, "I want hot chocolate."

"I'll get you hot chocolate when the rain stops."

I'd been right. It wasn't long until the rain began to let up.

"Daddy, look," Sam said.

"I am," I said.

"No, here. Daddy, look here."

I looked down. Sam showed me his arms and how his skin had goose bumps.

"It's from the cold air," I said, helping Sam on with his jacket. "It's something your body does to keep you warm."

By the time Anna Brody and Sophie Brody-Ashworth made it through the gate, the rain had turned to a drizzle. They were an hour late.

"You waited," she said, as if she hadn't expected me to.

Of course, I wanted to say.

"Do you know why you waited?"

I had my theories. "No," I said.

"Because, Tim Welch, you are a good, good man."

Hardly.

My proof: That night, with Kate working late and the boys in bed, I came up with some lame excuse to call Anna. But when her voice mail answered, instead of mentioning my reason for calling, I quickly hung up the phone. This felt rude. So I called back and listened to her recorded greeting.

Hi. Leave a message . . .

I loved the warmth in her *hi,* as if she were genuinely happy I'd called.

for Philip, Sophie . . .

She said Philip's name with an almost mock seriousness and Sophie's with warmth. Maybe she didn't love her husband. Surely she loved her daughter more.

Or . . . me.

Curious, the pause before *me* and the long pause after. The pause before suggested she was contemplating whether she should call herself *me* or *Anna.* And the long pause after? Either Anna Brody couldn't figure out how to work the machine, or she was comfortable with pauses, or she wanted to give callers a moment to compose themselves, gather their thoughts, and therefore speak sincerely.

I hung up mid-beep. Then, to my surprise, I dialed again.

That time I noticed something I hadn't heard before—it sounded as if she was about to laugh while saying *me*, so I hung up, waited for a dial tone, and pushed redial.

Early on that mid-November Friday night, I dialed I don't know how many times. Her voice became a kind of fix. Finally, I set the receiver in the cradle. Enough for one night, I thought, when the phone rang.

BEA MYERLY

"HELLO, MR. WELCH?"

"Yes?"

"Is something wrong?"

"Who is this?"

"Bea Myerly, Mr. Welch."

"Why, uhm, uhm, Bea?"

"Hello, Mr. Welch."

He paused. "What can I do for you?"

"What can *I* do for you?"

"Well, Bea, I can't think of a thing. I'm just sitting here working on my dissertation."

"That's funny. Didn't you just call?"

"No, no, why would I call you?"

"You realize that Mr. and Mrs. Ashworth have caller ID."

"Oh?"

"And the reason I'm calling is that someone with your phone number just called *seven* times." I paused for effect. "Would you like me to pass on a message?"

"How do you know my number?"

I felt sorry for him. "The box displays the listing *Welch, T.* Shall I say that you called?"

"I'd, uhm, rather you didn't."

"You know what, Mr. Welch? They'll know anyway, because the readout lists the last ten calls. Seven of which . . ." I neglected to say that

Mr. Ashworth would be away for the next week and that Mrs. Ashworth never checked the readout.

Mr. Welch didn't say anything. Then he laughed nervously and said, "I'm kind of confused right now."

Duh.

"I mean, Bea, what are you doing there, anyway?"

I explained, but Mr. Welch didn't seem to understand. So I said it again, slowly, as if speaking to a four-year-old. *"I'm their babysitter."*

KATE

CHRISTMAS CAME EARLY THAT YEAR.

On the first Wednesday in December, while we slept, the heavens dumped nineteen inches of snow. Like other families, we woke to a changed world. ("Not since the blizzard of '47" my historian of a husband kept saying, with such certitude that one would believe he'd actually been alive to survive the blizzard of '47.)

For the next three days, there would be no work, all schools would be closed, airports backed up, and the city, for the most part, shut down.

Of all the extreme weather possibilities, snow had become my favorite, especially here in the Heights, where, in those early hours after it stopped falling, everything was white and the cars were all covered. A Volvo could be parked next to a Volkswagen, and you'd have no way of knowing, which was what I loved most about it: Snow made us all equal.

I was working from home when Anna called.

"Am I interrupting you?"

"Yes, but it's good you are," I said. "Tim and the boys are expecting me." I explained that they'd taken the toboggan and gone over to the park near the base of the Brooklyn Bridge. "It has the best hill for sledding."

"So you're going there now?"

"Yes, as soon as I get dressed."

"Oh."

"What is it?"

"I have a favor to ask of you. Could you stop over on your way?"

I promised I would stop by.

One of the housekeepers opened the door. She looked at me with an annoyed curiosity. Maybe she couldn't recognize me under the stocking cap and ski goggles. And yes, admittedly, my bright purple snowsuit was a tad enthusiastic, but I was dressed for the hills.

"May I tell Mrs. Ashworth your name?"

"It's Kate. She's expecting me."

I did my best not to track in snow. I stood in the vestibule for at least five minutes and had begun to sweat from being indoors. When Anna finally appeared, she said, "Take all that off." Then, disappearing up the stairs, she said, "There's something I want you to try on."

I struggled to unlace and pull off my boots.

Anna called from somewhere on the second floor, her voice an eerie, faint echo: "Hey, Kate—we're pretty much the same size, aren't we?"

"Yes," I shouted, although I'd never thought of us that way.

Then she peered over the stair rail and said, like a teenager to her best friend during an all-night sleepover, "Don't be shy. We're the only ones here."

Just us and the housekeeper and who knows what other members of the staff . . .

"Okay," I said as I stepped out of my snowsuit.

I found Anna upstairs as she emerged from her changing room. She smiled at how I was dressed—long underwear and thermal socks—and she said, "Try this on." She was holding a bright red chiffon dress, which I soon realized was vintage Valentino. She led me into the master bedroom and hung the dress on the brass hook on the back of the door. "Let's hope it fits."

Alone in the room, I stripped down to my ratty bra and tired old underwear. I quickly slipped into the dress. The silk lining felt like a softer, smoother second skin.

"Ready," I said.

Anna came in the room, and we both looked at me in the mirror. It was, without a doubt, the nicest dress I'd ever worn. Even so, something about it was too loud, too garish.

"Do you like it?" Anna asked.

"Uhm. It depends, I guess, on what it would be for." I was hoping for some sort of clue as to Anna's intentions.

She sighed sadly. Maybe I had said something wrong. She left the bedroom. From her dressing room, I could hear the sliding of hangers as she frantically searched her wardrobe.

I thought I did the bold thing by following her.

Anna's dressing room was modest in size, considering. And yet the contents were anything but modest. She didn't own the typical Chanel lace dress, nor did she have an Yves St. Laurent royal purple over-the-top sex dress, nor did she, like Debbie Beebe, have her grandma's Edwardian wedding gown, now tea-dyed. No, her clothes were more elegant, unique, and eclectic, as if she knew herself as I was coming to know her—as a person with many moods.

A different Anna chose the second dress. She seemed chipper, all smiles, saying, "Maybe you'll like this one better."

"It's not that I didn't like—"

"Shhh," she said, "I know." She unzipped the garment bag and lifted out the gown. It was dark copper, of a pleated shiny silk. It was a one-shouldered full-length Grecian-goddess dress.

I was still wearing her Valentino, hoping, I suppose, that she'd excuse herself while I changed. But she stayed in the room with me, watching. Just as I was about to make a joke about my underwear, I thought of what Tim would say—*This is me. This is how I dress.* And even though I said nothing, at least I didn't make fun of myself or make some sorry excuse.

Once I had the second dress on, Anna said something about my looking regal, statuesque. I wasn't thinking about how I looked but how I felt, which was great. *This is why some people spend millions on clothes.* In my mind, I started to accessorize, imagining a gold Cleopatra coil to wear around my wrist, for starters.

Anna tilted her head, thought a bit. "We can do better."

"Why? What for? How can we do better?"

She disappeared into her closet and called out: "The dress. Something about it makes you seem untouchable."

Untouchable? What an odd word choice.

I joked, "All I know is this gown does encourage one to stand tall."

"Let's keep looking."

Each dress that followed seemed to raise the bar. I tried to act as if this were an everyday occurrence. But soon any subtlety on my part was gone. I was intoxicated. And her litany of compliments didn't help! "You have great bones," she said. "You have a great neck." "Clothes look great on you."

I caught myself smiling at my reflection, admiring how different each dress made me look, seduced by my own sense of myself, all the while thinking, *How good of me. What a good friend I am.* Because wasn't I the one, in actuality, doing her a favor? But what favor was I doing? Finally, unable to stand it anymore, I blurted out, "So you said you needed a favor. Surely this can't be it."

"Oh, but it is."

"Oh, but it's what?"

"Didn't Tim tell you?"

Tim, who's Tim, do I know a Tim? "Oh! No, he told me nothing."

"Well, Philip's out of town—Singapore or somewhere—and he won't be back in time."

"In time for what?"

"The Yuletide Ball. I'm going, and I want the two of you to be my dates."

I didn't tell Anna about my own awkward history with the Yuletide Ball. How, during our first year in the Heights, we hadn't known it was a coveted invitation. We were among the select to receive a handwritten invitation to attend one of several pre–Yuletide Ball dinners in people's homes. Our neighbors down the street had invited us, but Teddy had just been born, and we forgot to RSVP. The next few years we couldn't afford it. The one year I really wanted to go, we had even less money. We both knew the problem wasn't the Yuletide Ball, because it was a great tradition, and it benefited the Kindergarten Society, a most worthy cause. The problem was that we were perpetually broke.

Now, thanks to Bruno, we finally had the funds. But we didn't get an invitation. Claudia called to apologize, saying there had been a mix-up, somehow we'd been left off the list. Her explanation, a lie, was that so many people had fought over us at the organizational meeting. But they hadn't fought over us, not in the way they probably fought over Anna Brody and Philip Ashworth. Claudia had simply forgotten to put us on the list, which didn't really bother me. For once we could afford to go, but at least now I wouldn't have to worry about what to wear. Instead, we made plans to do what we always did—rent a movie and order in Chinese.

Anna was still trying to make sense of it. "He really didn't tell you?"

I shook my head.

"You must've been wondering what this was all about."

"Yes," I said.

"You'd be helping me, and I thought I could help you." She seemed terribly embarrassed. "Kate, I'm sorry, but when Tim said you wouldn't want to come because you had nothing to wear . . ."

I saw white. He'd talked to her about my clothes! I felt dizzy, hot in the face. Anna must have kept talking. I think she even left the room, because the next thing I knew, she was standing in front of me with another dress, which I had no interest in, no fucking interest in whatsoever until I saw it.

I could name the designer. Mariano Fortuny. I knew his singular style. I'd seen knockoffs in upscale stores. I'd seen the collection of his gowns at the Metropolitan Museum. I'd studied the craftsmanship, the artistry of his designs in my Fashion Trends and Cultural Influences class at Berkeley.

This particular gown was classic Fortuny, made of hand-blocked silks with a metallic sheen. And the colors! The silver gown was covered in random geometric shapes in two colors, a pale aqua and an ice blue. I'd read that Fortuny dresses were most likely to be in museums and that on rare occasions, they appeared for auction, usually in Italy, for a price equivalent to, at the very least, several teachers' salaries.

Anna helped me into the dress. With her cool hands, she zipped up the back. For her, it was just another outfit, while it was the dress of my dreams.

"You'd be helping me," she said. "I'd hate to go alone. And the truth is, I can only wear one of these dresses at a time . . ."

Everybody has a price. Anna Brody had just named mine.

"Kate, are you upset?"

Upset? Please. There I was, facing myself in a full-length gold-framed mirror. I forgot that my husband had been too forthcoming, and I forgot the stubble on my unshaven legs and the regrettable state of my underwear, and for a moment I even forgot about the mess we were making of this planet's future, because my mind raced with other thoughts, ranging from *I could stare at myself for hours* to *Damn, I'm hot* to the near certainty that *this dress was made just for me.*

BEA MYERLY

Dear Mr. Welch,

I'm sorry for your loss.

Sincerely yours,

Bea

P.S. Please disregard this letter if the homeless man who was found frozen to death on the steps of Plymouth Church was not the same homeless man who is/was your friend. My hunch and fear is that he's the same person. If he is/was, you must remember you did all you could. It was you who gave him money and food and showered him with clothes and athletic apparel—it was you who made him feel less alone in this cruel and brutal world.

Oh, it just occurred to me that there's a chance you haven't even heard this news. My apologies if you haven't heard!

I don't even know when it happened. Recently, I think. My father told me tonight during dinner. I had complained that we never have anything good to eat anymore. My dad mentioned that there were plenty of people in the world who would kill for pork chops like ours. "Like who?" I snapped. (Or is it *whom*?) "Well, that homeless man at the Clark Street subway station," he said. I said, "Fine, then, I have a good mind to march over there in the cold and give them [the pork chops] to him." That was when my father told me that a homeless man had frozen to death in the Heights.

Apparently, the janitor of the church was shoveling snow when he found the man curled up like a baby, stiff as a board. It's so sad.

It reminds me of the lecture you gave about how everybody has a history. And how most histories go unrecorded. Generally, I believe, people do the best they can, and if they don't do well, they don't do well for very good reasons.

I'm left with so many questions. Who was he? How did he get lost? If it's true what you taught us, that each of us is capable of doing anything, then you or I or anyone, for that matter, could end up homeless, on the street, buried under a ton of snow, having frozen to death.

If I'm so sad, Mr. Welch, I can only imagine how you feel. Please reach out to me if you need comfort.

P.P.S. I never told Mrs. Ashworth you called all those times. Your secret is safe with me.

TIM

HINDSIGHT IS, SADLY, AFTER ALL, ONLY HINDSIGHT. STILL, IF PHILIP ASHWORTH had been home to accompany his wife, and if Anna hadn't invited Kate and me in his place, and if we hadn't said yes, and, furthermore, if the lightbulb in our closet hadn't burned out, then what happened the night of the Yuletide Ball might never have happened.

On a night when there was so much to be bothered by, what would I claim bothered me most? Not the excess of food and drink before me; not the ornate chandelier hanging overhead, the numerous candles, the fires blazing in the matching marble fireplaces; not the din of smug chatter from the hedge-fund-rich or the mixing of so much cologne with so many perfumes or the threat of cigars; and not even the unspoken but well-known fact that soon there would be dancing in a building a few blocks from where a homeless man—and not just any homeless man but my homeless man—had frozen to death two days earlier. No, what would I say bothered me most?

The collar on my rented tuxedo shirt felt too tight.

Earlier, when I told Kate as much, she laughed, because she knew the collar was the least of my sadnesses. "Honey, I know this is a terrible time for a party."

"Yes," I said. "I think so."

"But if you don't feel like going, stay home. Anna and I will be fine . . ."

"No, I'm going."

"Okay, but then please don't be so glum."

I understood her point. If you're going to a party, be in the proper mood. And besides, hadn't I ruined the last party we attended? So I put on my best party face, determined to be a positive force despite the inner turmoil I felt. Kate made it easy. When she emerged from our tiny bathroom to model the borrowed dress, I had no words beyond "Wow." But she knew by my expression, by the way my eyes welled, that I was sincere. She appreciated, too, that I laughed at her little joke: "We need to be home by midnight," she said, "otherwise, I may turn into a pumpkin." I was even able to shake off the rude greeting given by the dinner's hostess, Abigail Hosford. She met us at the front door wearing an unfortunate bright red dress that made her look like a giant Christmas ornament. When she greeted Anna, Abigail seemed star-struck. However, her smile froze when she realized we'd come in place of Philip Ashworth. Later, when Kate whispered her annoyance that Anna hadn't forewarned the Hosfords, I said sweetly, "Aw, honey, don't be so glum."

Abigail Hosford clinked her glass with a fork and gave a succinct speech about the purpose of the evening. She mentioned the homeless man whom "several of us had befriended" and asked that we "all think of others less fortunate." We bowed our heads.

After an appropriate silence, Abigail explained why she had elected to seat the men in one room and the women in another, explaining to the gathered guests, "This is how they used to do it." *And it was a bad idea then, too,* I thought. But she would never know what I thought, because I welcomed her announcement with an easy smile and a gentle shrug.

"Poor Tim," Anna said as I was ushered off into the other half of the parlor floor, where I sat among the men, who talked about man things. Stocks. Alma maters. A rather boisterous conversation about the skills and dexterity required to excel at squash, a sport I knew next to nothing about, but who would know by the way I nodded and seemed to agree?

"You play?" one man said.

I smiled as if to say, *Oh, all the time.*

Sitting to his right, a pink-cheeked doughnut of a man in a shiny tuxedo stared at my untouched plate of seared salmon and broccoli rabe. "You aren't eating," he observed.

"That's correct."

"Why aren't you eating?"

"I haven't much of an appetite."

"Hmmm," the man grunted. "Well, I'm starved."

Normally, I'd have done the polite thing and concurred. But *starved* had a new meaning that holiday season. Besides, I'd left the company of the men (at least in my mind) and was staring across the double parlor to the opposite end, where Kate and Anna shared a chair.

If they were sisters, I decided—and that night they seemed like they might be—Anna would be the older, more worldly-wise of the two, who, for one night, stepped aside and let her younger sister emerge. For Kate had the better dress, and that was saying a great deal.

I decided then, if one were to start a new world, if the gods were to flood the earth and begin again, they should start there, with those two.

The pink-faced man looked where I was looking. "Lovely, aren't they?"

"Yes," I said.

A cater-waiter brought them an extra chair. Another brought a plate and a setting of silver. Anna waved them off, which made me smile.

"Do you know them?" the pink-faced man asked.

"Yes. One of them is my wife."

"Oh," he sighed. "A pity you couldn't marry them both."

As if on cue, Anna glanced to where I was sitting forlornly with the men. Then she leaned in and whispered something to Kate in such a way that I knew they were talking about me.

Later, when dessert came, the sexes were free to mingle. Kate and Anna plopped down next to me. Anna spoke first: "You must be in your own little circle of hell."

"No, I'm having a nice time."

Kate smiled because she knew I was lying.

Anna, after a pause: "I'm sorry about your friend."

"Who? Oh, well, I wasn't really his friend."

"Of course you were," Kate said.

"No, a friend would have done more for him."

Kate: "You did more for him than anybody else."

Oh, please, I wanted to say. *All I did was buy him the occasional slice of pizza.* The truth was I didn't do nearly enough for him, and whenever I did something, it didn't really help him; I used Lenny to feel good about myself. Besides, I hardly knew the man. Lately, I had avoided him. Part of me was relieved that he was gone. Lenny had snapped, he was insane. He was always going to live on the street. He was a lost cause. If he were an academic paper, he would be my dissertation. So much potential, lost, wasted.

When I was younger, I believed that special people would always find a way to rise up and fulfill their potential. But now I knew otherwise. Remarkable people, people like Lenny who would rattle the world if they were given a fair chance, these same people were starving to death, freezing to death, losing their way every day.

"Well," Anna said. "I hope this doesn't sound too in-the-clouds."

"Yes?"

"Even though it's difficult to lose someone, it's been my experience . . ." Anna put one of her hands on top of one of mine. Her hand was softer and smoother than Kate's, and colder. "With every death, there comes a gift."

KATE

MY HUSBAND IS A RIDICULOUS DANCER. BUT OTHER THAN TEACHING, IT MAY BE THE only time he enjoys an audience. Surely he knows how absurd he looks. He basically flails. He shakes his head wildly, he bunny-hops across the floor, pointing his fingers in opposite directions. He does a sloppy spin that causes the sweat from his forehead to spray in a circle. And I must confess, it would be all right if I never had to dance with him again.

However, my friends don't agree. They line up to dance with him, because their husbands are not much fun in that regard. Their men usually stand stiffly in the corner, drinking and talking shop. Still, I've often wished for a husband who moves with me, connects with me when we dance.

Be careful what you wish for, because that night Tim danced in an entirely new way.

First of all, when the usual suspects approached and tried to cut in, he wouldn't even acknowledge them. They must have thought him rude. But maybe they felt as I did—how refreshing to have a husband so smitten.

At one point Tim disappeared, claiming that he found the current song undanceable. That was when I went over to where Anna was sitting alone, watching. "You two are good," she said.

"Not always."

Now, I am a person who receives her fair share of praise. But nothing had prepared me for what followed. Wives, husbands, people I didn't know, people I didn't know even knew me, passed by our table, saying things like: "You look fabulous/you are stunning/my wife and I have been watching you/you are the belle of the ball."

I blushed. Anna laughed when I tried to attribute it to the dress. Once we were alone again, she took my hands and asked, "Where's your husband?"

"I don't know. Why?"

"I want to dance."

I didn't know where Tim had gone. I looked around the room. It was the first time I'd noticed the white paper lanterns hanging equally spaced from invisible wires. The rented white tent, the Christmas lights, and the bouquets of flowers at each table. It was impressive how the Heights Casino had converted their prime tennis court to a dance floor. The green turf had been rolled up, revealing a beautifully polished wooden floor. At the far end, a big band called Yesterday's Tomorrow played. The band was made up of only female musicians and a buxom African-American singer so beautiful she could be a plus-size model.

Since Tim had wandered off to I didn't know where, and because the music had changed to something great, I stood up, and Anna followed me to the dance area. Soon Claudia, Debbie, and some other mothers joined in. Weirdly, men began to appear on the sidelines, watching. Anna was barefoot. I thought it was a mistake for her to have taken off her shoes. It made her look shorter, ordinary. But she was comfortable. Soon my shoes were off, too.

When Tim returned, he joined us on the dance floor, where he was even more focused on me. I don't know how else to describe it: He was a human spotlight that night. I closed my eyes and began to spin. It felt as if everyone were watching me.

I stopped when I got dizzy, and Tim held me up. "Dance with Anna," I said.

"No, thanks."

"But she'd like to dance with you."

"I only dance with the prettiest girl here."

"All the more reason."

"And I'm dancing with her now."

Good answer.

During the next song, which was a slow song, Tim said he wanted to go home. I started to object. Then he whispered in my ear in the nicest way that he'd never been so erect. I wondered if the others noticed us leave. Anyone watching us must have known—soon there would be sex.

TIM

IT WAS THE KIND OF DRESS PERFECT FOR UNZIPPING. AND BECAUSE IT WAS tight-fitting, we both could hear the zipper as it faintly clicked down her spine, curving as her back curved . . .

"She wants me to keep it," Kate said. "Do you think I should?"

"What?"

"Anna. The dress."

I said nothing.

"You're not listening."

"Yes, I am."

"So should I keep it?"

"My only interest in this dress is how quickly I can get you out of it."

She seemed put off by my answer. "I really want to keep it," she said. "But I don't know if I should. It's much too much, way too generous. I'll always feel like I owe her. It's not like I can give her anything of comparable value. So that's it. It's decided. I'm going to return it. Okay?"

"That's probably best."

"You think? But she gave it to me. Now I don't know. I really want to keep it. Agh! I feel like I'm fifteen. Let me just say this—wearing it made me understand why, as a general rule, it's better to be rich. Tim, are you listening?"

Later that night, during a shared bath, the room lit by a lavender-scented candle, I was giving Kate a foot rub when she said, "I didn't say good night. Did you?"

I kept up the foot rub.

"Tell me you said good night to Anna."

Anna, Anna, please shut up about Anna. "No," I said, as if I'd forgotten, when in truth, it had been a deliberate choice. By ignoring Anna, I could avoid her kind words or warm smile or, even worse, another one of her patless hugs.

"That was rude of us. We were her guests. We should've thanked her."

I tried to shut Kate up with a kiss. As I lunged forward, the bathwater sloshed up and snuffed out the candle.

That kiss led to a series of kisses, which led to our bed, where—more so than normal—I tried to be especially in the moment: the touching, the moving together. Kate's skin. Her eyes. Her soft mouth. I'd never been so aware of her sweat, her hair, those hands, hips, her back. Her bones. I was awash in Kate and all her Kateness when the light in the closet (which was the only light on) suddenly went out, turning our bedroom pitch-black.

I froze. In the dark, Kate kept moving, saying, "It was an old bulb. I can't believe it lasted this long."

"Do you want me to replace it?"

"No," she said. "Please, it's nice like this. And don't stop."

Now the only light came from the red numbers of Kate's digital alarm clock. This had the distracting effect of accentuating time. And the time on the clock kept changing. My fear? This was taking too long. My solution? I turned the clock facedown. "So close," I kept telling her. "I'm so close!"

She wondered did I want to shift positions?

"No," I said. "So close, so close!" (Say it enough, and it must be so.) After I'd said that a thousand times, I switched to "Almost . . . almost."

Poor Kate, I thought. *She's going to be sore later.*

That was when I changed to a new approach: by any means necessary. No surprise, then, when Anna Brody came back into the picture.

A yoga teacher had once told me, "Let the thought in, let the thought out . . ."

So *in* came Anna, *out* went Anna . . .

It was that simple.

The yoga teacher's name was Megan. I liked when Megan used her hands to adjust my plow and downward dog. Even better, Megan wasn't Anna. I tried to picture Megan. Surely I wasn't the first person to have his mind wander during sex. But it felt that way. And the many faces began to fluster me, so I decided to bear down, give a laserlike focus to Kate.

By any means necessary.

I got serious about ejaculating.

Come! Come!

Now, because any thought was fair game, it became like twisting the stem off an apple— *Kate, Anna, Kate, Anna.* Or like pressing the remote on a TV so as to jump between two favorite channels: *Anna, Kate, Anna, Kate.*

"I'm about to come."

"Yes," Kate said.

"I'm coming!"

"Yes, yes!"

"Here I go—"

And that was when I said the wrong name.

KATE

I WAS STUNNED. I MAY HAVE LAUGHED. THEN I GATHERED MYSELF, CALMLY WALKED from our bedroom to our bathroom, where I closed and locked the door. I took a shower and scrubbed with lots of soap until I was clean.

Tim stood in the hallway, calling, "Kate, are you all right? Kate?" Over and over he said my name.

Little late for that, don't you think?

I wrapped myself in a towel and opened the door.

"I'm sorry," he said. "I'm sorry. Are you okay?"

"Why wouldn't I be?" Once you've been humiliated in your own bedroom, my advice is to stiff-arm the apology. The *feeble* apology.

"Come on, are you sure?"

What, did he expect me to weep, to fall apart?

I thought about how much to tell him. *Do I tell the truth?* How, during that sweet-seeming (but, in retrospect, protracted) exercise in the missionary position, my mind had wandered, too, although my thoughts were more chore-related, as in *Did I put away the dishes? Did I double-lock the door?*

I brushed my teeth as he tried to explain himself. He rambled on, something about how it had been mostly me in his thoughts. He felt terrible, and I was almost convinced, but then he complained that the complete darkness of the room hadn't helped. He'd felt bad that it was taking so long. Did he really believe this would make me feel better?

"Look," I said, "you're not the only person who thinks of other people." I spat into the sink. "The truth is—"

"What? Tell me."

I rinsed my mouth out. "I was thinking of someone else, too."

"Really?" Tim looked part relieved, part worried.

"But there's a big difference . . ."

"Yeah, you didn't moan out his name." He must have thought that was funny, because he kind of laughed.

"That, too," I said. "But the big difference is that while I can fuck Jeff Slade whenever I want, Anna Brody would never have you." Then I walked past him and climbed into my side of the bed.

Faintly, from the hallway, he said, "Ouch."

TIM

IT HAD BEEN TWO DAYS SINCE THE GREAT FAUX PAS, FORTY-EIGHT HOURS SINCE the blurting out of another woman's name as I came. This should have prompted some swift action on my part. But for whatever reason, I was stumped. Flowers, chocolates, even jewelry wouldn't cut it. That much I knew. But hadn't Kate committed a thought crime of her own? Jeff Slade, indeed! And while I'd been wrong for saying that other name, Kate had been wrong for thinking about a realizable person. My crime had been that I didn't protect her. Her crime? She intentionally and understandably hurt me. I was mulling all this over when Anna called.

"How would you and the boys like to—"

"Yes," I said, interrupting her.

She laughed and said, "You don't even know what I was asking."

"A playdate?"

"Mind reader."

The other line beeped, and I said, "Hold on."

It was Kate, checking in. "What's up?"

I told her the truth: that Anna had called with an invitation.

She was quiet for a time. "Do the boys want to go?"

Had I even asked the boys? "Yes, all excited," I said. So much for truth.

"Well, then. Dress them warm, it's very cold out."

After hanging up, I went to get the boys ready, only to find they had no interest in going over to Sophie's. They wanted to be in their house with their toys. I was usually able to bribe Teddy, so I offered a quarter if he cooperated and a dollar if he could get his brother to fall in line. But Sam didn't want to go. He refused to get dressed. He tensed his little body, clenching his small hands into tight fists. He fought walking down the stairs, so I carried him. "No, we're going, Sam, and we're going to have fun." He kicked and squirmed while I strapped him into his stroller. I thought he'd calm down once we got moving, but no, he pressed against the safety belt, his face red with rage. Teddy trailed along as we pushed across the Heights. I'd been so preoccupied with Sam that I hadn't noticed Teddy's bottom lip begin to quiver. Somewhere between Montague Street and Clark, Teddy defected. I crouched down, took both of them by the arm, squeezed more firmly than I'd have liked, and hissed, "What about what I want!" Teddy cried out, "Daddy, you're scaring me!" Sam was howling, saying something about wishing Mommy was there.

I turned us around, and we went back home. Inside, the boys were inconsolable. They continued to scream and cry until they finally fell asleep in Kate's and my bed.

I sat on the edge of the mattress and just looked at them. I'd hurt Kate, and now I was hurting our kids. What else would have to happen? That was when I knew it had to stop. The question was how. I could've been classier about it, but here's what I did: I went cold turkey. I cut Anna out immediately. That afternoon I didn't call to cancel the playdate. The messages she left over the next several days were immediately erased and phone calls never returned. Because I knew her routines, where she shopped and where she walked, I was able to avoid Anna Brody for two weeks.

Then, the day before Christmas, and in an effort to get Kate her favorite organic milk, I ventured over to Garden of Eden, where— *fuck!*—I bumped into Anna Brody in the produce section.

She saw me first, came up behind me, and said, "Tim, is everything all right?"

"Oh, hi. Yeah, sure. Why do you ask?"

"Well, because you don't call me back. I assume you're either too busy or you're bored with me."

"No, it's not that—"

"Then what is it?"

It took her a moment to realize what a wreck I was. She said, "Are you sure you're all right?"

"I'm great, I'm—No, I'm not."

"What is it?"

"I don't know how to say this, but you've made a mistake about me." It was all I could do not to drop to my knees and puke my toxic heart and guts out onto the floor. "I'm not who you think I am."

She just laughed.

I said it slower, clearer: "I'm not a good man."

"Oh, but you are, you *are* . . ."

"Listen," I said, grabbing her firmly. "A good man doesn't moan out your name when he's making love to his wife."

She froze at this news.

Bingo.

"Oh," she said, as if she'd suddenly noticed a big stinky smell. I thought, *I better get used to this.* Her cold stare, the instant hate in her eyes. It was that easy and awful. How quickly it had turned. Now I was dead to her. And I knew what was coming next. I could even say the words: *I don't want to see you ever again, Tim. I don't want to talk with you. You disgust me . . .*

But what did Anna say?

"I know you love Kate very much."

"I do." I laughed as the tears came. *Why do they always come?*

"I know you'd never want to hurt her."

"That's right."

"Even the thought of hurting her . . ."

"I better go."

"Tim."

"Yes?"

"So you're just going to cut me off?"

"I see no other alternative."

"Because you can't control your feelings . . ."

"That's right. And because I'm a bad man."

Anna took me gently by the wrist and said, "We can work through this. We can get past it."

"I don't see how," I said, grabbing Anna's grocery cart and starting to push it to I didn't know where.

"What are you doing?"

"I have no idea. I'm all mixed up."

"Tim, stop."

I stopped.

She told me to look her in the eye.

I did.

She seemed desperate, too.

"Tim, if it will help in any way . . ."

"Yes?"

"I'll give you a weekend."

FOUR

TIM

I'LL GIVE YOU A WEEKEND.

Five simple words—six if you count the contraction—strung together to form one simple sentence. But what did it mean? I spent much of January breaking it down.

I'll . . .

Notice what she didn't say: "I may." Or "I might. I could/should/would/can't/won't/don't/ haven't." Or "I would never, ever in a million years."

No, it was *I'll* . . .

Meaning?

I, Anna Brody, will . . .

Give . . .

As in a gift. Or as in: It is better to give . . .

You . . .

Seeing as it was my ear into which she had whispered, her *you* meant me. This led to the question: "Why me?" Granted, I'd been helpful. A friend. We'd had several heart-to-heart conversations. And I was really good with Sophie. So yes, I deserved a thank-you note, maybe an Armani tie or a holiday basket of fruit and cheese. Make me a tin of Christmas cookies! But to offer . . .

A weekend.

What, just the two of us alone? To be alone together for the two days that comprise a weekend? What was Anna Brody thinking? Was she even thinking? And was I to take her offer seriously? Surely she was joking. Or was it a game? A tease?

Truth be told, I couldn't even determine whether she was serious, because the day after our curious encounter in the produce section of the Garden of Eden on Montague Street, Anna Brody left the country with her husband and daughter for a trip abroad.

So for the time being, I was left all alone to wonder what she'd meant. I tried to put her offer out of my mind, to get on with my life, that sort of thing. But too often, random Anna Brody thoughts popped up, especially whenever I worked on my dissertation. If her intention had been to pervade my daily life, she'd succeeded. I wished it were otherwise, but her words, and the direct, almost desperate manner in which they'd been said, not only lingered, they burrowed their way in, deep.

This may help explain why I wrote the following letter.

1/13 3:13 A.M.

Dear Coach,

The greatest gift we can give our parents is to not make their mistakes. Would you agree? I suspect you do. So would you do me a favor? Please list your ten biggest mistakes in no particular order. Any explanation as to why these ten and not any of the many others would be appreciated. This is not meant to be vindictive or to hurt you. My sister and I both would like to benefit from your hard-earned life lessons. By making new and different mistakes, not only do we honor the past, it's how we also honor you.

Your son,

Tim

I addressed the envelope, sealed it, and affixed a LOVE stamp. The next morning I dropped it in the mail.

Two days later, our phone machine's message light was blinking. It was Coach: "What kind of bullshit is this? Mistakes? List my ten biggest mistakes? That's weakness, Tim. Plain and simple. Sissy talk. What's happened to you? I can't figure it out. I thought New York would toughen you up. What have you been doing, going to church?"

No, but it occurred to me: *Now, there's a good idea.*

If ever a person needed church.

That Sunday I woke the boys, plied them with Frosted Flakes, got them dressed, and took them along while Kate slept in.

I hadn't been to church in years. As a kid, I rarely went because my father loathed organized religion. According to the Gospel of Coach, God was a terrible dad. "What kind of father would let his son die on a cross?" (A fair question.) "No," Coach liked to tell me when I was little, "if I were God, and you were my only son, do you know what I'd do for you? I'd make you a winner. Every time out, son, you'd win!"

So which church?

I chose the closest.

Grace Episcopal was a beautiful gray stone structure, built in 1847, with Tiffany stained-glass windows, an ornate altar, and Sunday school/ child care for toddlers and preschoolers. A friendly usher pointed us to the basement, where I left my boys as they began a messy but fun-looking arts-and-crafts activity that consisted of gluing dried macaroni to paper plates. "Be good," I said.

I sat in the last pew. I spent much of that morning learning when to kneel and sit and stand, the complex switch from the black prayer book to the bigger dark blue hymnal to the church bulletin, and somehow, amid all the kneeling and standing and sitting and hymn singing, I managed to eke out a little prayer—something about wanting guid-ance, the nature of sin, and needing direction. During the closing hymn, when all the other parishioners were standing and singing "O God, Our Help in Ages Past," I dropped to my knees and prayed: *Please, I don't know what to do about Anna Brody's offer. So, God, if there's a God, just send me a sign.*

KATE

MOST PEOPLE BELIEVE THEMSELVES CAPABLE OF KEEPING A SECRET. TIM SAYS I'M one of the few who actually can. Even as a little girl, when my mother confided in me things no daughter should ever have to know, I prided myself, almost to the point of gloating, on my capacity for sealed lips. As long as I can remember, it has been one of my best attributes, or so I thought. In my dark period, that endless year before I met Tim, it was my raison d'être. So much so that I once considered having a T-shirt custom-made that would read: I AM AN ACCOMPLISHED KEEPER OF SECRETS.

I know that's what made Tim so appealing. His lack of secrets. That's what made our first days together so refreshing. Secrets, the kind I had kept, were exhausting. I was exhausted. And with Tim, I could finally rest.

Anyway . . .

I needed to get rid of Anna's dress. As long as I had it, I'd be haunted or, as Claudia suggested, cursed. (Perhaps it had been a mistake, but I told Claudia about Tim's blurting out Anna's name. Claudia cringed when she heard, then said, "We all think about other people from time to time, but who wants to be reminded of it?" For Claudia, there was no question as to whether I would return the dress. In her mind, I couldn't do it fast enough.)

I'd heard that Philip had taken Anna and Sophie to France for the month of January. My plan was to return the dress while they were away, leaving it with their housekeeper.

But to my surprise, after I knocked, Philip Ashworth opened the door. He was fresh from a shower and smelled of English soap. I remember thinking if this were an old black-and-white movie, he'd be played by Gary Cooper or a blond Henry Fonda. But the black-and-white part would be a pity, because his eyes were Paul Newman blue.

"Oh," he said, "I thought you were the car."

I handed him the garment bag and said, "If you could give this to Anna."

He looked puzzled. "What were you doing with this?"

"I'm returning it."

"Why did you have it?"

"Well, your wife gave it to me. But now I'm giving it back."

His jaw dropped slightly. He looked down. He sighed. "Won't you come in?"

"I'm late for work."

"Please, Kate. Please, come in."

That he remembered my name was what carried me inside.

We stood in the foyer with the light blue Egyptian tile floor and the ornate tin ceilings. Near the door, a leather carry-on was packed, ready for travel. Even though he spoke softly, the sound bounced around in the cavernous front room. He wanted specifics. He seemed most interested in the time frame as to when had she given me the dress. I told him that she'd lent it to me for the Yuletide Ball, that she hadn't wanted to go alone. He seemed pained by my saying it, but I thought it was better to be honest. Then I explained that she'd insisted I keep it. I said it was too much, I didn't feel comfortable receiving such a valuable gift. He thanked me for returning it.

Something was knocked over upstairs. He didn't seem to notice. A woman's voice called out, "Philip?" or at least I thought so.

"Was that someone calling for you?"

"No," he said. "We're the only ones here."

Then the doorbell rang.

"Not anymore," I said, my attempt at a joke.

"That's the car." He went for his bag. "I'm going into the city, Kate. Can I offer you a ride?"

Outside, he looked older. The light of day accentuated his wrinkles, proving that even Philip Ashworth had to age. I found this comforting.

The driver held the door for me as I ducked into the car. While Philip went around to his side, I glanced up and saw a woman looking down from the Ashworths' third-floor corner window. Not the house-keeper, and not Anna Brody, although the woman in the window had the same coloring. She was an older, duller version of Anna, pale, not pretty, an earlier, rougher draft. This was my sense of her, but it all happened fast, the way she raised her hand as if to wave good-bye, and then, as Philip climbed in the back with me, she pressed her hand to the glass. It was a sad gesture, I thought, and one that only I saw. She must have noticed me watching, because she abruptly stepped away, and the curtain she'd been holding open fell back into place.

"What luck," he said, "getting to spend some time with you."

"Well, I appreciate the ride." I tried to quietly connect my seat belt. It made a loud click. Philip Ashworth slipped his on without a sound.

"So, Hank, what do we got?"

Hank was the driver. "Ray Charles."

"I hope you like Ray Charles," Philip said to me.

"Yes," I said. "He was a compelling argument for being blind."

Thankfully, Philip let my comment go. I forgave myself the odd choice of words, because my mind was still focused on the woman in the window. *We're the only ones here,* he had said. Apparently, the woman in the window didn't count.

Ray Charles came over the car stereo—raw, soulful, at a soft volume—as we turned onto the Brooklyn Bridge.

"Comfortable?" Philip asked.

"Yes," I said as I sank into the soft black leather seat. "Very."

Philip was in the middle of explaining his whirlwind schedule—

back in the States for the day, a quick stop at the house to freshen up before an important meeting in midtown, then a rush to catch the last flight for Paris to rejoin Anna and Sophie in the South of France—when the traffic on the bridge came to a stop.

"Construction, sir, or an accident, I can't tell which."

Philip craned his neck to see the traffic situation on the bridge and said, "She talks about you all the time."

"Excuse me?"

"My wife talks about you all the time."

"No-o."

"Oh, yes, it's always 'Kate this' and 'Kate that.' She's always mentioning you and your husband."

"I wouldn't know why."

"She seems to think you have it all."

I couldn't help laughing. It was one thing for her to flatter me with such nonsense, but to brainwash her husband as well?

"How well do you know her?" he asked.

"Not very."

Philip sighed and said, "I was afraid you'd say that." He glanced out the side window. "It's her nature to inflate things. Sometimes she gets a wild notion in her head." He looked back at me with a mournful expression. "You really don't know her well, because she's tough to know. She doesn't trust easily."

Yes, but, Philip, maybe with good reason. I mean, who was that woman in the window?

"It's difficult to explain her. Suffice it to say she's a person of extreme sensitivity. Fragile, I think. It's what makes her Anna. It's what makes her vibrant and astonishing in my eyes."

No cars on the bridge had moved. In the van in front of us, a driver leaned on his horn.

"You better call ahead, Hank. Let them know we're running late." Philip turned to me and said, "Where were we?"

"You were telling me about Anna."

"If she likes somebody, she tends to idealize them. Like you and your husband. Also, she's extremely generous, almost to a fault."

"Yes, I know, the dress."

"You see, I never wanted to marry anyone. But she's not anyone. I couldn't have imagined Anna. I couldn't have dreamed her up."

A few years back there was an awards show on television where a noted philanderer received a lifetime achievement award. His much younger, almost as famous, very pregnant wife watched from the front row as he humbly thanked the many people who had aided/graced his career. The last part of his impressive speech was devoted entirely to a lengthy tribute he paid his wife. As if on cue, tears sprang from her eyes, and even a skeptic such as me felt something catch in my throat, the sudden rise of goose pimples. I turned to Tim, equally moved, and asked, "Do you think he loves her as much as he says?"

"We'll never know," Tim said. "One thing is certain, though: He's in love with the idea of us believing he's in love."

I wondered whether this was true of Philip Ashworth as he waxed on and on about Anna. "She's not made like you or me. She's unusual. Sometimes I think she has an extra set of nerve endings. She's complicated."

What I found funny, of course, was that Philip Ashworth was equally complicated. Maybe all of us are complicated, but because of our tenuous place in the world, our contradictory selves aren't indulged. And because they're not indulged, those interesting, inappropriate, shocking parts of us wither away, atrophy. Maybe Philip and Anna were complicated only because they could be.

At the same time, how like all husbands Philip seemed. Sure, he had too much money, too many houses, a driver who was his and his alone; he had his art collection, his wine cellar, his numerous business ventures (many that were mysterious), but underneath it all, he was just another husband afraid of his wife.

It was what endeared him to me.

"In her defense, she warned me. She did. Early on, after I proposed and she accepted, she said, while crying and smiling both, 'You do realize, Philip, that there are no brakes on this car.'"

He paused to check the traffic. Other cars were honking now, as if it would do any good.

"I was given fair warning, right? And it's what I love about her—the impulsiveness, the surprises. Even though some of the surprises lately—"

"You mean the dress?"

"Yes, the dress."

"It's beautiful. It must have been expensive."

"It's not the money. Please, that's not it at all."

"Oh. Sorry."

"It's that it was—it is—her wedding dress."

I wasn't sure if I heard him right.

"Tell me, Kate, why would she give away her wedding dress?"

I didn't know what to say. Then Philip laughed the laugh of a rich, confused man. "She's funny," he kept saying. "She's very funny."

I didn't say anything. I let him trail off. We were both quiet as Ray Charles crooned.

"Did she tell you the story of how I proposed? Probably not, because it's not a story she ever tells. The first time I saw Anna was at an opening in London. Now, here's all I know about art: The kind that I'm supposed to like is expensive. That night it was a group show of an 'exciting' new wave of artists—cows sliced in sections floating in formaldehyde, ice sculptures of the artist's frozen blood, lumps of cow dung covered with glitter glued to canvases—it was basically just ridiculous and indulgent, but what do I know about art? Everyone was young and excited. I felt like a very square dinosaur. Then I saw Anna, and I thought she was more spectacular than any painting ever painted. Soon we were dating. Or rather, *I* was dating. She was just having dinner with me because, I think, she was cash-strapped and hungry. Soon I was in love, and she was still just having dinner. We had many meals in those first weeks, and I was starting to get fat. I knew I needed to do something to get her attention. Because she loved art, I called one of my dealers and asked for something modest in size, very special, not overpowering, cost not an issue, something one-of-a-kind. He found a small painting, and I presented it to her after yet another dinner, and she knew the artist and seemed pleased. That night she kissed me for the first time. The painting she kept at her flat, resting on the mantel, leaning next to a small pot where she put her keys. I offered to have a security system/alarm installed for her, but she didn't want one. She said, 'None of us is safe.' More and more dinners. One day I stopped over on a whim and noticed that the painting wasn't in its usual place. I asked her, 'Where is it?' She said, 'Gone, Philip. It's gone.'

"Oh, wait," he said, "I skipped something. Anna is an avid grocery shopper. She loves, I don't know, squeezing fruit, figuring out what's ripe. Finding a good bargain. She may as well clip coupons, she's that frugal with food. Her one indulgence—and I hardly see it as that—is to have her groceries delivered. She had a delivery boy, a young man maybe in his early twenties—black, dreadlocks, but that's not important—who apparently was fond of the painting. Every time he made a delivery, he would stop and stare at it. They would discuss it. He loved it. He was possessed by it and, apparently, not because of who painted it—incidentally, it was by de Kooning."

"Oh, de Kooning," I said. "I think I've heard of him."

"Anyway, when Anna said it was gone, I knew immediately who'd taken it. I practically dove for the phone to call the police. Then she said, 'Philip, stop.' 'It was your delivery boy,' I said. 'I know,' she said, 'I gave it to him.' I couldn't speak for a moment. 'You what?' 'I like the painting, but not the way he does. And it seems to me, if somebody loves something so much, they should have it.'

"Well," Philip continued, "I almost lost it right there. But I didn't. Oh my God, I was angry, but I didn't yell or scream. No, I did the smartest thing ever. I went for a walk. During the walk, I remembered a deeply held belief of my father's—the successful person always tries to turn disappointment and adversity to his advantage. So that night, during what very well could have been our last dinner together, I gave her a note, which read: *My love, you were right to give away the painting. And it's true what you said. If somebody loves someone so much, they should have them. Will you marry me?"*

It was eerie how, when he finished the story, the cars on the bridge finally began to move. It was as if the whole world had stopped for him. A great effect. Part of me wondered whether he'd hired a bunch of drivers to stop in unison around us. But in truth, the accident up ahead had been cleared.

As I think back, even though he told the story in a clumsy manner, it had a certain smoothness, as if it had been told too many times.

Hank was now speeding up FDR Drive. He cut across two lanes and barely made the Houston Street exit.

"Tell me your opinion of the house tour," Philip said.

"Have you and Anna been asked?"

"Tell me your opinion."

The house tour is an annual fund-raiser for the Brooklyn Heights Association. Five houses are chosen for uniqueness of architecture, quality of restoration, and interior design. A few thousand people from all over New York City and the surrounding suburbs come and tramp through these homes. It's sweetly voyeuristic, and I found it fun my first years in the Heights, but it can leave a bitter aftertaste if you don't have a comparable home. I told all this to Philip. "Basically," I said, "if you want my opinion, I wouldn't do it. Not your house. Keep it a mystery."

"Well," he said. "I'm glad Anna didn't talk to you."

"Oh, why?"

"They asked her. They've been after her to do it. And I told her she should. So she's doing it. And it's a good thing because Anna needs something to do."

"In that case," I said, "sure, great. Good."

"You can let me out here, Hank, I need to walk a bit." Philip turned to me and said, "He'll drop you wherever you need to go."

"Thank you."

Before he got out of the car, Philip said, "And Kate—may I trouble you for one more thing?"

Trouble. His word, not mine.

"Please don't tell Anna about my friend back at the house."

TIM

"I JUST SPOKE TO YOUR FATHER."

"He's your father, too."

"Oh, right. Anyway, Tim, how are you?"

I sighed. Then my sister sighed. In the aftermath of our father's great unmasking, Sal and I talked nearly every day, trying to make sense of what we'd learned. But lately, we hadn't spoken much. We'd grown tired of rehashing the mess he'd made, so with each call, we tried to sidestep the myriad of land mines and talk small for a time. For me, these phone conversations proved single-handedly why every family should have at least two children. A good sister or brother can help keep one sane.

"How are you, Sal?"

"Been better."

"What's wrong?"

"Oh, the nerve of the man."

"Yes," I said warily.

"Their fiftieth anniversary. It's coming up."

"Can't be."

"Not for another year, but he wants to celebrate early."

"A whole year early?"

"Yep. Next year Mom won't remember anything, so he's probably right. It's just . . ."

"What, Sal, what?"

"It's hard to imagine throwing him a party at this point. Mom, though. Mom deserves a parade. Anyway, he kept saying how terrific you were at his retirement shindig. What an amazing MC you were. So I said, but probably shouldn't have, 'Let's have Tim organize your party.' "

"You didn't."

"I was kidding, all right? I know it's my turn. Don't worry. I'll do it all. But you have to be there. Okay?"

"Just postpone as long as you can."

"Why, are you hoping he'll die?"

"I didn't say it. You said it."

"So, brother, how are you?"

"I was just going to ask you."

"Don't ask."

"Are you smoking again? It sounds like you're smoking."

"Yep. Red broke up with me."

"No."

"She did. She left me for a man named Shirley. It's okay, you can laugh."

"I'm sorry, Sal . . ."

"I said you could laugh!"

We laughed.

"How are you and Kate?"

"Why?"

"Everybody's getting divorced or breaking up. It's just a disaster area out there. I don't know, it's probably wrong of me, but you and Kate have, like, the only relationship that I know of that actually works. And to think we have to celebrate our parents just because our feeble mom never had the courage to kick the feckless bastard out."

"Well . . ."

"You haven't answered my question."

"Forty-one years to go, that's how we are."

"Now, that's a party I'd like to plan."

I said nothing. The only sound was of Sal lighting another cigarette.

"So you guys going to make it? To fifty?"

"Well," I said, exhaling with her, "we're going to do our best."

After hanging up, I checked the kitchen clock. It was almost midnight. As I suspected, during my conversation with Sal, Kate had fallen asleep while reading *Jane Eyre*. Before turning off the lamp on her side, I studied her sleeping face. Her sweet features. The faint wrinkles around her mouth from smiling too much. The slight upturn of her near-perfect nose.

How will we be after fifty years?

Sleep was difficult for me that night. I took a bowl of Raisin Bran to the living room/dining room/toy room, turned on the TV, and channel-surfed. Finally, in desperate need for perspective, I returned to the kitchen. Because we'd married at a younger age than most of our friends—I had been twenty-three and Kate twenty-five—fifty years of marriage seemed a possibility. For me, it was a goal.

Yes, I had dueling fantasies: a golden-anniversary celebration with my would-be-seventy-five-year-old wife and the dream of a wild weekend with Anna Brody. But honestly, a weekend with Anna Brody seemed far from the realm of possibility, which made doing the math that night, at our jelly-stained kitchen table and without the aid of a calculator, all the more harmless. What if I had it both ways? Fifty years of marriage to Kate, one weekend with Anna Brody. What would it mean?

Listed below are my preliminary findings.

Over a fifty-year period, I will have shared the following . . .

2,600 weekends:
    1 weekend (Anna)—2,599 weekends (Kate)
18,250 days:
    2 days (Anna)—18,248 days (Kate)

438,000 hours:

    48 hours (Anna)—437,952 hours (Kate)

26,280,000 minutes:

    2,880 minutes (Anna)—26,277,120 minutes (Kate)

1,576,800,000 seconds:

    172,800 seconds (Anna)—1,576,627,200 seconds (Kate)

Viewing it from a purely numerical standpoint, the weekend seemed like not such a big deal. Barely a blip. But I've never been one to trust numbers. That was how I found myself back in church.

On the first Sunday in February, I arrived early because I needed extra time to pray. Attendance would be down, I heard one bald usher tell another, because it was Super Bowl Sunday. In addition to my primary reason for needing church, I had other concerns. First, there was a letter from Dr. Jamison Lamson, my mentor and dissertation adviser, telling me of his impending retirement and of his "regret" that my work was the only piece of "unfinished business" in his long and distinguished career. The second area of concern was ABC's post–Super Bowl airing of the family-friendly *An Angel and His Wings* series, starring Jeff Slade, that Kate had been threatening to watch along with an estimated forty million other viewers.

But no, that morning I stayed, as they say, on topic.

I prayed for what I wanted most: a sign. Then I made an important addendum to my prayer. Because it was my third Sunday at church, because of my elementary understanding of the Trinity (that somehow God is Father, Son, and Holy Spirit), because Peter denies Jesus three times before the cock crows, and because my boys had become big fans of the early and rentable films of the Three Stooges, I decided to make it tougher and up the ante.

I'd need three (3) signs before I'd do God's work and indulge/surrender to a weekend with Anna Brody. And I told God as much.

(Only an amateur churchgoer would dare challenge the Divine.)

Furthermore, I prayed: *Each of these signs needs to be clear, irrefutable, near miraculous.*

Imagine my surprise, then, when within the hour, the First Sign arrived.

It came after the minister finished his weekly announcements and told a rather funny joke about Jesus at the Super Bowl. The congregation was still laughing when the minister raised his arms and said, "The peace of the Lord be always with you." I joined the others in saying, "And also with you."

I began to greet the other parishioners around me—handshakes, a polite nod to an older couple down the row to my left—when I felt the sharp poke of a finger in my ribs. I turned upon hearing, "You're the last person I expected to see here."

"Hello, Bea."

She stepped up onto the pew, threw her beefy arms around my neck, and gave me a bone-crushing squeeze. I felt myself being pulled down, as if my spine might snap. She pressed her mouth to my ear and hissed, "Meet me over by the baptismal font after the service. We need to talk."

When she finally let go, I nearly fell backward.

"And Mr. Welch?"

I must have appeared dazed. "What, Bea?"

"Peace of the Lord."

As the rest of the congregation stood in line to greet the minister, I huddled with Bea near the baptismal font.

"*What?*" I asked.

"I have two matters to discuss with you. The first concerns your replacement."

"Oh, him."

"I always knew he was a bag of hot air. Ever since Thanksgiving, he's been the lamest teacher. You can't imagine it. Let me give you an example of the kind of thing we're doing. We are *memorizing* dates and time lines. He's preparing us for SATs, as if we don't all have private coaches already. So I've started a petition to get him removed."

"You're kidding," I said, trying to hide my pleasure with Bea's efforts.

"Unfortunately, I'm the only one willing to sign it."

Any momentary satisfaction I'd felt was quickly dashed.

Bea stared up at me, her fat eyes blinking slowly, and said, "Sir, don't worry. You—*we*—will prevail."

"What else? You said you had two things."

"Oh, right. I have something for you."

Bea dug around in her purse. Purse? I had never seen her with a purse. In fact, I'd never seen her in a dress, wearing hose, half heels, and was that a touch of rouge on her chipmunkesque cheeks?

"I really must be going, Bea."

"Wait, it's here somewhere." She produced a small cream-colored envelope. "It's from her."

"Who?

"Mrs. Ashworth."

"I don't think she goes by that name."

"She asked me to call her Mrs. Ashworth. When I asked why, she said, 'Because Mr. Ashworth is my husband.'"

The sealed envelope was blank. There was no stamp on it, no return address.

"She gave it to me to give to you."

"Wait—she gave it to you? She handed it to you?"

"Why, sure."

"I thought she was in France."

"Oh, no. She's back. She got back the other day."

I snatched the envelope from Bea's hand. I wanted to rip it open right there. But that would draw undue attention, so I slipped it into the breast pocket of my brown tweed blazer. I bolted for the exit as she yelled after me, "You're welcome!"

Outside I walked. I walked with the letter in my pocket. The letter in my pocket was heavy. It was a bullet in midflight. And it was from her. She was back, and she had something to say to me. She'd taken out pen and paper and written something down. With her tongue, she'd licked the envelope. Her spit sealed it. And she'd given it to an unlikely messenger.

I kept walking, waiting for the perfect moment to open it.

Finally, at home, after a rousing game with the boys of Bury Daddy, I ducked into the bathroom, where I closed and locked the door. I sat on the toilet with the lid down. I took the envelope out of the front left pocket of my blue jeans, which was where I had transferred it after changing out of my church suit. I took a deep breath. I tore open the envelope. I carefully read what Anna had written. It didn't take long. Then I reread it to make sure I hadn't missed anything. Then I stared at it until her words became blurry, and not because I was crying, but rather, because my hands had begun to shake.

ANNA BRODY

May 9th–11th

KATE

MANY OF OUR FIRST GRANTS WERE EARMARKED FOR CHARITIES EITHER ST. LOUIS–based or autism-related. This was wise politically. I had other lists for later days: the Quite Possiblys and the Very Much Want to But Not Sure Yets.

Four months into this job, and still my favorite part remained the discovery of a new charity. Every Friday Bruno and I would order in lunch and eat at my desk.

Plopping down in my high-backed swivel chair, Bruno liked to ask, "What's got your heart this week?"

"Pretty much everything, but this week's winner is . . ."

Ever since I'd first worked for him, Bruno had held a deep belief in dream time. Friday lunch was the hour when anything was possible. Forget the constraints of life and the limitations of reality. This was way-down-the-road-assuming-all-goes-well time, when we could award grants to every group we believed worthy.

". . . Red Flag."

Bruno's interest was piqued.

"Since I'm a mother of two boys, this one caught my eye: Red Flag is a Stanford-based research group studying the alarming feminization of the male species in all classes of vertebrate animals, including people. Phthalates, flame retardants, PCBs, and a host of new chemicals in the environment are most likely the cause. Lower sperm counts are one by-product. In a lot of cases with these animals, the male genitals are shrinking."

Bruno: "That has not been my experience."

"What else? There's a Nigerian-based charity devoted to distributing bed nets for malaria prevention, aptly named Nothing but Nets. There's also Soles 4 Souls and Adopt-A-Minefield, the International Breast Milk Project . . ."

So, all in all, it had been another terrific week at work when Claudia called. "Can you talk?"

"I'm all ears."

"Well, can I just say: If Dan took me to France for a month, I sure as hell wouldn't come back looking like that."

"What do you mean?"

"Guess who put on some pounds in Paris?"

"Anna Brody?"

"Aka Miss Porky Pig."

"I'm sure it's not that bad—"

"Don't be so sure. We're talking *oink-oink*."

I like to believe that I'm above gossip. But with Claudia, it was cheap, easy, and abundant. It was a nice break from the problems of the world, and I began to crave her daily updates.

The following Monday:

"How are you?"

"Busy."

"Then I'll be quick. Miss Piggy waddled her way through the health club this morning. Debbie asked if she wanted to take a spinning class with us. She said, 'No, I don't feel like working out.' Then she just stood there, so I asked, 'Are you all right?' Said she: 'I don't know why I'm here.'"

Later that week Claudia called with a series of reports about the arrival of an unfortunate-looking Chihuahua that had been delivered to the Ashworth-Brody house.

"Apparently, the dog has the runs."

"How do you know?"

"The house tour committee met with Anna for a preliminary tour.

In every room they went, the little dog—which isn't a dog at all but a rat that barks—had shit or peed. The stench."

Soon Claudia had other news. "Did you hear about the biting incident?"

"The dog?"

"No, the kid. The girl." Claudia went on to recount how Sophie Brody-Ashworth had bitten Angus Strubel and broken skin. Then she said, "Oh, about the dog. It had worms. That was why it was puking and shitting everywhere. Well, as of last Thursday, the dog? Gone. Anna probably drowned it."

When Claudia stopped laughing, I asked why she despised Anna Brody. "Oh, I don't, not at all," she said. "I actually quite like her, especially now that she's fattened up. It's just that you hate her, and I want you to be happy."

This caused me to stop. Did I hate Anna Brody? What had she done to me? She'd been kind. She'd said nice things about me to others. She'd even given me the most beautiful dress I'll ever wear. Okay, so it also weirdly happened to be her wedding dress. Her greatest crime had been to be—through no fault of her own—the momentary subject of my husband's fantasy life, but if that was reason for hatred, then I'd need to add her to a list that included a certain Victoria's Secret model, a cluster of movie stars, and most notably, the late Donna Reed.

I had no problem with Anna. So to prove it to myself, I called her up and asked her to lunch.

TIM

IN THOSE FIRST WEEKS AFTER HER RETURN FROM FRANCE, I DIDN'T HAVE MUCH contact with Anna Brody. Whenever we crossed paths, we were cordial but distant. Each time I saw her at preschool drop-off, we'd make minimal eye contact, and if I happened to be with other mothers, she'd greet them warmly but pretty much ignore me. I took this to mean she was covering her tracks. Except for the note (which I admit to hiding in my wallet and frequently taking out to smell its lavender scent), there was no evidence of anything between us. This was to be our secret. Or, I don't know, maybe she was telling the world. All I knew was she had offered me a weekend, and May ninth was eight weeks away.

One morning after drop-off, Anna and I found ourselves alone, heading in the same direction. As we walked, my heart raced. *Thump thump thump.* I could feel my pulse in my neck.

Anna spoke first. "What, you don't like me anymore?

"I'm sorry?"

"You don't talk to me. You ignore me. You won't even look at me."

"Wait a minute. I didn't leave the country for a month."

"True," she said.

"I didn't send a cryptic note with dates on it."

"Cryptic? I thought I was rather clear. Is there a problem with the dates?"

"It's not that."

Something was different about Anna Brody. Yes, she'd gained

weight, but it made the sharp, hard angles of her face seem softer. There was also something more human, more vulnerable, about her.

"See, you can't even look at me."

That's because now you're even more beautiful!

"Sorry," I said, my eyes locking with hers.

"Is this making you uncomfortable?"

Yes.

"I don't mean for you to be uncomfortable. It's the last thing I want. The whole point of this is so you can get beyond your feelings. So we can get back to what we had."

I believed her.

"I love our talks," she continued. "I love being with you. I love that you're funny and sweet. And I love the way you tear up whenever you talk about Kate. It happens every time. I especially love that just the thought of having a weekend with me is ripping you up inside. That's the kind of man you are. If it were easy, then I would have been wrong about you."

What was I supposed to say to that?

"Maybe you don't even want the weekend. Or maybe you can't handle it, which is also fine. But if it's going to make you act weird around me, then we should forget it."

Me weird? Who offered the weekend? But did I ask that? No, instead, I stammered, "How would it, uhm, work?"

"It's simple. We both clear our schedules. We meet somewhere. A hotel. We don't speak of it to anyone, because we don't want to hurt anyone."

I must have looked perplexed.

"You know, our spouses."

"Oh. Oh, right."

"For one weekend, we forget everything and leave our lives behind. For one weekend, we do anything and everything. Whatever we feel like."

Anna was cool and collected. We may as well have been planning a trip to Costco. "But you have to stop acting weird."

Half a block back, Claudia called out, "Hey, you two, wait up!" She and Tess, dressed for Pilates, were hurrying to catch us.

"We'll cover the specifics later. For now, Tim, just don't think about it. It's something we'll do in May, if it makes sense at the time."

"Okay, sure."

"Anything you want to say?"

Oh, there's plenty.

"Because at the speed they're moving, you have about thirty seconds . . ."

Here's what I wanted to say: *I haven't been naked in front of anyone other than Kate since I was twenty-two. Also, strange rogue hairs grow on my body. I have the beginnings of man breasts. I don't have much body hair, although some of my pubic hairs are gray. I could pluck those. And what about sexually transmitted diseases? I can't bring anything home! Did you read that article online about the recent proliferation of anal warts?* But all I could muster was this: "Spoons. Do you sleep in the spoon position?"

Anna laughed, reminding me of the pleasure I got from making her laugh. "Now, Tim, it's not until May. So put it out of your mind."

The girls caught up. "Hey, didn't you hear us?"

"Oh," I said. "Sorry."

"You guys must've been talking about something important."

"Not at all." Anna sighed. "We were just scheduling a playdate."

KATE

WHILE WALKING TO TAZZA ON HENRY STREET, I TRIED TO DETERMINE MY REAL reason for having lunch with Anna Brody. Between Philip's claiming that Anna talked about me all the time and my prurient interest as to whether there was any truth to Claudia's gossip, I felt torn between the friend I was thought to be and the nasty neighbor I was becoming. I'd invited Anna to lunch out of both guilt and a desire to help her through this hard time. Another part of me was just plain curious about how she would look.

Great. She looked great. And the weight she'd gained made her look healthier. The most surprising change to her appearance was that she'd hacked her hair off at chin level. It looked like she'd done the job herself. Why anyone would cut off hair like hers is beyond me, but I didn't even have a chance to ask her why, because Anna started talking right away.

First she told me about their trip to the South of France, where she had rented a rustic cabin. "Philip got all fidgety after three days. So it was mostly Sophie and me roughing it. No amenities. No dishwasher. It was the kind of place where you and Tim would stay."

Yes, but not by choice! It's the only kind of place we could afford! "So where was Philip?"

"Oh, he was wherever Philip goes. Here, there."

Anna moved on to the re-redecorating (if that's a word) of her house. "Philip has given me carte blanche to do whatever it takes."

"Whatever it takes to what?"

"To make me happy."

"It seems to be working. You seem happy. Very, actually."

"I'm redoing *everything*."

The more she talked about her house, the more I thought about her marriage. I wondered if she knew about her husband. Maybe she was just another one of those smiling wives who put up with untold betrayals and disappointments. Maybe she knew that the real reason Philip was letting her redecorate was so he could carry on with someone else, or many others.

But she seemed so positive about everything, I couldn't tell what she knew. So I pressed and asked if it was hard to be married to such an important man.

"What are you talking about? You're married to an important man."

"What I mean is, Philip's a public figure."

"Big deal."

"Well, that can make things complicated. You see, I was once with a famous man. Before Tim. So I have some idea what you must be facing." I lowered my voice and said, "I hate it when people name-drop. But I used to be lovers with Jeff Slade."

Anna didn't say anything.

"It was very passionate, purely physical, but somehow raw in that end-of-the-world way."

(Hopefully, I wasn't this ridiculous, but this is the conversation as I remember it. Maybe I knew that you don't get something unless you give it. So I came prepared to sacrifice, to open up in hopes that she would follow. But clearly, I tried too hard to make her feel comfortable, to impress her. How else do I explain the series of weak segues that led from "How have you been?" to a frank recounting of my Jeff Slade experience, in which I neglected to mention that I had dated him twelve years before he became famous, so my intimation that what we had in common was powerful, famous men was a complete and utter lie.)

"Jeff Slade? Should I know him?"

Nothing worse than having to explain the name you just dropped.

"You'd recognize him. He's on TV all the time."

"I don't watch TV," Anna said sweetly.

"Oh, well, neither do I."

From that point on, our conversation went off track. Something I said sounded like a criticism of Tim. I had mistakenly thought it would encourage Anna to open up about Philip. Instead, she came to Tim's defense, arguing that he was a unique and special man.

"Look," I said, "I think you idealize him. Us. Our marriage."

"I think you're a lucky woman."

"I don't know if you see us in the right way. We have our troubles."

"Well, are you worried about him?"

"Am I worried, what? That Tim would cheat?"

She nodded.

"No, I'm not. The truth is, I'd be much more concerned about me."

"How so?"

Understand I was realizing these things as I was saying them. "There is someone else that I think about from time to time . . ."

I didn't tell her everything. I didn't tell her it was Jeff Slade. Instead, I signaled to the waitress for the check.

Anna leaned in and said, "What's stopping you?"

I'd revealed too much.

"For starters, I'm *married*," I said.

"Yes, but it could be fun. No one has to know. And it doesn't have to mean anything."

Not mean anything? Is she whacked? I'd come to offer her encouragement, and now she was encouraging me to have an affair. I should have just ended the conversation. Instead, I asked, "But what if it did mean something?"

"Just decide in advance that it won't."

The bill came, and I started to calculate the tip. "Is it that easy?"

"I'll know soon enough."

I looked at her.

She gave a slight shrug and said, "I'm in the process of taking a lover."

That was when Anna leaned forward, took my hands in hers, and said with complete compassion, "It's okay, you know. Sometimes it's what we need."

TIM

DURING THOSE STRANGE, UNCERTAIN WEEKS, I BECAME A BETTER THAN USUAL DAD and a kinder husband. Kate even said so. It proved to be an unexpected benefit from the Anna Brody of it all. However, one part of my life had been neglected. This was made all too clear when Dr. Jamison Lamson called and left an emphatic message on the phone machine: "Timothy, do you read your mail?" The stern yet hurt tone in his voice stung. That was when I remembered the letter he'd sent, a letter I'd skimmed and then tucked away behind the unpaid bills.

It took a few minutes to find and reread the letter. Dr. Lamson had written to all his students, past and present, announcing the end of his "invigorating" and "satisfying" teaching career. He thanked all of us for "the privilege of witnessing the wonderment of history catching fire." He wrote that he would miss us, his students, and that we had been his teachers, too. It was an exquisite letter, graceful and self-deprecating, worthy of framing, except in my case, he'd hastily scribbled across the bottom, *Timothy—I need to see you ASAP!*

As soon as possible was the following morning. After dropping Teddy and Sam at preschool, I caught the R train to Queens and sprinted across the St. Bernard campus to Dr. Lamson's corner office on the third floor of the J. Arthur Kresge History Building.

I found Dr. Lamson packing up his office, standing among the stacks of books and half-filled boxes. He had the stunned look of someone who'd only just realized he had way too much stuff.

Seeing me, he squinted in disbelief and said, "Was beginning to wonder if I'd ever see you again, Timothy. Thought you were dead."

I laughed nervously as he cleared a place for me to sit.

Never one to mince words, he got right to the point. "You're not going to finish in time, are you?"

I hemmed and hawed.

Dr. Lamson sighed and threw up his hands in surrender. "It's a pity."

Me, faintly: "Yes."

"What's frustrating, Timothy, is that in all the years I've been doing this, your dissertation is one of the few I actually wanted to read."

It occurred to me that he believed in me more than I ever would. It was probably cruel to continue this conversation, but he seemed upset, so I said, "Sir, not that it's possible, but when would be the last day that I could turn it in?"

Dr. Lamson didn't need to consult a calendar. "April twenty-third."

I flinched. April 23 was only six weeks away, and what I really needed was six months. "That early?"

"Please understand why I want to laugh. I want to laugh because of perspective. What you find to be early, I view as much too late. You are funny. Early. That's funny."

But neither of us was laughing.

Me: "There's no other possible—"

"Not if you expect the committee"—the committee: Dr. Lamson, Dr. Rita "The Noodle" Lovejoy, and Dr. Rejandra "Killer" Kanwar, the Elvira Krause Professor of German history—"to have enough time to prepare for your defense."

"My defense?"

"Tell me you weren't expecting to have that part of the doctoral process waved."

"No, sir." The truth was, I had blocked out the whole idea of a dissertation defense. Clearly, Dr. Lamson had been more hopeful than I. He admitted as much, saying he had saved the last remaining time slot just for me.

I had to ask. "Sir, what day would my defense have been?"

"The morning of the ninth."

"The ninth? May ninth?"

"Why, yes."

I nearly fell out of the chair. "You saved the morning of May ninth just for me?"

"Yes, but it's a moot point—"

"I can do it."

"What did you just say?"

"Not only can I do it, sir. But I will."

Perhaps this was the Second Sign. I didn't know yet. But I believed it was no accident. Here was an opportunity. Life was colluding. I never thought I would actually have a weekend with Anna Brody. And I'd been wondering, *Why me?* But now it kind of made sense. Maybe the real purpose of her offer (and little did she know) was to motivate me to finish my work. You see, everything was pointing toward May 9! I was so excited that I quivered like a piano moments after every key had been pounded.

I turned, looked Dr. Lamson dead in the eye, and said, "Pencil me in."

Back in the Heights, heading toward home, I felt a perceptible shift in my thoughts. Already Anna Brody was less present in everything—in the black patches of unmelted snow, in the gray winter sky, and in the ash-smudged foreheads of the parishioners filing out of St. Charles Borromeo on Sidney Place. With each exhalation of my cold, steamy breath, I felt her leaving me, so that by the time I hit Oak Lane, I felt like a new and improved version of my old self. I was Tim Welch again.

And thus began a period of unprecedented productivity.

Day and night I worked, fueled by Coca-Cola and loud music that I blasted through headphones plugged into Kate's portable CD/tape player. Incidentally, any music with lyrics distracted me, so I began each night with Pachelbel's Canon in D cranked at full volume—then later, Bach, Vivaldi, Beethoven. Under these influences, I slashed my work, moved entire sections, edited with abandon.

Like old Thomas Edison, I didn't sleep much. I took brief naps, sometimes lying down under my worktable. I didn't shave. I showered at odd times. I began to look like a savage. I didn't recognize myself. I didn't go to the gym as planned, so I didn't do the sit-ups and the push-ups and the pull-ups and the full-body crunches. There was no time, which may explain why I began to speak more quickly, my words and phrases clipped. I stood a bit straighter. Still, I loved the simplicity of my life. During those hours the boys were in preschool, I worked. When they bathed, I edited. When they watched a video or the Cartoon Network, I revised. And after an all-nighter, my eyes raw from no sleep, my caffeinated body shaking from all the Cokes, I'd stop in time to make breakfast for Kate and the boys—pancakes or oatmeal, turkey bacon, apple slices, cantaloupe cubes—an early-morning feast. Then I'd hurry them out the door, do the dishes, and get back at it.

My goal? *Just finish the fucking thing.*

KATE

UNDERSTAND THAT I WAS THE LEAST DRUNK OF THE VERY DRUNK, BUT ONLY BECAUSE I arrived late. Had Debbie Beebe stayed, she would've had clearer, more reliable memories of what has since become the most notorious of those evenings that we call Girls' Night Out. But since Debbie had given birth to twin girls a few months earlier—in fact, this was her first night away from them—she was eager to get back home, which conveniently happened to be just upstairs. The Beebes lived on the top three floors of a two-family brownstone co-op they shared with Claudia and Dan Valentine.

When I got there, Debbie was preparing to leave. I asked, "Why so soon?" She shook her head and indicated her chest, where her breast milk had leaked through her blouse. "I guess it's a sign I better go," she said. "Too bad," I said. "Truthfully," she told me as she slipped on her coat, "I may be getting out just at the right time." It was an odd thing for her to say, considering she'd spent the afternoon making margaritas for the rest of us.

I arrived late for the same reason I'd missed in recent weeks Debbie's baby shower, Claudia's birthday brunch, and book club (*Jane Eyre*) at Rebecca's house: work. Long days reviewing grant proposals and seeking out ideal grant recipients.

It had been a hard week. I was still rattled from my lunch with Anna Brody. When Friday finally arrived, I was late leaving the office, tired, and definitely not in a party mood. I went to Claudia's because—and this is my only complaint about her—if you miss one of her events, she takes it hard. She pouts. She punishes you in small ways. And Claudia had been particularly insistent this time, swearing, "You'll be glad you did." "Why?" "There's someone coming you need to meet." "Who?" "A writer friend. You'll see." "Whom does your friend write for?" "I don't know. *Cosmo,* probably."

Needless to say, by the time I made it to Claudia's, I was ready for a drink.

The girls were in the back part of the garden floor, which was the Valentines' family room. I could hear them laughing loudly. Someone was smoking pot, which was rare in our circle. Debbie's margarita mix was on the dining room table, and I poured myself one, sat down, and drank it fast, wanting a good buzz to come quickly. I carried my second margarita down the hall, stopping to admire the way Claudia had framed the school pictures of her boys, noticing how Otto's (age nine) permanent teeth had overwhelmed his baby teeth, how his mouth was in transition. I thought of Teddy and how soon this would be happening to him.

I was met in the hallway by Rebecca, who was hurrying to the bathroom. "Hey, Tess's sister is here. She's a writer."

"Ah, the writer. Claudia told me . . ."

"Yeah, well, we were telling her all about you."

"Really."

"She writes puff pieces, mostly for *The Wall Street Journal.*"

"I didn't know the *Journal* did puff pieces."

"Well, it's their own particular kind of puff. Aren't they great?" Rebecca indicated the margarita pitcher. "I've had three!"

Clearly.

"Anyway, we've been telling Lacey all about you, your work, all that you're doing." Shamelessly, Rebecca lowered her jeans and sat on the toilet. I pulled the door closed. She kept talking. "I'm so proud of you! So many people talk about making a difference, but you're making a difference!"

"Oh, I don't know." But I smiled because it was true.

A woman hooted in the back room. Other women cheered.

"What's going on back there?" I said.

"How many have you had?" Rebecca called out from the bathroom.

"Margaritas? I'm working on my second."

"You may want to finish it before you go back there. That would be my advice."

The door to the back room swung open, and Claudia poked her head out. "Rebecca, get your butt in here! Oh, Kate, just in time. I want you to meet Lacey. She's a wr—"

"Rebecca was just saying."

"But first, hurry, you two. Intermission is almost over."

In the back room of the Valentine duplex, a state-of-the-art home entertainment system had been installed to project movie-theater-equivalent images on a large flat screen. Speakers hung in all four corners gave the viewer a Dolby-surround-sound feel.

Dan the Bear was a movie buff. He loved John Ford westerns, Frank Capra's *Mr. Smith Goes to Washington,* and Billy Wilder's *Some Like It Hot,* and he had a particular passion for the disaster films from the seventies, *Poseidon Adventure, The Towering Inferno,* and *Earthquake.*

What the girls were watching that night probably was not what Dan the Bear had in mind. *Bend Over Boyfriend* had been more instructional. I knew this because Claudia had drunkenly shouted it in my ear. "It was more educational. We learned about the anatomy. How much lubricant!"

She said *lubricant* in such a way that it was as if she'd been waiting her whole life to say the word. In fact, she kept saying *lubricant* or *lube* or the verb form, *lubricate,* as she got me up to speed.

"This sex therapist and her not-too-shabby husband have made this video series where women fuck their men. We already watched the first one. It was all about the mechanics, the anatomy of the asshole, some terrific foreplay techniques." Claudia inserted the evening's second DVD. Then she continued, like an announcer at a sporting event, "These are real people. Real husbands and wives. Real girlfriends and boy-friends. This isn't porn for porn's sake. It's educational. It's instruc-tive." She held up the laminated case. "Unlike most sequels, *Bend Over Boyfriend Two* is better than the original." She read the blurb on the back of the box: " 'More Rockin', Less Talkin'.' "

Lacey, the *Wall Street Journal* reporter, cozied up next to me with a joint in her hand. "What you're doing sounds incredible."

"Yes, I think it is—I mean, it could be. We're a young foundation."

"Tell me about it."

We shared the joint as I described my work with Bruno, his illness, and the ticking clock. And Cortez. She said she knew of Cortez (who didn't?), but she hadn't heard anything about the Lucy Foundation. It so happened that she'd begun work on a long-lead piece about the New Philanthropy. She had interviewed Bill and Melinda Gates and George Soros, among others, but had been looking for a smaller foundation as a point of contrast. She seemed to think the Lucy Foundation might be what she'd been looking for.

Maybe it was the pot, maybe it was the margaritas kicking in (or the mixture of both), and maybe it was an effort to avoid what was up on the home movie screen, but I felt an almost giddy sense of hope. Here was a reporter—young, eager—who wanted to make a mark, and she wanted to make a mark with me.

We agreed to exchange numbers, but during our mutual search for pen and paper, we were distracted by what was up on the big screen.

Claudia: "Now watch how much she uses, because apparently, you want to lubricate his asshole real good . . ."

"Can we watch something else?" someone said, laughing.

The man reached back to help spread open his butt cheeks.

"Look how bad he wants it!"

The room grew eerily quiet as the blond wife slowly worked the head of the dildo into the man. When the woman gave a sudden thrust, only Claudia cheered.

Lacey to me: "You were saying."

"Oh, I don't know, something about the future."

Later, as we were leaving, Lacey asked for my card. She said she'd be calling me Monday morning. "And Katie?"

I liked that she called me Katie.

"I know you think I'm drunk, but actually, I think very clearly when there's more booze in me than blood. And what I'm saying is, I'm going to write about you and your foundation."

"It's not my foundation," I protested.

"Yes, but you know what I mean!"

I was happy when I got home. Tim was still up, back from his boys' night out, sitting at the kitchen table working, or at least pretending to. He asked how it had gone. I started to drunkenly tell him about my day, and I was fully intending to compliment Debbie's margarita mix and even render in detail the porno movie experience when he interrupted with a simple "TMI."

TMI was an acronym he'd picked up from his students. Too much information. "Oh, right, so I don't have to tell you everything?"

"I'm actually asking that tonight you don't."

"Okay, then. The upshot? *The Wall Street Journal* is going to write about my work. Can you believe it?"

"That is terrific," he said, genuinely excited.

I started a shower to wash the smoke out of my hair. But before I shut the bathroom door, I called out to Tim: "So how was your boys' night out?"

Tim shrugged and mumbled something.

"What did you all talk about?" I asked.

He looked at me as if to say, *You don't want to know.*

I smiled back at him and said, "Oh, right—TMI."

TIM

I DIDN'T WANT TO GO. KATE MADE ME. SHE WAS GOING OUT WITH THE GIRLS AND HAD a sitter, so I reluctantly met up with the Weasel and his men—Dick Beebe, Dan Valentine, Tom Manker—who were having their monthly meal together at Peter Luger in Williamsburg. I sat on the end with another man who was (thankfully) also a newcomer. Initially, the talk was small, although my ears did prick up when Dan the Bear made passing mention of a risky investment that had gone sour. It had been a hard day for Dan. He'd lost a bundle. I asked him if Claudia knew.

"Yes," he said glumly. "But she's not as upset as I am."

Easter was two weeks away, and if Dan's investments didn't rebound, Claudia was going to strap one on and have her way with him. I didn't let Dan know that I knew. But clearly, he was dreading the day.

All in all, I found the evening interesting, from an anthropological point of view. A night out with a bunch of steak-eating men, sans wives and kids. What might these meat eaters discuss? Their good fortune. Tom Manker, who worked for Brown, Harris and Stevens, bragged that while the nationwide housing bubble had recently burst, the Heights seemed immune to falling prices. For fun, I referenced past speculation-driven debacles: Tulipomania, the Panic of 1837, the junk-bond high jinks of the 1980s, and, for good measure, I tossed a sub-prime smoke bomb into the conversation. "No," Tom said. "*This* is not *that*. House prices in the Heights are only going up, up, up!" Dick Beebe snorted in agreement. The Weasel kept saying, "Yawn. Yawn." Meaning, I suppose, he wanted to talk about something else. When our slabs of steak arrived, the Weasel got his chance: "So, who's hot?"

I managed an "Excuse me?"

"Who would we like to bang?"

Before I could change the subject, someone offered up that all of our wives were hotties. "Especially Tim's wife," someone said. *Agreed.* Fortunately, for the purposes of the discussion, all of our wives were off-limits. But other wives, nannies, and babysitters were up for grabs.

The beer flowed. I soon concluded the steaks all must have come from the same angry cow, because the men got ornery. They kept punching one another in the shoulder to emphasize a point. It was like a junior high locker room. At any moment, one of the guys might have started snapping the rest of us with a cloth napkin.

Out of respect for the fine women of the Heights, I'll refrain from sharing the names of the most desired. But it was a curious mix of the older/highbrow and the younger/funky. As the conversation went on, I found it odd that a certain someone had not been mentioned. Off-handedly, I brought up in my best oh-by-the-way tone, "What about Philip Ashworth's wife?"

The Weasel turned toward me, bared his beaver teeth, and said, "Don't kid yourself, Welch. She's completely out of your league."

Loud, manly laughs. Another round of beers.

The other newcomer—an unassuming man on all counts—had said nothing up to this point. With his pale skin, tortoiseshell eyeglasses, and an ill-fitting dark blue sport coat, he looked like the kind of man who'd played too much chess as a kid.

The Weasel asked if the Newcomer had anything he'd like to add.

"Why, yes. I'm reminded of a guy I know."

I was grateful this man was speaking. It took the pressure off me.

"For our purposes, let's call him the Happily Married Man."

The other men turned and listened in.

"The Happily Married Man doesn't like to travel, because he hates to be away from his wife and kids. This man loves his wife the way one should love one's wife. But he has to make a living. So he goes on a business trip to a major American city. He and an associate are going out for dinner, as they've just closed a major deal. The Happily Married Man will be going home in the morning. He's feeling great. He's taken care of business. He's in the shower, lathering up his body with soap, shampooing his hair, when his cell phone rings. He steps out of the shower, answers the phone, and his business associate says, 'Don't leave your room. I'm sending over a gift.'

"The man finishes showering. He slips on the nice terry-cloth robe the hotel provides. At eight on the dot, a knock comes on his door. He opens the door, and the most beautiful woman he has ever seen is standing in the doorway. She is a knockout. Perfect skin, exquisite breasts, a tattoo of thorns around her ankle. She asks if he'd like her to come in."

All of us stopped midchew while the Newcomer took a sip of seltzer.

The Weasel couldn't stand it: "Keep going."

Newcomer: "Well, the Happily Married Man invites her in and proceeds to have unbelievable, astonishing, best-ever sex with this woman. They do it in the bed, in the shower, on the cold tiles of the bathroom floor, in every position imaginable. He comes so many times, he loses count. He comes so much, he wonders if there's any come left inside him."

The gist of the story is that the man catches his flight, gets home to his wife, makes mad, passionate love to her, and remains to this day a Happily Married Man. He's never told his wife, feels no remorse, has absolutely no desire to cheat again, and to top it off, he's certain the whole experience made him an even better husband.

Genius.

When the Newcomer finished his story, all of the men spoke up at the same time. "Bullshit!" "Didn't happen." "Too good to be true."

Pause, then the Newcomer: "Oh, it happened."

Dan the Bear: "How do you know?"

The Newcomer said nothing but smiled smugly.

The Weasel: "Oh my God. You are that guy?"

Me: "It's not our business."

"I'm not saying anything."

But clearly, he was that guy.

"I'm neither confirming nor denying!"

Me, practically shouting: "Waitress, check, please!"

Here's what I learned that drunken night: The only difference between me and those other men was that I had an opportunity with Anna Brody that they'd never have, a once-in-a-lifetime chance most of them would never pass up, except for maybe the Newcomer. But he'd already had an Anna Brody moment of his own. Most important, I learned that not only was it possible to pull off the Weekend, it very likely could make me a better, more loving husband and also improve things at home. My upcoming Weekend with Anna Brody was the kind of sacrifice I was willing to make.

I was drunk enough that I almost had myself convinced.

KATE

MAYBE IF THE FIRST THING HE SAID THAT MORNING HADN'T BEEN "I PULLED AN all-nighter," I would've been kinder. But this was his third report in as many days. The previous two were "Wow, I got in six hours" and "I typed so much I can't even move my fingers." On those mornings I managed a "Good" and a mildly enthusiastic "Oh, honey, how great." Now it felt as if he was expecting me to burst into applause.

When Tim first started on the history of loss, I was eager to help. I read every word he wrote. And I think I weathered well the theme shifts, the new approaches, and the complete rethinkings. But as the years went by, I began to wonder if I was helping. My interest seemed to make him tense. Which made me tense. So I tried to detach, deciding that I didn't know anything, and I didn't want to know anything. Better, then, to ask nothing and eventually, hopefully, be pleasantly surprised.

But that morning I worried we were headed toward the all too familiar place of last-second panic. "I pulled another all-nighter," he said, looking especially tired and frazzled. "And I was on fire!" As he protested too much, an old fear of mine came rushing back: Tim won't ever finish.

Later that same morning, Teddy's kindergarten class made a presentation for the parents. For six weeks they had been studying space. Teddy had learned a great deal. The sun is hot. Jupiter has a red spot. The *M* planets are Mercury and Mars.

He told me all this and more as we stood next to his three-foot-by-five-foot space mural. He'd painted a piece of the sun in an upper corner; he'd cut out planets of various sizes and glued a gold and purple glitter ring around Saturn; he'd painted in comets and asteroids, and we'd taken his picture and his teacher had taken our picture, all of us proud. I gushed about the planets that he'd stuck on in no particular order—or, to be scientific about it, an order understood by him alone.

I smothered him with praise: "Oh, Teddy, that's beeeeaaaauuuutiful." "I love the colors." "You did this by yourself!" "Look, Sam, at what Teddy made. He made the galaxy!"

I noticed the time. "Okay, Mommy has to work." I gave both Teddy and Sam hugs. "Bye, boys. Mommy loves you."

"Can't you stay longer?" Tim asked.

"No," I said as I hugged him.

He looked rattled. "Do you know what you just did?"

"What?"

"You patted me."

"I did?"

"You patted the back of my shoulder while we hugged. Don't you realize what that means?"

"Stop it, Tim. All it means is I'm going to be late." Backing away, I blew kisses to the boys, and then I turned and was gone.

When I got to work, two messages had already been left on my voice mail. Both were from my new reporter friend at *The Wall Street Journal.* The first message had been left at the ungodly hour of 5:57 A.M. It went: "It's Lacey, calling from home. I'm ready to get started. Are you?" The second message came at 9:05 AM. "It's Lacey Windsor." She sounded serious. "I'm at my office. Did you see the paper?"

I hung up my coat, replaced my shoes with my fuzzy slippers, pulled out Lacey's business card, and dialed her work number. She answered her own phone. I said, "In answer to your questions: Yes, I'm ready to get started. And second, I haven't seen any newspaper of any kind."

"Oh," she said.

"You see, my older son's kindergarten class gave a presentation on outer space. They even baked these moon cookies." I heard the sound of Bruno sitting down in my big squishy office chair. "My boss is here. Can I call you right back?" I hung up and turned toward Bruno.

"Outer space," he said, trying to smile. "That sounds promising."

Bruno looked pale, ghostlike. His baggy, brightly colored clothes could no longer hide the fact that he was now mostly bones and skin. His eyes seemed twice their healthy size. He needed cheering up.

"You're going to be a happy man," I announced. "I have some interesting news." I began telling him about my "almost unbelievable chance meeting" with a "rising star" at The Wall Street Journal whom "I was just talking with on the phone" when Bruno extended a section of The New York Times and let it drop on my desk. The paper flopped open. The headline of an article in the top right-hand corner read: COR-TEZ STOCK PLUMMETS, UNDERFER OUSTED.

I began to read the article but didn't get far. I knew it wasn't good for us.

"I'm sorry, Kate."

"Did you know about this?"

"Louis gave me a heads-up last Friday."

"Why didn't you tell me?"

"I didn't want to ruin your weekend."

"Bruno, what does it mean—"

"The foundation was endowed with Cortez stock. Which is now worthless. So, basically, we have nothing to give away. It's over, Kate. Louis is sorry about it. We'll be paid what we're owed, but he needs us to go away quietly."

I stared out my office window, noticing the dirt on the glass. "Is that all he said?"

"No, he said he hoped I was feeling better."

I was too stunned to cry.

"I feel especially bad for you, Kate. You've done so much work."

I put on my best face. "Don't worry about me."

"I do."

"I wouldn't trade away all that I've learned."

"That's my girl." Bruno pushed himself up to a standing position and gingerly crossed toward my office door. "Thanks, Kate. You could've taken this hard."

I took it harder than he will ever know. I took it hard at first, snapping at our intern, Jessica, while we made the long list of people to call. Around noon, I took it hard when I headed out for lunch and couldn't decide on what and where to eat. Around three o'clock, I took it especially hard when I realized Bruno Schwine & Associates was finished and the Lucy Foundation was no more.

Funny thing was that Bruno seemed relieved.

I went home early that day, so I wasn't there when Bruno collapsed headfirst and tumbled down the stairs. Jessica called 911. She rode in the ambulance with Bruno, who was unconscious. I got to St. Vincent's as quickly as I could, and it was during those three continuous days when I stayed at the hospital that it occurred to me I'd been wrong. Maybe I hadn't been hired to try to save the world. Maybe I'd been hired to help my old friend die.

ABIGAIL HOSFORD

KATHERINE . . . YES . . . IT'S ABBY HOSFORD, WITH THE HEIGHTS ASSOCIATION . . . calling again. I left a message earlier with your sweet, sweet son . . . such good manners, too . . . I worried you might not have gotten my messa—

KATE

"I GOT YOUR MESSAGE."

"Hello? Katherine?"

"In fact, I've gotten all of your messages."

"Are you screening?"

Yes. "No, I was sleeping."

"Oh, I'm sorry. I can call back. I just hate to keep calling you."

"Then stop. Stop calling."

"And I know you've been at the hospital. I spoke with your friend Claudia. I'm sorry about your loss. Your boss, I mean."

"He's actually doing better."

"Is he?"

"I mean, he's stable, they think."

"Oh, good. Good."

"Abigail, why don't you tell me why you're calling?"

"Yes, well, we have a situation which might require your help—"

"Just tell me what you want."

"Okay, basically, it's this."

As she explained her "predicament," my first impulse was to hang up the phone. Instead, I listened as Abigail Hosford described "a delicate situation" that needed "prompt attention" and a "savvy touch." At the end of her spiel, and to my surprise, I said in a voice not my own, "Why, yes, I'll be glad to help. In fact, why don't we pay a visit to Mrs. Anna Brody-Ashworth this very afternoon and straighten out the entire matter?"

———

The reason for this meeting had to do with the proposed brochure for the Brooklyn Heights Association's annual landmark house and garden tour: twelve pages in length, a glossy cover with colored photographs, a brief history of the Heights Association, a map of the Heights with the tour houses clearly delineated, the extensive list of house tour patrons, and most important, an entire page devoted to each featured house that year, including a detailed (five-to-six-hundred-word) description of each of the five homes.

Abigail filled me in on the particulars as we walked toward the Ashworth-Brody house. Months before, when Anna agreed to open her home to the community, she did so on one condition: She wanted approval of the copy. The Heights Association was happy to give her approval, because they always gave approval, and in the past, there had never been a problem. But there also had never been a house quite like hers. (Oh, there'd been 84 Remsen, and 70 Willow, and countless others, but no house in the Heights rivaled, really, the Ashworth-Brody house.) And now the brochure was a week late getting to the printer for one simple reason: Anna Brody was not pleased.

I stood off to the side as Abigail Hosford reintroduced Pamela Wyeth-Bacon. Then Abigail indicated me, saying, "And of course you know—"

Anna turned and looked startled. Clearly, she hadn't been told I'd be joining them.

"Hello," I said. "It's good to see you."

Anna Brody had cut her hair again, but this time it was extra short, like Mia Farrow's in that movie where she gave birth to the devil. Anna wore a big-collared cream blouse under a powder-blue cashmere sweater, caramel-colored slacks, and no makeup. She appeared nervous, jittery, as if highly caffeinated. (This didn't seem like the same woman who'd had lunch with me two weeks earlier.) She didn't look me in the eye. Instead, she focused on my forehead as she whispered, "It's been a while."

Anna didn't make eye contact with me the entire time all four of us were in the vestibule, nor did she later in the sunroom, where we sat around a glass table as her maid served tea and a tray of bitter Italian cookies. In fact, during the entire forty-seven minutes I was with her, she looked at me only once, and only at the end, and only because I made her.

It was all very polite at first. Pamela Wyeth-Bacon had never been in the mansion, and she gasped and praised and fawned over the spaciousness, the colors, the curtains, the Biedermeier tables, the 1920 English stove, the Tuscan-style emblature.

I hadn't been in the house since Anna had done her newest redecorating. Needless to say, it was always exquisite, but now it was more so.

While the three of them discussed the "situation," I reviewed the most recent draft of the proposed description. Whoever had written the copy had done a wonderful job. In my opinion, *One of the most striking and distinct features . . .* was a phrase that could not be overused. It could apply to the *hand-carved moldings* and the *ornate tin ceilings* and the *one-of-a-kind Honduras mahogany circular staircase* and the *truly grand parlor entrance hall with its huge pocket doors and marquetry paneling with black walnut inlay.* It was true that her bathroom floor *sparkled with a mosaic of muted green and yellow encaustic tiles,* and how could she object to *a border of limestone frames the bathtub* or quibble over *serenity fills the finished space . . .* ?

"Something's missing," Anna said.

"I don't know," I said. "This copy seems pretty good to me."

"I don't mean the brochure. The house."

We were confused.

"Something's wrong with my house."

The ladies objected, but that was all part of Anna's power. The more you complimented her, the more it appeared to hurt her.

"Maybe you could find another house," Anna said. "A better house."

Abigail laughed, clearly terrified at the thought. I began to feel sorry for Abigail and Pamela. They were trying to please Anna, and there was to be no pleasing.

Anna leaned toward me and said, "Let them use yours."

Now she was being cruel. (Only later did I realize she was being sincere.)

A faint wail came from I didn't know where. Was it from upstairs or the basement? Was it in the walls? Had it been going on the whole time we'd been sitting there?

Anna must have sensed me listening because she said, "That's Sophie."

"Is she all right?"

Avoiding my eyes, Anna spoke directly to my neck. "Of course she's all right. She wants to go the playground before it gets dark out."

The wailing unnerved me.

Anna said with a creepy Stepford smile: "Look, I hope you all don't think I'm being difficult."

Abigail: "Oh, my word, no. Never."

Yes! You're being impossible!

Pamela: "You want it to be perfect, that's all."

Abigail: "We do, too. We do, too."

I asked the ladies to leave us alone for a moment. With them out of the room, I told Anna to look at me. When she resisted, I took her by the wrist and squeezed hard, saying, "Goddammit, Anna, look at me."

When she finally did, Sophie's wail from upstairs eerily started up again, this time louder, more insistent. So shrill, in fact, that I thought it might very well shatter glass.

"Now," I said, "listen good—"

Five minutes later, I found Abigail Hosford and Pamela Wyeth-Bacon standing nervously in Philip Ashworth's library.

"Mrs. Ashworth agrees to the copy as written. She looks forward to being a part of the house tour. And she apologizes for any inconvenience she may have caused. Now, ladies, if you'll excuse me." And I left the house.

There was so much I had wanted to say to Anna Brody. With all the real problems that real people are facing in the world, it was hard to care about the description of her house. So I told her to stop behaving like a child. I told her to get over herself fast. I told her to stop crying, and when she said, "I can't," then I told her to cry softer. I told her to get off her privileged ass and take her little girl to the playground.

Finally, when I was done, she asked me to wait a moment, but I said, "No, I'm afraid I'm already late for a date with my husband."

Of course I wasn't late at all. Tim was. Half an hour late, and by then the Heights Café was packed and I was finishing my vodka tonic. I had already asked for the check when Tim rushed in. He looked at me with a puppy-dog expression. He was the embodiment of an apology. But I was in no mood for excuses. It had been over a week since my work had ended and Bruno had collapsed. It had been the worst week of a very trying year. Tim had suggested we go out, just the two of us, like old times.

The moment he sat down, I noticed how bad he looked. Bleary-eyed. It was if his eye sockets had sunk an inch lower on his face. He hadn't shaved in days, and he had scraggly patches of facial hair. His beard was blond and brown, but all I noticed were the flecks of gray.

He said, "How was your day?"

"Not good. So pile it on. Your dissertation. You're not going to fin-ish on Friday, are you?"

Tim diverted his eyes to the menu. He sighed and said, "No, I won't."

Funny, no matter how ready I was for this disappointment, I didn't feel ready.

"Kate, you gotta let me explain . . ."

What I couldn't handle was some sort of explanation, another grand excuse. "I don't want to hear—"

"There's a reason I won't finish on Friday."

I covered my ears.

"Because I finished it today."

"What?"

He unzipped his backpack. He removed a gray cardboard box that had been wrapped in a blue ribbon. He set it on my plate. "It's done."

In disbelief, I pulled at the ribbon, and it came off easily. I lifted the lid. I saw the cover page. "Done?"

"Done."

There it was. All those years of work. Five hundred and forty-two dense pages. Endless footnotes. All his. I flipped through it, amazed at the weight of it. He didn't point out the dedication page. I found it on my own. It read:

to Kate
sorry for the long wait

"That's something," I said. "That's real nice." I didn't care if it was good, I realized. I even forgot how long it took to finish. I loved that it was done. And we would've celebrated longer if Debbie Beebe hadn't hurried into the Heights Café and said, "Did you hear?"

"Maybe," I said as I dried my eyes.

"Did you hear what happened to Anna Brody's little girl?"

TIM

THAT NIGHT WE FOUND OURSELVES AT PIERREPONT PLAYGROUND SMACK IN THE middle of a band of other mothers. There were Claudia and Tess and Joan Manker and Suzanne, mother of Trevor and Jack. There were fathers, too—the Weasel, of course, and Dad Without a Clue.

If one were to listen to the many conversations going on around the playground that night, here was what would be learned:

Earlier that night Sophie Brody-Ashworth tripped over/slipped off/fell headfirst from the top of the circular slide at Pierrepont Playground. Her mother, Anna, saw the whole thing happen/didn't see a thing/wasn't even at the playground. Sophie's injury was just a scrape/a deep cut/a nasty gash that exposed her skull bone. She received four stitches/twenty-three stitches/eighty-four stitches and her jaw was wired shut. Finally, when the ambulances arrived, Sophie was fully conscious/unconscious but not yet in a coma/brain-dead.

The only aspect everyone could agree on was they had never heard so many sirens or seen so many flashing lights. "That's the good part of it," Tess Windsor said, already clinging to the bright side. "You call 911 in the Heights, say a child has been hurt, and they send the world."

Indeed, two fire trucks, two EMS wagons, an ambulance from Long Island College Hospital, and another ambulance from Kings County Hospital all had arrived within minutes. My favorite person that night was Claudia. Normally a gossip artist of the first rate, she told those gathered, "We don't know. Nobody knows. And until somebody knows, maybe we should, I don't know, just shut up and pray."

Prayer works, or so it seemed. Four stitches under the chin. The kind
that dissolved. A battery of tests given by the best of St. Vincent's Hospital. The diagnosis? A much earned headache that was treated with
over-the-counter children's Tylenol. A two-night stay "just for observa-
tion" in the Frederick J. Ashworth Pediatric Wing.

News that good didn't stop people from talking. Rumor had it that
Philip Ashworth was out of town. But rumor also had it that he'd beaten
the ambulance to the hospital. Rumor had it that Philip had insisted on the
barrage of tests that, according to rumor, may have been his way to allevi-
ate any guilt for having been with his mistress/lover when Sophie fell.

Before questioning the ethics of what I was about to do, consider
how, prior to the eighteenth century, children were personas non grata in
nearly every culture. Keep in mind how the Aztecs would sacrifice children to ensure a good harvest, and how in London during the late nine-
teenth century, the lucky children slaved away in factories while the
orphans begged and stole in the city streets. Contemplate the various
cultures where infanticide was commonplace, or even old China, where
girls' feet were bound, and contemporarily, consider those young Indo-
nesian children who use their small fingers to sew the seams of Nike
soccer balls. This was not the coal mines of Kentucky, nor were live gre-
nades about to be taped into my boys' hands before they were sent into
enemy Vietnamese territory, nor would my boys be pierced by hooks
and hung by their nipples on their twelfth birthday like the Sioux Indians
of South Dakota. The truth was that in the history of children, few children had ever had it as good as Teddy and Sam Welch. This made it possible for me to dial the phone and force Teddy to speak into the receiver.

Teddy said in a shy voice, "Can . . . uhm."

"Say, 'This is Teddy. May I speak with Sophie, please?'"

Teddy said, "Hold on, my dad's yelling at me."

"I'm not yelling . . ."

Teddy dropped the receiver and ran out of the kitchen. I sheepishly
picked up the phone and forced a laugh. "Hello?"

"Yes, who is it?"

"Oh, Philip, it's Tim Welch." *Is it true? Were you with your mistress?* "It's not really me calling. My boys have been asking about Sophie, so . . ."

Anna, in the background, faintly: "Who is it?"

Philip Ashworth didn't cover the phone well. "Go back to bed. It's nobody." To me, he said, "Anna's resting right now. I'll let her know you called."

"But I'm not calling. It's the boys . . ."

The boys who are down the hall playing with their toys.

"The boys want to speak to Sophie . . ."

"She's resting, too. We're all trying to rest."

"Of course . . ."

A second phone was picked up. When Anna spoke, she sounded fuzzy, foggy, as if underwater. "I got it, Philip. You can hang up."

It took him a moment to hang up.

Anna sighed and said, "We need to talk."

The study of history has taught me many important lessons, but none more important than to be prepared, since the unlikely will likely happen. Which was why three days later, as I crossed the Heights toward our agreed-upon meeting place, I went over numerous, various conversation scenarios in my mind. What should I say? How best to say it?

It depended, I decided, on which of the various Annas I might find.

Sad Anna would be met by Funny Tim.

Cold and Distant Anna might need to have the ice broken first. A witticism, perhaps, as in: "So what brings us to this part of Brooklyn?"

Angry Anna would require a Thick-Skinned Tim.

Distraught Anna might prefer Bright Side Tim or It Could Have Been Much Worse Tim.

Her choice of where to meet proved curious.

The Fulton Street Mall was a short walk from the Heights. Just head down Joralemon, cross Court Street, keep going past the courthouse, and enter the Fulton Street Mall, Brooklyn's oldest and largest outdoor mall. It's a kind of gateway to the Other Brooklyn. Real Brooklyn. Black Brooklyn. If this were the South, one would have just crossed the railroad tracks to the other side of town.

Kate and I shopped there every so often. Modell's offered great deals on tennis shoes. The Toys "R" Us had closed, but they had a Macy's. It just wasn't Madison Avenue. And the elite, like Anna Brody, never set foot there, or so I thought until that day.

We need to talk, she had said. I didn't care where. A talk was long overdue.

The deserted second level of the Arby's was where I found them.

Anna and Sophie had already ordered.

I focused on Sophie first. She looked bigger since I'd last seen her. She'd lost a tooth. She wore an antique-white dress with large wooden buttons. The white of her bandage matched her dress. I sat down across from them and said, "Hey, Sophie."

Sophie slid off her chair, climbed up on my lap, and wrapped her arms around my neck.

"Somebody missed you," Anna said. The whites of her eyes were spiderwebbed red from crying or lack of sleep. She offered me her french fries. I motioned a no-thanks.

All that practice, and I still didn't know what to say, except: "So what brings us to this part of Brooklyn?"

"The bargains," Anna said, not missing a beat. She smiled.

Good, I thought. At least she can still smile. "I didn't know you liked Arby's."

"This is Sophie's favorite place to eat."

Judging by the untouched food left on Sophie's tray, she'd lost her appetite. And now she was asleep.

"You've still got the touch."

I looked away. On the floor, a plastic packet of ketchup had been stepped on, making an irregular circle of red. I blurted out, "It could happen to anyone, you know that, don't you? Any of us, any parent, one little turn of the head, one glance in the wrong direction . . ."

That was all it took for Anna to crack open. Mostly, she blamed herself. It was heartbreaking. She also blamed Philip. "We didn't need all those doctors and medical tests. Two MRIs. Just because he paid for half the hospital."

"You can never be too careful—"

She even blamed Kate.

"What did Kate do?"

"She came to my house, got so mad at me. Squeezed my arm so hard I can still see the finger marks."

"I don't understand . . ."

"I was sitting there at the park, trying to figure out why she was so angry at me, and I wasn't paying attention to Sophie . . . does she suspect something?"

"Kate? No, I don't think so."

"You didn't tell her about us."

"Never."

"Then why was she so rude?"

"She's had a hard time lately. Lost her job. And she really liked her job."

"Oh, that explains it," Anna said. She seemed relieved. "So, Tim, let's talk about our weekend."

Our weekend? "Oh my God," I said, "I'd forgotten about it." It was sort of true. Since I'd been sitting there, I hadn't thought about the Weekend once.

"You seem pleased with yourself."

Yes, it was one of those moments when you realize you're not an entirely bad guy. I *was* pleased with myself.

"Tell me, Tim, why do you think we're meeting?"

"Well," I said, "I thought you might need a friend."

"Oh, no." Anna laughed. "Hardly." She glanced at her watch. "There's a new hotel in the city I'd like to try."

Oh, here we go.

"Unless you have another idea," she said.

"No, sounds fine, great."

"Should I book us a room?"

"Whatever you think is best."

This is really happening.

She asked if I had any concerns. *Many,* I wanted to say as I put the sleeping Sophie back in her stroller. "No concerns," I said.

"Well, then, there's just one other matter to discuss."

"Okay," I said, forcing myself to make eye contact.

"I have only one rule, and it's not negotiable."

"Not negotiable, I understand."

Anna used a wipe to clean her hands. "We'll do anything and everything," she said. She crumpled the wipe into a ball. "But I only kiss my husband."

"Okay, sure."

How come in that moment Anna suddenly became all mouth? A Giant Mouth.

"I hope that's not a problem for you."

"Why would it be?"

I only kiss my husband. This, I quickly rationalized, was a good thing. It meant that for both Anna and me, our spouses were, and would always be, our priority.

Truth be told, my latest Anna Brody fantasies were exclusively about kissing. I had made elaborate plans.

Anna must have sensed my disappointment. "Are you sure it's not a problem?"

"Believe me. Not a problem."

After Anna left, pushing Sophie in her stroller, I stayed behind because I needed to think. Tim the Realist had expected Anna to cancel. But now the Weekend was more real than ever. Noble Tim felt great for having forgotten about it. Pissed Tim hooked up with Insulted Tim and began to rant on behalf of Ashamed Tim and Tim with Petty Thoughts: *Who ever said there had to be a Weekend? Maybe I'm not interested anymore. Maybe I used you, Anna Brody, to light a fire under my ass to finish my dissertation! Maybe I don't want you and your complicated life filled with soft landings!* Spiteful Tim began to chime in. *Maybe I won't even show up. Maybe I'll go to the movies. Maybe I'll cuddle up with my wife, renew my wedding vows.* Then Pragmatic Tim seized control of the moment. *This all may be beside the point. Let's not forget, friends. There hasn't been a Third Sign!*

In that spirit my many selves and I walked home.

"It's been a weird afternoon," Kate called out from the kitchen.

"You're telling me," I said, heading toward her and the smell of baking cookies.

"You want to go first or can I?"

"You, please," I said.

"Phone rings," she said, spatula-ing the last of the peanut butter cookies off the baking sheet. "It's a headhunter calling. She specializes in nonprofits. She's gotten my name from that *Wall Street Journal* reporter and wonders if I'm looking for work. 'Maybe—possibly—yes,' I say."

"That's not weird. It's wonderful."

"Here comes the weird part. The phone rings again. Guess who it is?"

"I wouldn't know."

"Jeff Slade. Calling from the coast. He has big news, he says, and a proposition. Honey, please eat a cookie. They're warm and chewy."

I took a bite of a warm and chewy cookie.

Kate called the boys and they came running.

"Because, honey, I think it could be a good opportunity, if you're open to it."

As Kate explained the reason for Jeff's call, as she detailed the offer he was making our family, my mouth must have hung open. I was stunned just by the thought of it: *You've got to be kidding! Jeff Slade, bearer of the Third Sign?*

KATE

"DISNEY WORLD? YOU'RE GOING TO DISNEY WORLD?"

My *yes* was barely audible, because I couldn't believe it, either.

The eerie silence that followed made me worry. Then the kimono-clad Bruno shrieked with glee, "You've got to be kidding."

"No, Bruno, I'm not."

He took my hands and said, "What fabulous news. I couldn't be happier for you."

Funny, I couldn't have been happier for him. It had been three days since my last visit, three days since he lay semiconscious in his hospital bed, writhing in pain, his hands strapped down so he couldn't yank out his IV line, three days since the parade of doctors—the oncologist, the pulmonologist, the endocrinologist, and the infectious disease specialist—each of whom knew for certain but wouldn't say: This was it.

Now, somehow, Bruno was back, propped up in the hospital bed, barking out orders to the plump nurse. No longer a grim gray room with its drips, bleeps, and numerous tubes, his surroundings had been Bruno-ized: His bed was framed by numerous bouquets of flowers. Oriental pillows had been brought from home. He wore his fuzzy bunny slippers. A stack of glossy magazines shared his bed. He had his color back, and he was speaking as if to a packed house, even though it was only the two of us in the room, and Rica, the nurse.

"If anyone deserves a trip, Kate, it's you."

"But Disney World? I thought you might object."

Rica refilled the ice in Bruno's mauve hospital water pitcher.

"Why would I object? You see, later this afternoon my sister is going to arrive with a handful of *hospice* brochures, hoping to get me to accept the inevitable. Oh, I accept it. I just don't want to die here, in this place, this house of horrors."

It was as if he were an old actor giving his last performance after a long run. He'd found his light, and I watched as he exaggerated every gesture, savored every word, stretching each moment so the curtain might never come down.

He went on, "So I'm happy to hear about your trip, because I'm going on a trip, too."

"Is that a good idea?"

"Probably not. My friends Carl and Doug have a boat that actually floats. It's anchored off St. Croix. They have a macrobiotic cook who also does deep-tissue massage. And I've told them, should I die between islands, they're to toss me overboard and sail on. Oh, Kate, stop crying."

It had hit me. Bruno was saying good-bye.

"Stop it or you'll make me start," he said. "And I don't want my makeup to run."

Four of Bruno's male friends came into the room. They smelled of leather, faint cologne, and cigarette smoke. They were all my age or younger, one balding, one bearded, but all of them impeccably dressed and oh so handsome.

"Ah, back for more," Bruno said. "Boys, this is Kate."

They smiled and nodded, as if they'd heard all about me.

"Hi," I said, giving a half wave.

"Kate's going on a trip to . . . *Disney World!*"

"Oooh," said one of the men eagerly.

"It's no big deal," I said, but from the way everyone began talking, it apparently was. "Can I just say a great ride? Pirates of the Caribbean—"

"I like Countdown to Extinction!"

"Splash Mountain. Space Mountain. Any ride with a *mountain* in it."

The cutest of the cute asked: "Are you going with kids?"

I nodded.

"Then eat at Cinderella's Castle. She'll greet you all at the door."

"Toontown is the best place to meet the characters . . ."

"Listen closely to the most important word I'm about to say. Are you listening?"

"Yes."

"*Fastpass.* Otherwise you'll be in line all day."

Too bad I didn't have a pen and paper, because their suggestions were golden. One man spoke of how he admired that Disney was the first major conglomerate to give full benefits to same-sex partners. Two of them fought over whether Goofy was gay. Bruno told how all his guy friends growing up had wanted to schtup Annette Funicello from the Mouseketeers. Not Bruno: He had a thing for Cubby. "He was cute. An angel. We were perfect for each other."

Watching Bruno revert to those first-crush feelings was sweet. We all took it in. Someone began to hum "It's a Small World." I was the content observer of a Disney Magic Moment. After it passed, Bruno was quick to ask: "Will you promise to bring me back a set of mouse ears?"

Later that same day I was riding with Claudia in her new Range Rover, running errands. We were hurrying to beat the rain. I thought I'd explained the story clearly, but apparently not, because she kept asking me the same questions. Here was what I'd told her: Jeff Slade had called the day before to share his good news. He had proposed to a "wonderful woman" who, "as fate would have it," was also named Kate. This particular tidbit kept Claudia from hearing the rest, which was simple: Jeff and his fiancée, Kate, had made plans to visit Disney World, and, yes, it was last-minute, but Jeff wondered if Tim, the boys, and I might like to join them. I objected, saying maybe he and his fiancée needed some time alone, but he said that Tim and I were role models for him and that he wanted the other Kate to get to know us, and ever since Disney had acquired ABC a few years back, they'd made "D-World" pretty much carte blanche for people like him (meaning: stars of a super-successful Sunday-night family show like *An Angel and His Wings*). Claudia couldn't understand why I would even consider going. "You hate everything about Disney."

"But Tim loves it," I said. "And since it was an all-expenses-paid offer, with first-class airfare, three days and two nights at the Wilderness Lodge, a personal guide provided by Disney, and free babysitting, I didn't see how we could refuse. The drag is Tim can't go."

Claudia smelled blood. *"What do you mean?"*

"He's got his dissertation defense. So he's letting the boys and me go. He'll be staying home."

"Well, it's either kind of him or really stupid. Dan would never let me travel with any of my great loves."

"But this is to meet the fiancée."

"Whose name is Kate, I might add!"

"Please, Claudia. It's not like that," I said, laughing.

"No?" Claudia swerved to avoid the new Grand Canyon–like pothole on Hicks Street. The windshield wipers batted away the fat drops of rain that, only moments earlier, had begun to fall.

"My thing with Jeff was a long time ago."

"Which makes it worse."

"How do you mean?"

"It makes you nostalgic."

Claudia hit the brakes and skidded on the wet pavement. She pounded the car horn at a man who had stepped stupidly out into the street. "You coulda been killed, you ditz!"

As the man crossed, he gave a vague look in our direction. It was Philip Ashworth, in a gray raincoat, holding one of those cheap umbrellas you buy at a newsstand.

"Well, will you look at that. Even Philip Ashworth gets wet," Claudia said. "Hey, have you heard the latest?"

"No."

"He's been having affairs for years. He's notorious for it. I mean, who hasn't that man fucked? But karma, it seems, really is a bitch. Because apparently, she's taken a lover." Claudia turned left onto Pineapple Street. "I say, 'You go, girl.' But Philip's all bent out of shape over it. Leave it to a man. The hypocrisy. My hunch? It's about to get very ugly." Now the rain was falling hard and fast. Claudia turned on her hazard lights and pulled over to wait out the sudden storm.

I wanted to change the subject to something more positive. "Actually, I feel the opposite with Tim. He surprised me. To let us go without him to the place he wants to go to most. That's really generous of him. Frankly, it gives me hope."

"I was saying something like this the other day."

"What?"

"Husbands. How we never really know them."

TIM

IT WAS THE NIGHT BEFORE THE WEEKEND, AND I WAS ABOUT TO BETRAY THE PERSON I most loved. While Kate and the boys were dreaming of Disney World, I couldn't sleep. How could I? I fretted and paced around our living room/dining room/toy room, finally ending up in our bathroom, where I sat on the toilet with the lid down, staring at myself in the mirror, not recognizing who was there.

I turned off the bathroom light and sat in the dark. I don't know how long I sat there. I needed the counsel of a friend. For obvious reasons, I couldn't turn to my best friend (Kate), so I turned to history for perspective. Who from history might understand how I was feeling? One person immediately came to mind. Neil Armstrong. Yes, I know it seems a bit of a stretch. What did Neil Armstrong, the commander of *Apollo 11*, the first man ever to walk on the moon, and I have in common? Normally, I would argue, not much. But this was not a normal night.

If I'd had Neil Armstrong's home phone number, I would've made the call myself.

Mr. Armstrong—may I call you Neil? What were your thoughts in those last hours before blastoff? Were you too excited to sleep? What if you didn't make it back to Earth? Did you worry about your life after the moonwalk? Were you concerned that the rest of your life would be a letdown? And as you descended the steps of the lunar module, did it occur to you that you could simply refuse to walk on the moon?

Neil Armstrong: "Why would I refuse?"

Because you don't walk on the moon and not have it affect the rest of your life in every conceivable way. Is every step afterward a lesser step?

In those last hours before the alarm went off and Kate and the boys dressed and ate the breakfast I would prepare and climbed into the car Jeff Slade had ordered that would whisk them to the airport, where they'd fly United at a cruising altitude of thirty-five thousand feet, heading toward Orlando, I had no illusions about being Neil Armstrong.

I *knew* I wasn't Neil Armstrong, but here was my fear: What if Anna was the moon?

FIVE

KATE

THAT MORNING I WAS IN A FUNK. AND TIM KNEW IT. BUT HE DIDN'T KNOW THE REAL reason why.

He had tried to cheer me up by saying, "It's just a few days. You'll be back in no time." He even joked, "Maybe you'll have your own Disney Magic Moment!"

But nothing he said seemed to help. It felt wrong to leave him right before his dissertation defense. "Honey," I said. "If you want, we can stay."

"No, no!"

"Are you sure?"

"It's just a weekend, Kate."

"That's true," I said. "Maybe it's a good thing we're going. Give you a little space."

"Yes, exactly."

"Will you do me a favor and treat yourself?"

Tim looked as if he'd been electrocuted. "What does that mean?"

"Sleep late. Rent a movie. Eat a lot of chocolate."

"Oh," he said, not smiling.

"Reward yourself for a job well done." Then I said something lame like "But don't have too much fun."

Later, we stood on the curb, locked in a hug. "Good-bye," he said, his arms wrapped tightly around me, not letting go.

The boys were already seat-belted in back of a gray sedan from

Promenade car service. Their small matching suitcases had been stowed in the trunk. They were ready, I was ready, but Tim was the one hanging on.

This reminded me of how we used to say good-bye in our first days together. Back then, whenever we parted, I'd walk a bit, sense that I was being watched, turn, and find that he was still standing there, watching me. I'd wave, he'd wave, and we'd both walk on. We'd keep turning and waving until we were terribly small, an eyestrain, until the last possible second. It was our way, I suppose, of letting the other know we'd always be there.

"Okay, honey, I love you," I finally said, which was code for *Let go*.

He released me and stepped back. He leaned into the car and kissed the boys and held them and whispered into their ears, not stopping until Sam squirmed and Teddy said, "Daddy, don't." When Tim pulled back out, he couldn't look at me. "You're going to miss your flight," he said.

Now I was the one hesitating. Here's why: The day before, Jeff Slade had called to tell me bad news. He and his fiancée had split up. I said, "How sad." He said, "Better now than later." He sounded upset, but I couldn't tell if he was acting. When I asked what had happened, he said there were reasons that he'd explain some other time. Then he said he hoped the trip could go on without his fiancée. "Let me think about it," I said. I pretended to think about it and said, "Yes."

"Ma'am," the driver said.

"Honey," I said, in a sudden panic right before getting in the car, "I just got a great idea. When your defense is over, go straight to the airport. Flights to Orlando leave like every hour. Just get a ticket. Cost not an issue."

"Your seat belt, honey . . ."

"Did you hear me? Come be with us—"

"By the time I got there, it would be time to come back."

"Please," I begged.

"There'll be another chance. Disney's not going anywhere." He helped me with my seat belt. "I mean, with what happened with your job, you deserve this trip. Go have a great time. Promise?"

I promised.

"And whatever you do, don't think about me."

"Okay, okay," I said. "Boys, say good-bye to your dad." The driver asked which airport. "Kennedy," I said as the car took off.

Why hadn't I told Tim? Shouldn't he know that Jeff was no longer engaged and that I would be the only Kate on the trip?

Here's what I told myself: I didn't want him to worry. Besides, it wasn't like anything was going to happen.

As we drove away, I had that familiar, distinct sense Tim was watching us go. But by the time I looked back, we had already turned the corner.

TIM

LATER, THERE WOULD BE MUCH TO REMEMBER: THOSE EARLY, AWKWARD MO-
ments; the somber mood of the committee; the poorly lit conference
room and the squeaky pale green plastic chair where I sat sweating; the
meandering opening statement wherein Dr. Jamison Lamson, who had
misplaced his notes, had to wing it; my surprise at Dr. Lamson's pro-
nouncement that he'd never had a more frustrating student; my confu-
sion, then clarity, regarding his strategy, for my mentor had deftly
anticipated the criticisms of the other advisers, and he battered me in
such an aggressive way that it must have engendered sympathy in the
others, because within minutes it wasn't a defense, it was a love fest, a
party of my now-peers, and what a pity I wasn't entirely present for the
experience, how unfortunate that I only half heard my harshest critic,
Dr. Rejandra Kanwar, cop to having had years of skepticism and say, "I
never thought a dissertation could straddle Rosa Parks and Pliny the
Younger, but somehow, Mr. Welch, you've found a way!" and Dr. Rita
Lovejoy, who was in awe of my use of minor players to illuminate the
"great stage of world history" and how my dissertation "went down
like a milk shake but boasted the sharpness and finesse of a complex
wine," and while the three doctors struggled to outdazzle one another,
this thought occurred to me: *I wish Kate were here to witness this. She
would've liked it.* But that thought gave over to other, more pressing
concerns, how I was dizzy from lack of sleep and weak from lack of
food, and most especially, how I had gas. All of which kept me from

confronting what I most feared. I'd been told that very often during a dissertation defense, the exchange between advisers and advisee evolves to a more personal expression of thought. Out slips the un-known, never-spoken, real motive for the years of research, leaving the doctoral candidate exposed, as if having been subjected to a full-body X-ray—as if to say, *Here, these are my bones.*

I wanted to avoid that moment. Could I get through my defense without it? If only I'd kept quiet after Dr. Lamson asked, "Is there any-thing else you'd like to say?" See, part of me didn't believe their uni-form praise. *Look at them,* I thought. *Surely they have a criticism or two—it can't all be completely wonderful—have they even read what I wrote?* Maybe they didn't understand it. Maybe they didn't know anything. Maybe *I* needed to teach *them*!

So instead of thanking them and exiting fast, I stood motionless, stared incredulously, and said, "Is that it? Is that all?"

They looked back at me. Smiling. Satisfied. "It's been a delight." Dr. Kanwar grinned. "Like Christmas in May," Dr. Lovejoy cooed.

That was when I figured it out. I might've been the feather in the cap of Dr. Lamson's career, but the other two couldn't have cared less. They were humoring Dr. Lamson, and they wanted me gone. How quickly their kind-seeming smiles turned into patronizing sneers. I de-cided to fight back, to prove myself and convince them. I began to speak without thinking, rambling, really, trying to reiterate a key point about history being an endless succession of mostly minor moments that ac-cumulate and how intention was all that could be controlled and how meaning well didn't always mean doing right, and even now I worry about what slipped out, what was exposed, because all I remember is the way the committee laughed and laughed until they hurt from laugh-ing, leaving me with the distinct impression that whatever I'd said had been all too revealing and how, when I felt the blood rush to my face, my knees buckled . . .

Flop.

When I came to, they asked if I remembered fainting or if I'd felt the crack of my mouth against the table's edge. "No," I said, fingering my newly chipped front tooth. "I don't remember any of that." Which was true. All I remembered was the moment before I fell—the buzzing lights, the blur of laughter, and me saying, "Please don't tell my wife."

KATE

PLEASE KNOW I WASN'T EASILY IMPRESSED. I RESISTED THE LURE OF THE EMPHATIC 3-D billboards that lined the network of Disney highways as we approached, and I felt no awe at the fact that Disney World wasn't one place, as I'd previously thought, but actually four theme parks, three water parks, and two huge areas that were designed for adult nightlife. And yes, I'm sure our accommodations at the Wilderness Lodge were lovely, but I didn't jump up and down like my boys when they saw the Lincoln Log–like lobby and the eighty-two-foot fireplace that blazes all year round, or the pool that begins indoors as a hot spring and then flows into a winding creek, culminating with a waterfall into the rocky caverns of the outdoor pool. It was kind of Jeff to be waiting for us when we arrived, and how sweet he was to get down on his knees as he greeted the boys, and how thoughtful he was to insist they be covered with sunblock, and how nice to have our own Disney chaperone named Darla to guide us through the complex series of options. All this was fine, but I wasn't convinced, not even as we floated on the launch toward the Magic Kingdom and hurried after the boys as they ran ahead down Main Street. It was simple, however, my conversion, and its cause was obvious. Cinderella's Castle. I'd avoided looking at it, but when I yielded and saw that familiar turret towering above, I began to scream.

TIM

IN THE HALF HOUR SINCE RETURNING TO OUR APARTMENT, I'D CHANGED OUT OF MY dissertation defense costume (the brown tweed blazer, the khaki pants, the scuffed penny loafers) and put on something more casual yet, I hoped, flattering (my new jeans, a purple linen shirt the color of a bruise, my bright red Converse high-tops). Then I checked the chip in my tooth. Not pretty. But I discovered it would be barely noticeable so long as I didn't smile, or talk, or basically open my mouth. Then I brushed and flossed and mouthwashed, I facial-creamed, body-lotioned, redeodorized. Checked my face for beard stubble, found none. Double-checked my ears and nose for long, unsightly hairs, found one. Rechecked my overnight bag, taking special care to unzip the secret pocket where I'd stashed a light blue box of a dozen Trojans, found them. Twelve seemed an overreach, I know.

I left the breakfast dishes in the sink (Sam's uneaten Lucky Charms, Teddy's plate of toast crusts). I passed by the boys' bedroom/closet and barely glanced at their matching spaceship bedspreads and the recently applied glow-in-the-dark stars stuck in constellation patterns on the ceiling. I mostly managed to ignore the shelf of family photos, catching just for a moment a picture of Kate and me and the boys all wearing the same L. L. Bean striped pajamas, smiling, from Christmas morning the year before. However, what I couldn't avoid was the blinking message light on our phone machine. Someone had called. Who? I stared at the blinking light for longer than I'd like to admit.

———————

Quite possibly it was Kate. Maybe there had been an emergency. Or maybe Kate couldn't help herself. Maybe she wanted to hear how my dissertation defense had gone. Maybe she wanted to be the first to call me Dr. Welch.

I stopped in front of the phone machine and pushed *play*.

"This is Jack with American Credit Services. Don't worry. Your accounts are fine. I'm calling with a unique offer, a onetime opportunity—"

"Exactly," I said as I pushed *erase*.

KATE

AS WE APPROACHED THE CASTLE, A DISNEY EMPLOYEE IN A DAPPER OUTFIT OF knickers and a blue hat came toward us with camera in hand. "Would you like a picture of the family?"

I started to wave off the photographer, but Jeff said, "What a great idea."

When I mumbled something about it probably costing a hundred dollars, Jeff just laughed.

The photographer positioned us so that Cinderella's Castle was the backdrop. I knelt down in the middle, Sam on one side, Teddy on the other. Jeff coached us as Darla, our guest-relations guide, filled out an order form.

I expected to feel ridiculous, the typical tourist. But it was nice, the boys and me, the backdrop.

The photographer focused the camera and appeared ready to snap when Teddy, of all people, blurted out, "Can't Jeff be in the picture?"

That afternoon the Magic Kingdom was jammed with people—predominantly white and on the heavy side—taking their place in lines that seemed to stretch in every direction for every attraction. Jeff insisted we start at Fantasyland for the simple reason that this was where we'd find the greatest concentration of kiddie rides. Dumbo was our first stop. The line was endless, but Darla led us past those waiting, through a gate, down a corridor, where somehow we bypassed everybody and were ushered immediately onto the ride. Jeff went with Teddy and Sam. I stayed behind with Darla, who explained as they boarded that the altitude of their Dumbo flight was controlled by a joystick. She added, "That's what makes it an appropriate ride for any age."

Teddy and Sam had the same look as they circled the sky—pure, unadulterated, mouth-open awe. Meanwhile, Darla offered up a wealth of Disney World information. I learned about other celebrities she had escorted (Robin Williams, Muhammad Ali, the Sultan of Brunei) and that every ride/attraction at Disney World had a secret entrance that we would be availing ourselves of, and that of all the celebrities she'd escorted, she'd never seen one take a greater interest in the itinerary than Jeff Slade. "He had several conversations with the head of guest relations," she whispered. Realizing Darla was clutching the itinerary, I asked to see it. She smiled and shook her head, saying, "I'm not supposed to show you."

"Oh, come on."

"He doesn't want you to have to think about a thing. Let me just tell you that what he has planned is ambitious—difficult but doable—and if we stay on schedule, you're in for an unforgettable few days."

"Yes, but we're not here for me," I found myself saying as the boys and Jeff flew above us.

Soon we raced from Dumbo to the train of boats for the Small World ride to the white horses of Cinderella's Golden Carousel to the spinning pastel cups of the Mad Tea Party, then the miniature pirate ships on Peter Pan's Flight, and, finally, the honeypot-shaped cars of the Many Adventures of Winnie the Pooh.

Later, when the boys and I emerged from the nearest bathroom, Jeff was waiting with official Disney autograph books and Donald Duck pens. We hurried toward Toontown, where a tour of Mickey's House was aborted when Teddy saw his favorite Disney character of the moment (Aladdin). While Teddy got Aladdin's autograph and Sam got all shy around Captain Hook and Brer Rabbit, I tried to pull Jeff aside for a private chat. I asked that he slow down with all the kindnesses. From the way he glared at me, I knew I better explain: "I guess I'm just not comfortable with all this special treatment."

Jeff said with a smile, "Then you better go home."

TIM

TRUTH BE TOLD, I'M MORE OF A RED ROOF INN/BEST WESTERN/MOTEL 6 KIND OF guy. I would've been more comfortable at any of those places. I'm fond of the noisy ice makers at the end of every hall, the Gideon Bible in every room, the cheap polyester bedspreads, the floral shower curtains, and the little rectangles of dry-out-your-skin soap. But that afternoon what I missed most were the large neon signs.

I worried I'd written down the address wrong because I'd been up and down Greenwich Street three times. Was this some sort of joke? I asked a handful of people if they knew of the hotel in question, and no one had even heard of it.

It didn't help that I'd overpacked, stuffing my bag with every conceivable clothing combination. If it rained. If it suddenly got cold. Casual pajamas, flannel pajamas. Something about the overwroughtness of my bag gave the impression that I was a man who was never coming back. The more I carried it, the heavier it became. I was tempted to start emptying much of it out onto the street when I saw the two gray industrial doors with thick half-moon handles. On the handle, faintly embossed, the following was spelled out from top to bottom:

t

h

e

i

n

f

i

n

i

t

y

Apparently, I'd asked the four people in the Village who hadn't heard of the Infinity. Inside, it was designed to speak to the ultra-hip, the über-cool. The lobby was a long craterlike structure, gray with stuccoed walls. It felt lunar. Brightly colored lamp shades. Mammoth mirrors hung from thick ropes. This was a moonwalk for the earthbound. I imagined at night the place hopped with the young and chic, decked out in black, sitting around the glass-topped moon-rock tables as they talked and drank and bantered about art and movies and the newest in high fashion.

I knew I was out of my league. But I didn't care! And I was early. But I didn't care! I approached the concierge, named Mahogany, a frothy British girl with a stud in her tongue. "Yes?" she said.

"I'd like to check in."

She was harried, or else unimpressed, because she snapped, "Sir, your room isn't ready."

"Well, could you check?"

"I know your room isn't ready because none of the rooms are ready. You're very early. Check-in isn't until three."

What? Check-in at three?

"Well," I said, "it's nearly two."

One thirteen, to be exact, according to the clock sculpted into the lobby's back wall.

"And it would be a terrific help . . ."

You see, I'm meeting Anna Brody at six.

Mahogany pecked hard at the keyboard, searching for a room. "Do you have a reservation?"

"I do. Would you like to know my name?"

"Just a minute, sir." She *sssssssss*'d the *sir* with such derision.

Admittedly, I wasn't the regular Infinity clientele, what with my red high-tops and my canvas overnight bag, a gift my mother had ordered from a catalog, monogrammed JTW (John Timothy Welch). But I was a person, goddammit. *I'm a person, too!*

"Your name?"

"Trammel. I'm Mr. Trammel."

At the eleventh hour, I had called Anna to suggest we check in using fake names. Just in case. I could tell she was put off by my idea. She said she was coming as herself, but I could be whoever I wanted. I told her that I'd be checking in under the name Trammel.

"I'll need a major credit card, Mr. Trammel," Mahogany said.

"I don't think you will."

"We always ask . . ."

"I was told everything had been arranged."

Which was true. Anna had arranged everything, even for me to be Mr. Trammel.

"By whom?"

"Anna Brody. Or I suppose it could be under the name Ashworth."

Mahogany sighed, clicking the tongue stud against the back of her front teeth. She typed on her keyboard, and whatever came up on the computer screen had a transformative effect on Mahogany, whose features softened. She practically purred when she said, "Oh, yes, Mr. Trammel—you'll be a guest of Mrs. Ashworth. She's taken care of everything."

Soon enough, a bellman/model/actor decked out in black appeared with a cart.

"Mr. Trammel, this is Nils. He'll show you to your room."

Nils gestured toward a candlelit elevator that was open, waiting.

As we went up: "Is this your first time staying with us, Mr. Trammel?"

"Yes, and it will be my last."

"May I ask why?"

"I'm only doing this once."

Nils hesitated, then began his spiel about the Infinity and how, for a year, it had been a well-kept secret, then after a change in ownership, someone pressured *Architectural Digest* into doing a sixteen-page spread, and ever since last spring, the hotel had been booked full. "You have to be someone to get a room."

"Really," I said, in an attempt to appear interested.

The elevator sprang open on the seventeenth floor. The floor was dark, and it snaked along like an ear canal, a fallopian tube.

"Everybody stays here. We sign a confidentiality agreement because of the rock stars and other famous types. Like I can't tell you who's here now, for instance."

"That's a relief to me."

"It is?"

"I wouldn't want you talking about my business."

"I would never . . ." Nils stopped in front of room 1701. Upon seeing its placement—the center door at the end of the hall, no doors to other rooms nearby—I braced myself for what was to come.

Nils unlocked and held the door as he gestured for Mr. Trammel to step inside, which I did.

"Yes, fine," I said.

"Are you unhappy with the accommodations, sir?"

I shrugged. "Just out of curiosity, what would this normally cost me?"

"You know what they say. If you have to ask . . ."

Ha ha ha ha ha.

"If you would prefer another room . . ."

Room? How can you call it a room? It's the size of Rhode Island.

I couldn't believe it. No way could I ever afford it. What a place. I noted the minimal, high-end furnishings in the roughly thousand-square-foot L-shaped room. The bed. The view. The bathroom. The bed.

The white fluffy sofas. The white comforter and the big square white pillows on the bed. The bed, the bed, the bed.

"Here we have a complimentary fruit plate."

"Yeah, whatever . . ."

"This folder outlines the many services you'll find at your disposal—"

I noted the folder.

"This door here opens onto your own private wraparound terrace—"

"Lovely."

"And this is my favorite feature." Nils showed me a computerized screen next to the bed. He demonstrated how, with the simple touch of a button, the various lamps and recessed lighting fixtures could be dimmed and brightened to one's liking, resulting in a myriad of looks.

"I have a question," I said. "Where might I find the ice machine?"

"Sorry, sir?"

"Ice. I like to get my own ice."

Nils, the actor/model/bellman, seemed stumped.

"It would be next to the soda machine and the candy machine. Surely you have . . ."

"No, but we do have a well-stocked minibar."

Nils used a small gold key to open the minibar, where an array of overpriced candies and nuts and cookies could be found. A price list in the tiniest type: Life Savers—$3.50—Snickers Bar—$6.00—Cheese Sticks—$12.00—Intimacy Kit—$20.00!

"No!" I said, waving him off. Then I proceeded to yank open every dresser drawer.

Nils again: "Is something wrong?"

"Well, Nils, I make it a point to always put the Gideon Bible next to my bed. I will be in great need of a Bible by the time I leave here. But I [drawer slam] can't seem [drawer slam] to find [drawer slam] a Bible anywhere!"

"Shall I have one sent up?"

"Could you? Would you?"

"I'm sure it can be arranged."

"You're too kind." I gave him an eleven-dollar tip. Why eleven dollars? I figured he'd had bigger tips and smaller tips but probably never an eleven-dollar tip.

Finally alone, I explored the room. In the marble bathroom, I noted the basket of high-end lotions and soaps. I opened the glass shower door. Staring up at the Frisbee-sized showerhead, I wondered if Anna was a late-night bath person or an early-morning shower person. I could be either. I could be both.

Using the touch pad next to the bed, I experimented with different configurations in a quest to find the most flattering light. Nils had said, "It takes some getting used to, but once you get the hang of it, there's no going back."

No going back.

I debated with myself over whether I could justify having a fire lit in the fireplace in mid-May at the same time I practiced closing the thick cream curtains, which, amazingly, blocked out all light. I tested out the state-of-the-art stereo and the flatter-than-flat-screen TV. I did not test the bed. The bed, I decided, would remain untouched until . . .

My heart banged against my ribs. Dizzy, I needed fresh air. I unlatched the glass door that led to the wraparound deck, which was more like a full-fledged terrace, with a gray slate floor and designer table and chairs. I leaned over the ledge, looked down all seventeen stories, and had that rise in my stomach that comes from realizing how easy it would be to fall.

KATE

DARLA AND I STAYED BACK AS JEFF AND THE BOYS RAN AHEAD. IT WAS SWEET watching them race toward the Magic Kingdom. Jeff had arranged for prime seating at the three o'clock character parade.

"Mr. Slade has given me back my faith in actors," Darla said.

"He's been really nice to my kids, it's true."

"I mean, after what he's done the last three days . . ."

I didn't know what Darla was talking about. "What has he done?"

"Uh-oh," she said. "Wasn't supposed to say that."

"You may as well tell me."

"Well," Darla said, obviously wanting to tell me. "There's a boy from Iowa named Charlie Boxer. He's only six, and he has a rare form of leukemia, months to live, basically. Charlie had two wishes. Like the majority of Make-A-Wish kids, he wanted to visit Disney World. But he also wanted to meet the actor who played Angel Alex on *An Angel and His Wings*. When Jeff heard about Charlie, he said something like 'Let's make all his wishes come true.' Jeff came three days ago to spend time with Charlie. 'I'm here,' he said. 'Use me.' And we have. He's been all over the park with a number of the Make-A-Wish kids. These kids really face hard stuff—it's all pain and hospitals most of the time, and Jeff has given them more than a little bit of happiness."

I couldn't believe what I was hearing.

"But, please don't say I said anything. I think he wanted it to be a surprise."

"I promise," I said. "I'll be surprised."

———

While Darla was on her cell phone, I bought myself a small Sprite served in a plastic Mickey Mouse cup. I sat down on an empty bench, and that was when it occurred to me: There is no litter in Disney World. No cigarette butts, no candy wrappers, no warm wads of gum waiting to stick to tennis shoes. If only the world were this clean. And to think thousands of people moved through Disney World every day. Where was the mess? How was it possible?

I was determined to find out. So I finished my Sprite, left my cup on the bench, and crossed to another bench twenty feet away, where I sat down to wait. I wondered who would do the job. Was it an actual person, or was there some kind of machine, or was there a cluster of gnomish midget people who scurried out of a tree trunk, jabbering in their helium voices? I needed to know.

Just then a young father passed me, pushing his baby in a stroller, followed by a man my age, pushing his dad in a wheelchair. All of them were wearing mouse ears.

I looked at them for all of five seconds. When I looked back at my empty cup on the bench, it was gone.

They've thought of everything at Disney World. For instance, when Jeff and I emerged, drenched, from Splash Mountain—the kids were off with Darla getting ice cream—we had to go through a store devoted exclusively to selling Splash Mountain memorabilia. Splash Mountain pencils, Splash Mountain T-shirts, a Splash Mountain snow globe. Better still was how each person who went on the ride was photographed halfway down the longest and wettest of the three drops. There we were, Jeff smiling slightly with the quiet confidence of a diamond thief. I, on the other hand, had my eyes squeezed shut, my mouth open in midshriek, my arms above my head, as if to surrender.

TIM

IN THE FINAL HOUR BEFORE ANNA BRODY'S ARRIVAL, I SAT WATCHING THE DIGITAL numbers of the sleek hotel clock blink past minute by minute. My clothes had been unpacked, my toilet kit set out. My wedding ring had been removed and respectfully hidden from view. Using a small hand towel, I'd given myself a birdbath and recleaned my privates.

With nothing to do but wait, I plopped down in the squishy chair next to the baby grand piano. And because I didn't have a Bible, I took out my small black Moleskine notebook and began to review my notes.

Confession: I wasn't a particularly adept or innovative sexual partner, which may explain why Kate and I had settled for traditional and limited expressions of our physical love. It was good, what we had. Comfortable. But the word for it was vanilla.

My hunch was that with Anna Brody, it would be anything but vanilla. With her, I would have to expand my sense of the possible. I would need to read up. So on the Saturday before the Weekend, I had taken the boys for story time at the Barnes & Noble on Court Street. While an eager employee read several Dr. Seuss classics, I ducked into the Relationships/Sexuality section and began filling the pages of my notebook.

It was astonishing, the amount of new information one could acquire!

Positions included the old standards, missionary and doggy-style, of which there were many variations. Also: the Butterfly, the Lotus, the Cowgirl, the Reverse Cowgirl, the Viennese Oyster, the Suspended

Congress, the Leapfrog, the T-square, the Modified T-square, the 69 (also known as the Congress of the Crow), the Piledriver. I learned there were nine positions for fellatio, ten for cunnilingus. I learned that an Altoid had special powers beyond being a simple breath mint.

Later, online, I continued my studies, where I learned there were names for things I never dreamed could ever be done.

We could Snowball, she could Snowblow, and we could Toss Each Other's Salad. We could Shrimp, Felch, Flog, Fist, have a Nooner, use a Ball Gag, a Bit Gag, or a Butt Plug. I could Teabag, leave a Cream Pie, or hang a Pearl Necklace. We could make Foamy Beer. I could ride Bareback or do a Shocker. She could do a Female Shocker. We could go ATM or do the Angry Dragon, the Dirty Sanchez, the Donkey Punch, or the Danza Slap. We might even invent our own signature moves.

We'll do anything and everything. Whatever we feel like.

Her words, not mine.

It was time to put away my study materials. I gave one last flip through the notebook. I didn't know what part of anything and everything was going to happen. All I knew was I felt ready for the test.

KATE

MICKEY AND MINNIE, CINDERELLA, SNOW WHITE, BEAUTY, THE BEAST . . .
I couldn't write them down fast enough. Our goal—while Jeff helped the boys into their swimsuits—was to remember every Disney character we had seen that day. *Peter Pan, Captain Hook, Simba, Tarzan, Donald Duck . . .*

Later, as the four of us walked in our flip-flops to the Wilderness Lodge's pool, the list-making continued. *Aladdin, Ariel, Buzz Lightyear, Cruella de Vil . . .*

The list had been Teddy's idea. "This way," he said, "we can tell Dad."

Tim had suggested it, but I'd been quick to agree. We were not to call each other that weekend unless there was an emergency. What happened with Teddy had me reaching for the phone. But then I hesitated. I'd like to think it was because I wanted to honor our pledge/pact. The truth was that if I did call him, the conversation might get around to the other Kate, and I'd have to explain her absence. But as soon as we'd pulled Teddy out of the water, I had reason enough. I grabbed my cell phone and dialed home, and when the machine answered, I said, "Don't worry, I'm not calling." Then I handed Teddy the phone.

TEDDY

HEY, DAD. DAD, THERE'S A POOL. A BIG POOL. AND GUESS WHAT I DID. YOU KNOW what I did? I put my head under. And Jeff showed me how to. I put my head all the way under. And Dad. I was swimming, Dad. I was swimming.

TIM

TRAFFIC. A BABYSITTER MIX-UP. A SNAG IN THE HOUSE TOUR PREPARATIONS. ANY of these seemed reasonable. But a tour glitch was the most likely explanation. Maybe something to do with where to place a vase of flowers. Something to do with beauty, something she couldn't help but do, evidenced by the care she'd taken in choosing this room. Getting it right was important to her.

Maybe she missed the stop. (As if she'd be taking the subway.) Maybe the titanium battery in her watch wore out and she wasn't aware of the time. Maybe she bumped into an old friend and was forced to make small talk on a street corner just as the brakes went out on a city bus, mowing down thirteen pedestrians, including her.

Ridiculous.

Then again, maybe not.

Anything was possible.

Well, not anything.

Yes, anything.

If I could be where I was, waiting for her, then yes, anything was possible.

Or maybe . . .

A last-minute bikini wax.

Or . . .

A pigeon pooped on her shoulder and she went back home to change.

Or . . .

Outside the Pink Pussycat Boutique, a chauffeured town car with tinted windows idled, while inside, a woman of astonishing class and style picked out a discreet and expensive battery-operated sex toy . . .

Or . . .

Maybe she got lost. Maybe she changed her mind. She wasn't coming. But a person didn't book this kind of room and then not show. Maybe she was already here, hiding. Maybe it was a cruel joke. Maybe the Infinity was filled with men like me, all waiting for her to arrive to indulge in their weekends. Maybe she was watching it all from a command center in the basement, a bank of television monitors displaying images from hidden cameras. I was being watched! How many times had my mother said it? "Always behave as if your ancestors are watching."

"Why?"

"Because very likely they are."

Well, then, Grandma and Grandpa were having a fine time right about now.

What did I know? I didn't know. I didn't even know what I knew. Oh, wait—I knew one thing. She was late.

Just breathe.

How late? I'd have to do the math.

Breathe, you dummy.

I double-checked the small, sleek digital clock at the side of the bed—my God, what a bed—and yes, I was right, she was late. Four minutes late.

KATE

THE BOYS AND I WERE HAVING A LITTLE DOWNTIME IN OUR SUITE WHEN JEFF knocked on the door. He was dressed in jeans and a blazer. He smelled of cologne. Darla was behind him, holding her rainbow-colored clipboard pressed to her chest.

"There's a thing I'm going to do," Jeff said. "It won't take long. Wanna come?"

I glanced at Darla. From the way she smiled, I knew this was my surprise.

"I'm game," I said.

Darla looked after the boys as Jeff and I were driven in a high-speed air-conditioned golf cart to our destination.

"Last December," Jeff said, "when we had dinner in Brooklyn, and I heard about the work you were doing, your *charity* work, I got to thinking how selfish I'd been. How everything always was about me. So I decided to do something. I got involved. And this is the result." The golf cart came to a stop. "This, Kate, is all because of you."

We had arrived at Give Kids the World, a nonprofit resort on the outskirts of Disney World, a wonderland paradise for any kid, especially those who were terminally ill.

GKTW handlers ushered us quickly into the Wish Café, where a big reception was in full swing for twenty Make-A-Wish kids and their families. These kids were all ages, shapes, and sizes. Some looked very sick. Several of the kids had no hair; others wore scarves. Many had faces bloated from steroids and anti-rejection drugs. One boy had a ventilator attached to the back of his wheelchair. The ventilator had been covered in skateboard decals.

Jeff stopped at the first Make-A-Wish kid he saw. He knelt down beside her and said, "Hey, Carla, it's Jeff Slade."

The Cleveland chapter of Make-A-Wish had sent Carla; her parents, Donna and Buzz; her brother, Scott; and her sister, Beth, to Disney World. I was introduced to them and learned that Carla had hypoplasia, a medical condition affecting the development of her arms and legs.

Jeff gently stroked Carla's cheek as they talked about his show. She asked him questions: "Do you believe what your character believes? Where do we go when we die?"

Jeff leaned forward and did his best to answer. From his pocket, he produced a small pewter angel coin. He pressed it into Carla's frail hand and said, "Squeeze this, and the angels will hear."

Yes, it was a cheesy thing to say, but it was kind, and the look on Carla's face made me want to believe.

Imagine twenty more different conversations but all the same in one respect: Jeff was bringing these kids hope and happiness that they didn't get to feel most days.

He was like Jesus to these kids. He knew each of their names. He hugged them, high-fived those who could raise their hands. He posed for pictures. And I watched him proudly.

In one hour, he did more for the world than I'd done in a whole year.

"Here goes nothing."

"No," I said, "you'll be great."

And great he was.

As Jeff approached the podium, everyone in the Wish Café started to cheer.

"You're too kind," he said, gesturing for them to stop.

One of the Make-A-Wish kids screamed out, "We luuuv youuu, Jeffff."

"I love you, too," he said.

The room erupted a second time. Jeff took a folded piece of paper out of his back pocket, opened it, and began to read. "I'm not an angel," Jeff said.

Silence.

"But I play one on TV."

Big laugh.

"When I look at out at you all in this room tonight, all I see are . . ." Jeff started to choke up. "Angels." He looked down at his speech and was overcome with emotion. He tried to keep reading what he'd written, but he couldn't see through his tears. It was raw, unexpected. Genuine. At one point he shouted out something. I don't know what he said, but the force of it gave me a chill.

The ovation was still going on when he sat back down next to me and asked what I thought.

I had to shout over the cheering. "Pretty much everyone was crying!"

"Really?"

"Not a dry eye!"

"But my speech that I worked so long on . . ."

"It doesn't matter." The truth was, I couldn't remember the words. "What it felt to me like you were saying—*without saying it*—was that there are some things that go beyond words. Some things words aren't for."

Jeff seemed to like my take.

The applause started to swell again and the crowd began to chant, "*Jeff! Jeff! Jeff!*"

Before he stood back up to take a second bow, he looked at me and said, "You hungry?"

TIM

EIGHT O'CLOCK. STILL NO ANNA. I TRIED TO THINK WHAT KATE WOULD DO, WHICH was difficult in a literal sense, because she would never be in this situation. I thought about how she handled our boys' frequent meltdowns and freak-outs with exceptional grace. Her secret? Distraction. So I thought like Kate and came up with a solution. I channel-surfed until I settled on Animal Planet.

What I'd learned so far: The long-eared hedgehog, despite her cute face, is actually a swift-footed predator. Her diet consists of insects and small vermin, including the highly poisonous yellow scorpion, proving an important fact of nature: Either eat or be eaten. Hunt or be hunted. This was nature's way.

On the screen, a hedgehog was in pursuit of a scorpion. It was a classic chase scene, rife with that age-old question: Will the hedgehog catch the scorpion?

Close on the hedgehog sniffing and moving fast.

Close on the scorpion skittering across a rock, not moving as fast as the hedgehog.

Cut back to the hedgehog, picking up speed.

Cut back to the scorpion . . .

The hedgehog. The scorpion.

I didn't have a good feeling about this when—

There was a knock on the door.

I froze as the hedgehog lunged for the scorpion, catching it in its mouth. I turned the TV off. That was better.

Mirror check.

During the 137 minutes that I'd been concerned/worried/crazed out of my mind, I had learned something, and now that Anna was finally knocking, I felt grateful for the delay.

Second mirror check.

There will be no recriminations, I told myself.

I popped a breath mint in my mouth.

No sirree. All is forgiven . . .

My heart was racing as I opened the door.

"Mr. Trammel?"

"What!" I groaned.

"I hope I'm not disturbing you."

"What is it, Nils?"

"Your Bible, sir." Nils extended the Bible. It was a deep gold color. It was the "Good News for Modern Man" version. "We didn't have one on the premises. So on my dinner break, I went to a Christian bookstore. The cashier recommended this one. She asked if you were a devout believer. I said I didn't know but that you were very disturbed about the lack of Bibles at the Infinity Hotel. She sold us this for half price."

I opened my wallet.

"You can charge it to your room."

"No, here." I gave Nils two twenty-dollar bills.

"Thank you, sir."

"No, thank *you*, Nils."

"You must be a religious person, Mr. Trammel."

"No, but I might be very soon."

Nils and I stood before each other.

"Are you all right, sir?"

"Oh, sure. I was just watching the telly." (I noticed that Mr. Trammel had begun to speak with a faint British accent. Perhaps he had lived for a time in London.) I went on, "Did you know that over the course of seven years, every cell in each of our bodies is replaced?"

"No, sir," he said, "I didn't know that."

"I learned it earlier this evening. Every seven years—a whole new set of cells. Isn't that astonishing?"

Nils smiled like he had a secret.

I had to ask, "What is it?"

Nils: "I like knowing odd facts and information, too. For instance, did you know that Brazil is the only country named after a tree?"

"I didn't know that," I said.

"The little parallelogram above your top lip is called the philtrum. Five years—or half a decade—is a lustrum. George Washington's teeth were not made of wood; they were made from hippopotamus, deer, horse, and human teeth screwed into an ivory base. Oh, and an opossum does not play dead. He gets so scared he faints!"

"Well done, Nils," I said, laughing. "You're distracting me, and I am most grateful."

"I can keep going!" And he did, speaking even faster, like an auctioneer. "According to the World Health Organization, there are more than one hundred million acts of sexual intercourse each day. The following men had or have one testicle: Fred Astaire; former president Jimmy Carter; the late, great race-car driver Dale Earnhardt. And my all-time favorite: Eighty-five percent of men who have heart attacks and die during sex are doing what?"

"Hmm, interesting. Let me think." *Eighty-five percent of men who have heart attacks and die during sex are doing what?* "I give up."

"They're cheating on their wives."

KATE

IT TURNED OUT I WAS HUNGRY.

Jeff and I were sitting at a prime table at the California Grill, which sits atop Disney's Contemporary Resort. The boys were in my room back at the lodge, already asleep in my bed. (We went back after Jeff's triumphant speech to say good night, and Jeff told them a long story about a magical fart machine, which they loved.) While we ate, the boys were being watched by a Disney-approved babysitter named Heather. I'd been provided with a beeper that I had clipped to my purse. I could be contacted if needed.

I admit, it was nice to be out without the boys and away from the Disney characters assaulting us every time we turned around. I was torn between wanting to gush about Jeff's speech, his work with Make-A-Wish, and wanting to hear about what had happened with the other Kate. But Jeff wanted to tell me a story.

"One time I was here and there was this guy—I guess you could say he was kind of a Disney freak. He had visited many times, and he knew that at Disney, things happened when they were scheduled to happen. Anyway, he brought his girlfriend here for dinner, and at eight fifty-nine P.M., he got down on one knee, raised a ring box, and proposed. His timing was perfect. The moment he finished asking, the first of that evening's fireworks burst in the sky behind him. When she said yes, the others in the restaurant broke into applause."

"That's kind of queer."

"You think so?"

"Yes, I do."

"Oh," he said gravely. "Well. It was me."

"It was you? No wonder she broke it off."

Jeff was quick to correct me. "But she didn't. I called it quits."

A family approached our table. They were from Sioux Falls, South Dakota, and wanted their picture taken with Jeff. They promised that as long as no one's eyes were closed, they'd make it their Christmas card.

After they left, I asked Jeff to tell me about the other Kate.

He did at some length. She sounded like a catch. Smart, sexy, kind to animals, a member of a progressive church, very sexual, a happy childhood. She loved Korky, his dog. I kept waiting for the downside. But she was curious, a good athlete, active in social causes.

I couldn't take it anymore. "So what was the problem?"

"She wasn't you."

I'd fallen for it. He was sneaky. And I was tipsy, but not so far gone that I couldn't manage "Yes, and it's a good thing she isn't me."

"Why? Why is it a good thing?"

"Because I'm married."

Could he tell in that moment I wished I weren't? I ordered another drink, and when it came, I quickly drank it.

Jeff got this serious look on his face. And oh, what a face. He struggled for the right words. I told him not to say anything. See, I was worried he was about to say something I knew we'd both regret.

Instead, he extended a small rectangular box wrapped in a red velvet ribbon. "When I saw it, I knew you had to have it."

It happened exactly this way. As I untied the ribbon, I heard the first whistle of fireworks being launched. As I lifted the box, there was a burst of purple light over the Magic Kingdom. Inside the box, resting on a rectangle of cotton, there it was—a Goofy wristwatch.

"You may be wondering—why Goofy?"

"Yes, I actually am wondering—why Goofy?"

"His hands go backward."

It was seminal. The Goofy wristwatch. Reversing time. Me, the drunk one. Jeff, all sober. Me, married but still yearning. He, single and still yearning, too. And the fireworks going on behind him were spectacular.

Later, back in his room at the lodge, we had sex.

TIM

don't ask   don't ask what time she got heredon't ask what she
was wearing

because she's not wearing anything now and don't don't don't ask
what was said

because nothing was said   as we fell on the bed
                                                    there will be no kissing

okay so no mouth kissing but there was plenty of mouth her mouth
on my neck on

my stomach and elsewhere pitch-black dark her hands, my mouth

her tongue so dizzying, this   can't remembertalking no hello
or how are

you or would it be all right if I or would you mind terribly if my penis

no, it was whatever whenever however   she on top   me on top
     her on the bed

on the floor   don't ask what time, don't ask how long we'd been
going at it no idea

only sound is her breathing, me breathing   we are sex
                                                    nothing is forbidden

nothing is said   nothing need be said
   and then oh God and then!

ring where was I   ring (fumble around in the dark) ring "Hello?"

   "Yes, I'd like to leave a message for Mr. Trammel in room—."
   "Uh—this is Trammel."
   "Oh, I thought this was the front desk."
   "Go ahead," I said, barely audible in a disguised voice.
   "I'm really sorry for waking you."
   Louder, in the same disguised voice: "Not a problem."
   "I'm calling on behalf of Mrs. Ashworth. She's been delayed."
   "Uh—clearly."
   "Wait—Mr. Welch, is that you?"

BEA MYERLY

AROUND MY HEART, PICTURE A TEN-CAR PILEUP. THAT'S HOW IT FELT LISTENING TO my ex-teacher breathe on the other line. "No, it's Trammel," he said, trying again to alter his voice. But I knew who it was.

Needless to say, I was confused.

I had done what Mrs. Ashworth asked. But the hotel operator mistakenly connected me to the room! And now I was freaked out. My head was spinning. It didn't make sense! (Because when you think of Anna Brody and you think *lover*, you definitely don't think of Mr. Welch.) I was smack in the middle of something sick and tawdry. I suddenly knew too much!

Oh, Mr. Welch. The great Mr. Welch. Now you're not so great.

I carried on as best I could: "The message is . . . as follows . . ."

What did I want to say? *I am so disappointed in you, Mr. Welch. You were my model of possibility. You were Bono if he were a schoolteacher in Brooklyn. You were my church.*

What could I have said? The facts. How that evening at the Ashworth-Brody house, as final preparations for the following day's house tour were finished, Anna Brody rushed around frantically trying to finish packing for a secret weekend away. But no—wait—Mr. Ashworth returned home unexpectedly and confronted her. Cue cymbal crash. Watch as the two of them have a knock-down, drag-out fight all the way up their mahogany staircase, Mr. Ashworth pleading and Mrs. Ashworth screaming. Finally, Mr. Ashworth collapses at Mrs. Ashworth's feet, begging her to not go see her lover. Inane dialogue like

"I'll give up mine if you'll give up yours." Mrs. Ashworth stood strong until Mr. Ashworth broke down like a baby. He cried and cried, and Mrs. Ashworth melted at the sight of her weeping man, looking up to the heavens and crying out, "At last!" Cue cheesy piano music. It was embarrassing! It felt like something from a bad nineteenth-century novel. Yuck! It went from this sappy weep-fest to a mad, sloppy kiss, culminating with the two of them disappearing into the master bedroom, where, from the sound of things, it seemed they wouldn't be coming out any time soon.

But no! Moments later, Mrs. Ashworth, all flushed, sweaty, and half-dressed, rushed into Sophie's playroom, pressed a piece of paper into my hand, and told me to call the Infinity Hotel and have them relay this message to a Mr. Trammel in room 1701.

What should I have said? *Grab your bag and get out of there. Mrs. Ashworth has used you.*

But what did I say? What did I tell Mr. Welch, my once great, now pathetic excuse for a mentor? With the door upstairs closed, and the Ashworths in the middle of a marathon of makeup sex, with the sounds of lovemaking echoing throughout the Ashworth-Brody house, I told him the furthest thing from the truth. "Mr. *Trammel*," I said. "She's on her way."

KATE

I WANTED TO TALK. PROCESS WHAT HAD HAPPENED. WHAT IT HAD FELT LIKE. MAYBE even do it again.

But Jeff was already fast asleep, lying facedown, his body (oh, what a body) splayed out in all directions, and his face (oh, what a face) deep in a pillow.

Naked, I sat on the edge of the bed and watched him breathe.

I needed to talk. But Jeff wasn't for talking. So I kissed his bare shoulder. He began to stir. I started to kiss down his back, when in his sleep, he slightly raised his left hip, and I heard a faint whisper of wind. Jeff had farted. Eggs came to mind. Sulfur.

Perfect, I thought, as I waved the smell away.

I used the spill of light from the bathroom to find my clothes and get dressed. As I picked up my bra and blouse, I remembered something. How earlier that night there had been more he'd wanted to say. So I went through his pockets and found his crumpled-up speech, which I took as a memento.

Besides, sleep was not going to be easy for me that night, and I needed something to read.

JEFF SLADE

I'm not an angel. But I play one on TV.
    (Beat. Hold for laugh.)
But when I look out at this room tonight, here is what I see: angels. All
of you are . . .
    (Choke up.)
Angels.
    (Cry here.)
I'm sorry . . . I wrote a speech, but words don't do justice . . .
    (Put speech away. Cry more.)
So let me just say—*KEEP WISHING!*
    (Beat. Let the moment land. Then look at Kate.)
Because that's how dreams come true.

KATE

"MOMMY, ARE YOU OKAY?"

Middle of the night, I was on my knees, hunched over the toilet bowl, Jeff's speech still clutched in my hand. I had just thrown up.

"Mommy . . ."

"Mommy will be okay, sweetie. I just ate something that disagreed with me. Go back to bed."

After Teddy went back to bed. I got in the shower. Water so hot it was practically scalding. I soaped myself. Scrubbed myself clean.

TIM

1:16 A.M. Okay, so if she was "on her way," as of 10:35 P.M., then where is she? *Where is she?!*

3:05 A.M. Still no sign. Rehearsed telling her off. "I'm not your pet. I'm not some play toy! Also, how foolish could you be, involving a third party (and one of my former students, no less) in our seedy enterprise? Bea could have ruined everything. Good thing I was able to disguise my voice!" Etc., etc.

4:22 A.M. Stared at self in mirror. Facing corner of bathroom, I saw a succession of reflections, my reflection of my reflection, so that I didn't see one of me, I saw countless, endless identical shrinking mes.

5:01 A.M. Checked phone machine at home. Kept replaying the only message. Teddy's little voice. *I was swimming, Dad. I was swimming.*

KATE

THE NEXT MORNING I TOOK THE BOYS DOWN TO THE WILDERNESS LODGE'S LOBBY, where we found Jeff and Darla huddled in the corner, reviewing the day's itinerary.

Darla chirped, "You thought yesterday was something, wait till you see what we've got planned—"

I walked right up to her, snatched the itinerary from her hands, and told her how it was going to be.

"I don't get it," Darla said. "Are you worried they're having too much fun?"

"No," I said.

"Oh, I see," she said. "You want them to learn something."

"Not exactly," I said. That was when I turned to Jeff and said, "I just want them to see something real."

TIM

TIMES I WANTED TO LEAVE: 5:02 A.M., 5:15 A.M., 5:52 A.M., 6:05 A.M., 6:36 A.M., 6:57 A.M., 7:10 A.M., 7:32–7:41 A.M., 8:01 A.M., and most every moment from that point on. But did I go? No, I stayed. I sat stuck in the cushy white chair. Apoplectic, but too tired to move. It was 9:47 A.M. when the room phone rang. Jolted out of my catatonia, I reached for the receiver. "Hello?"

She didn't say anything at first.

"Yes, I'm here," I said. "I'm still here!"

She said nothing.

"I've done my part. *Where are you?*"

No answer, but I could hear her breathing.

"Is this is some big joke to you? You find it funny? It's no joke!" I was quiet for a long time. "I'm giving you five minutes to get here— Wait, I'll give you an hour. Then I'm gone. You have one hour, do you hear me? One—!"

Click.

I should've left. Right then. Who am I kidding? *I shouldn't have even been there.* What kept me there? This part is hard to admit. I had said I'd wait an hour. So I clung to this idea that I was a person of my word. In the fog of my own moral war, I'd somehow worked out that I was the honorable one. I was holding up my end of the bargain, forgetting that I was violating a much bigger vow—the biggest vow of all—my vow to Kate.

I was disoriented when I heard the knock. It was more of a banging, really. The daylight streaming into the room made me squint. I half stumbled to the door and pulled it open only to find . . .

BEA MYERLY

CLEARLY, I WASN'T THE PERSON HE EXPECTED. STILL, THERE I WAS, ALL PUFFED UP, full of outrage and disgust. But seeing him, the shame/shock look in his eyes, just made me *sad*.

"Mr. Welch," I said.

He said nothing at first. The only sound was of this once great man deflating. Finally, he managed a faint "Hello, Bea."

"May I come in?"

He sat on the edge of the bed. He'd made an effort to look his best. He smelled of cologne. But he was like a shell of his old self. I stood near a large potted plant. Neither of us spoke for the longest time. *My hands, my knees, were shaking!*

Finally, me: "What are you doing here, sir?"

"I've been sitting here asking myself the same question." Then he scrunched his face. Then he sighed as if he'd been shot. Then he looked down at his feet and said, "You must be disappointed in me."

I was. I'd had such high hopes for Mr. Welch. But to tell him that would only have hurt him. And I was in the presence of a man who was already in far too much pain. That was when I thought, *Remind him*, so I said, "Here's what you taught me: History is full of people doing the unthinkable. And each of us is capable of doing anything."

Mr. Welch looked up, staring vaguely in my direction. I seemed to be having an impact. *Keep going, Bea*, I told myself. "And there is always a place for mercy."

"I taught you that?"

"Actually, no, but it's something I believe." I blurted out, "I won't tell anybody about what you've done here."

"Bea, thank you. It would be awful if it came out."

"Yes, I would think."

"Besides, nothing happened."

"Mr. Welch, I'm sorry, but that would be an incorrect statement, wouldn't it? That nothing happened?"

Who was the teacher now? He'd forgotten his own core belief. History—even if it is forgotten—is always happening.

Mr. Welch nodded. "You're right," he said slowly. It was as if he'd ingested mass quantities of sedatives and they'd just kicked in.

It was time to explain why I was there. "Sir, last night when I called, I was stunned. You see, I recognized your voice." *It's only my favorite voice ever.* "And I was so caught off guard that I said something untrue."

"Oh?" he said.

"I, uhm, lied."

"Go on."

"Mrs. Ashworth wasn't on her way."

He looked puzzled.

I explained about Philip and Anna's big fight, the begging and the tears, the makeup sex, and mostly, how I'd failed to deliver the real message.

"And it was?"

I handed him the piece of paper Mrs. Ashworth had given me. It was folded in half.

But he didn't move. He just sat there holding the piece of paper. I think he wanted to read her note in private.

I excused myself to use the bathroom. Before I closed the door, I caught his reflection in the mirror. *How do I give this man comfort?* I wondered, just as he opened the note.

ANNA BRODY

Go home.

TIM

GO HOME. YES, THAT WAS THE RIGHT IDEA. OF COURSE, I WISH I'D GIVEN MYSELF
the message. Hell, I wish I hadn't signed up for this pathetic adventure.
But I had. And now it was up to me. Go home.

With Bea in the bathroom, I quickly packed my bag. Tossed the
condoms in the trash. Unlocked the minibar and retrieved my wedding
ring from under a high-priced chocolate bar. As I slipped it on, I felt a
wash of relief. *This will never come off again.* I had dodged a big, fat bullet.
Yes, Bea had the goods on me, but I believed she would tell no one. And
I was grateful that she'd lied to me the night before. By leaving me to
stew in room 1701 of the Infinity Hotel, she had done me a great service.
I had met myself, and I didn't like the man I'd found myself to be.

So . . .

I couldn't get home fast enough.

I was stuffing my pajamas into my bag when Bea emerged. I was
slow to notice the way she was standing, her arms outstretched, as if
making an offering of herself. Only then did I realize she was naked.

KATE

THE QUEST FOR SOMETHING REAL TOOK US TO THE ANIMAL KINGDOM, WHERE THE Kilimanjaro Safari was more authentic than anything we'd seen in two days. As we jostled along in an actual lorry, I pulled Teddy and Sam in close to me and tried to speak over a confused Jeff. "Look," I said. "Do you see that giraffe? It's real."

No response.

"Oh, look, real zebras!"

No response.

I pointed out the rhinos and the hippopotamuses, but the boys were miserable. They were about to cry.

"What is it, you guys?"

"We miss Dumbo."

"Yes, but over here, what we have is a *real* elephant . . ."

"We want to see Dumbo."

"Hey, guys, look: These are all real, live animals that we're seeing . . ."

"But Mommy, Dumbo is real! Mickey and Minnie are real!"

BEA MYERLY

COULD HE TELL I WAS NERVOUS? THAT MY BODY WAS SHAKING? I SQUEEZED MY eyes shut, even though part of me wanted to look and see his expression. Another part of me wondered which part of me he would touch first.

I heard him moving closer.

Be open to what comes next, Bea. Be open.

I could feel his breath.

I am yours, Mr. Welch.

Before I knew it, he was behind me.

I have always been yours.

He draped a hotel robe over my shoulders . . .

Huh?

And gently told me to get dressed.

I don't even think he looked at me. That he ever saw me. I really tried not to cry. But he gave me Kleenex.

Later, on the subway, he said a lot of things I think he meant. He felt bad I had gotten mixed up in his mess. He was flattered by my offer. "But it would be wrong," he said. *Of course it's wrong!* But that hadn't stopped him! He told me we were kind of the same. He talked about how he'd gone too far with Anna Brody. How he'd lost himself. And how I was in danger of doing the same thing with him. He told me not to make the same mistake. He said it would make what he'd just done less terrible if I learned from it. And I promised I would do my best.

We were quiet for the rest of the ride to Brooklyn.

He walked me all the way to Baltic Street, and while I climbed the steps to my house, he waited, like a gentleman, until I was safe inside.

KATE

WE HAD BEEN TRANSPORTED BACK TO THE MAGIC KINGDOM IN RECORD SPEED, AND now Jeff wanted to know what was next. I think he meant in terms of us. But I wasn't biting.

"Now we stand in line like ordinary people," I said.

"But the line for Dumbo is an hour and ten minutes!"

I insisted we stand there and inch along with the others. A frustrated Jeff, who hadn't stood in any kind of line in years, tried to entertain the boys, who were hot and cranky. He pulled me aside and asked if I was upset about last night. He said he had lots to say about what had happened, and I told him to put it in a speech. Then he disappeared. He returned with a stuffed Eeyore for Sam and a *Jungle Book* whirligig for Teddy and a long strand of cherry licorice for each of them. Over the next hour, he spent more money than I'd seen him spend the entire trip. We couldn't carry all the trinkets and memorabilia, the T-shirts, the plastic whistles and light-up saber-swords, the Tarzan clubs, the Aladdin lamp full of jelly beans. This was war. And Jeff wanted to win. My boys? They kept saying "I want this" and "I want that," and Jeff kept reappearing with it and more.

"Stop," I said. "Please stop."

"But, Kate," Jeff said. "They have the rest of their lives to be disappointed."

Late that afternoon, at the epicenter of the Magic Kingdom near the life-size bronze statue of Mickey and Walt, a mother freaked out. Poor woman. She had lost her mind. Well, it was understandable. It was hot, and her children were tired and sunburned and overstimulated from having consumed mass quantities of sugar and soda and chocolate. Maybe her younger child wanted to ride all the rides all at the same time. Maybe her older child, weighed down from all the souvenir gifts and Disney pins, had just moaned, "How come I never get what I want!" Maybe a maintenance gate had opened briefly to let a Disney cast member drive through in an electric cart, and maybe the mother had caught a glimpse of the backs of the facades facing Main Street and had been stunned at how it looked like the back of any strip mall in any city in America. Maybe she'd told her boys to come quick—look—for this, she thought, they should see.

It's a relief when it's some other mother who has snapped a tether, when you're not the one making a scene. It's a relief until you realize that it's actually you. You see, I was the person raging at her children, the one who lost her bearings, my way of behaving, my sense of perspective, so that amid all the clamor and the approach of security guards, I didn't have the wherewithal to negotiate a graceful denouement—no, all I could do was shout, shout until I was hoarse from shouting that same word, the only word: *Enough. Enough.*

TIM

I WENT HOME TO A PLATE OF TOAST CRUSTS.

Sam's cereal dried to the sides of the bowl.

The height marks on the pantry door.

Kate's hairbrush.

The glass with four toothbrushes in the bathroom.

Then I got out a small screwdriver and started to fix the broken cabinet door.

KATE

"I DON'T BELIEVE IN REGRET," JEFF SAID IN OUR FINAL MOMENTS TOGETHER.

Well, sure, if you live in your own private Disney World, you can excise mess and garbage and even regret. But for me, regret was all too real.

"I don't know what happened," Jeff said. "Am I now some sort of monster to you?"

"No, Jeff, you're not a monster. You're an actor." Then I stuck out my hand. "Good-bye."

"So that's how it is now?"

"Yes, that's how it is." And we shook hands.

Later, forgoing the limousine Jeff had provided, the boys and I boarded the Disney shuttle and rode it to the airport. It felt good to blend in, to be just another mother traveling with her kids.

On the flight home, a woman sitting across the aisle leaned in and asked if I was all right. I turned and looked at her. She had gray hair and kind eyes. *Of course I'm all right,* I wanted to say. But she seemed to know better.

"What are you reading?" she asked.

"My husband's dissertation."

"What's it on?"

"Loss."

"Is that why you're crying?"

"Well," I said, pausing to wipe my eyes. "I'm halfway through, and it's obvious he doesn't know what he's talking about."

She smiled.

"But that's not why I'm crying."

I reached over to give Sam a different crayon. Teddy had lifted the shade and was stretching up to look out the window. He named the clouds. Popcorn. A doggie.

"Good, Teddy," I said. "That's good." I turned back and found the woman waiting with a small packet of tissues.

"You were saying?"

"Oh," I said, and this I whispered: "I cheated on my husband."

"I see."

From her lack of reaction, I could've said, "I'm from Northern California" or "I like the color green."

"It was a onetime thing," I said, opening the packet of tissues. "And it's over."

"Do you still love your husband?"

I nodded.

"So what's the problem?"

I didn't have an answer. All I could come up with was "Somewhere it went wrong."

"Well, did you die?"

"I'm sorry?"

"Are you dead?"

"No."

"Is he dead?"

"No."

"Well, then . . ."

I waited for her to say more. But she went back to her reading. Then the pilot came over the intercom and said we'd begun our descent.

During the taxi ride from the airport, the boys fell asleep. This gave me time to gather myself for my reunion with Tim. I decided not to tell him what I'd done with Jeff at Disney World. This was a go-to-the-grave secret. Never to be told. What would it serve to let him know how nice it was (because at first it was) to kiss Jeff again and do other things again? This was my plan. Could I (the astonishing keeper of secrets) keep this secret? Yes. Would he be able to tell when he looked into my eyes—would he know that something had happened?

When the taxi pulled up in front of our building, I didn't see Tim sitting on the stoop. But there he was, waiting. He looked unsettled, wild-eyed. I signaled that both boys were asleep, and we busied ourselves getting them up to the apartment, careful not to wake them.

Our apartment was spotless. Cleanest ever. Tim had sorted through papers. Cleared shelves. Organized our overcrowded medicine chest. Bagged up outgrown clothes for Goodwill. He had fixed the broken cabinet door.

He could see I was pleased. He smiled at my reaction. And that was when I noticed.

"Honey, what happened to your tooth?"

He didn't want to say.

The story of the chipped tooth was told, and I was laughing, we both were, until it led to the other, bigger story, the story he didn't want to tell, but for some reason he couldn't stop, and as he talked, as it slowly dawned on me where this was all headed, I was filled with an intense mix of feelings—sick and achy, sad. It was kick-in-the-gut painful. I even felt a strange admiration for him as he fumbled his way through the details, for this was why I had first loved him. Mostly, though, I tried to listen as the tears fell, *just listen,* all the while knowing that when he was done telling me everything, it would be my turn to do the same.

BEA MYERLY

WHEN MR. WELCH APPROACHED ME ABOUT ADDING MY VERSION OF THINGS TO THIS story, I told him I would only participate on one condition: I get to write the end. I thought he would refuse. Instead, he agreed immediately. I assumed Mr. Welch or his ex-wife would want to have the last word. (Point of fact, I'm not sure if she's an official ex-wife yet.)

No one is more surprised than I am that I'm left to finish telling this story, that I'm the one chosen to make sense of all this ruin.

On a personal note, when Mr. Welch gave me what he'd written, I found a cozy spot in my room and began to read. I didn't get far. *Pug-nosed little chunk of a girl? Barrel-chested? A cluster of pebble-sized pimples dotting my fleshy forehead?*

I couldn't believe it! So I confronted Mr. Welch. "How could you distort me this way? This is how I look to you?" "Of course not," he said, "but at that time you were an annoying student, and that's how all annoying students look to me."

Needless to say, I didn't read any more.

So the end.

The BHA Annual House and Garden tour was a huge success. They kept the Ashworth-Brody house open two extra hours to accommodate the record crowds.

The next day Anna Brody and Philip Ashworth left the Heights for good. Within days, a fleet of moving vans arrived and the house was emptied. For a while, it was all the talk—*where did they go, why did they leave, was it something we did?*

All anybody knew was they were gone, and their empty house was on the market. Frida Fabritz got the exclusive, but my dad says now no one can afford the house, *so good luck, Frida.* By the fall, everybody was talked out about the Ashworths. Maybe because the whole world had started to fall apart. My mom and dad ask me all the time if I'm worried about the future. They can sense I'm upset—and I am, but not about what they think.

I'm upset about what happened with Mr. Welch and his ex-wife.

There were such clear lessons in this story. Mr. Welch tries to cheat on his wife, and she kicks him out. I assumed she kicked him out. I didn't know. It was my fantasy. (Obviously, they weren't meant for each other. Right? He was meant for me! Joking. *Not.*) All I knew was that when Mr. Welch was scrambling to find a place to live, I got my parents to rent him our garden apartment at a reduced rate. Meaning: for free.

He moved in on the first of August, the same day Mrs. Welch took their boys out of state for a two-week vacation. At night I could put my head up to the radiator and hear Mr. Welch's muffled crying.

Now that he's back at Montague, kids ask me what it's like having a teacher living in the same house. I say, "He's a tenant, and he's in the basement with his own entrance." I don't explain that having him under the same roof feels right.

I see Mrs. Welch sometimes, although I don't know if I'm supposed to call her Mrs. Welch anymore. She got a new apartment. She tries to put on a good face in her new job at the Public Library. But she doesn't look the same. Tired. Worn out from it all.

Truth is, I don't know what to think. I don't understand people! Next year I go to college, and I'm more confused than ever!

I'm sorry for that outburst. I'm . . . I'm having a hard time . . . oh God.

You see, this morning my dad told me that Mr. Welch said he would be moving out soon.

I didn't see it coming. "Where's he going?" I said, in a panic. "Where?"

"I didn't ask," my dad said. "I don't think it's our business."

So I made it my business.

I waited until he left the house, and I followed him. I kept my distance, but I didn't let him out of my sight. He didn't walk toward the Heights, as usual. Instead, he went the opposite direction, through Cobble Hill, deep into Carroll Gardens. As he walked, I saw him in a new way. Or maybe he was always small and I just never noticed.

When he disappeared around a chain-link fence, I waited a bit before crossing the street. Here's where I saw the most baffling sight in the short history of my life.

Mr. Welch was sitting on a bench talking to a woman whose face I could not see. I pressed up to the fence to get a closer look. The woman was Mrs. Welch. What were they doing? This is where it gets hard and confusing. He was saying something, she was laughing, and they were *holding hands*.

Now would someone please explain that to me.